OFFICE MONSTERS

To: Charlne,

Best Regards,

Lorraine Helena

Lorraine Helena

ISBN 978-1-64140-206-4 (paperback)
ISBN 978-1-64140-208-8 (hardcover)
ISBN 978-1-64140-207-1 (digital)

Copyright © 2018 by Lorraine Helena

All rights reserved. No part of this publication may be reproduced, distributed, or transmitted in any form or by any means, including photocopying, recording, or other electronic or mechanical methods without the prior written permission of the publisher. For permission requests, solicit the publisher via the address below.

Christian Faith Publishing, Inc.
832 Park Avenue
Meadville, PA 16335
www.christianfaithpublishing.com

Office Monsters is a work of fiction. Names, characters, places, and incidents are the products of the author's imagination or are used fictitiously. Any resemblance to actual events, locales, or persons, living or dead, is entirely coincidental.

Printed in the United States of America

DEDICATION

This book is dedicated to my family and friends, who have given me the encouragement to produce this work. To my best friend, Tom, who cherishes my spirit and believes in me, and to all women who labor in the work force.

PROLOGUE

The long walk seemed more like a hop, skip, and a jump for little Lorie Richards and her sister, Emma, as they trekked along to the bus stop. Lofty pines and maple trees, hosting a choir of chirping feathered friends, lined the old country road. Lorie was particularly interested in the birds and tried to identify them as they walked along. Stopping for a few seconds, she shouted, "There are two robins, and over there"—pointing to another tree—"I see a bobwhite! Do you hear him, Emma?"

Emma looked at Lorie in bewilderment and thought, *Why in the world would anyone be so interested in birds?* But not wanting to sound scornful, Emma responded, "Yes, yes, I see them. Now let's get moving or we'll miss the bus."

Climbing onto the crowded bus, Lorie managed to find a seat next to another girl. Emma strolled down the aisle to the back of the bus. As Lorie glanced around, she saw Emma smoothly slide onto the long seat in the back. Next, she checked to see if her homework was in her school bag. *Yes*, she thought. Lorie liked school, but this year seemed to be different, mainly because of the new girl, Gail Zeller. Gail had recently moved into the area with her mother and older brother. Gail was not a particularly pretty girl. Actually, she was a bit on the homely side with an attitude to match. When Lorie found out that Gail's dad had passed away, Lorie tried very hard to be friendly to her. But all her efforts seemed to be in vain. As time went on, Lorie got the impression that Gail did not like her at all, but she couldn't figure out why. Lorie thought, *When someone is nice to me, it makes me feel good, and I like them and appreciate their kindness. Gail seems so unpleasant and disagreeable that I don't think she will ever change. Mom says that I have to be kind to her because that is what Jesus would want me to do. Mom wants me to invite her to spend the day at our house on Saturday and to ask her to stay for dinner. Oh my, this will be hard, but I'll try.*

Finally, they arrived at the school. The kids all hurried off the bus and to their classrooms. As Lorie walked into her classroom, she saw Gail talking to a few other girls. One of the other girls was Lorie's friend, Mary Lou. *Oh well*, Lorie thought, *I'll wait until recess before I ask Gail about coming over.* Lorie went over to her desk and started to put her books away.

"Hi, Lorie," Mary Lou said with her usual big smile.

"Hi, Mary Lou," Lorie returned. Mary Lou was good at reading people. Even though Lorie was trying to act normal, she could tell that something was bothering her.

"You don't seem like yourself today. What's wrong?"

Lorie sighed, "Oh, it's my mom. She wants me to ask Gail to come over on Saturday and stay for dinner. I think Mom feels sorry for her because she lost her dad, but I get the feeling that Gail does not like me, and I can't see how having her over is going to change that."

Mary Lou suddenly lost her smile. She spoke softly, not wanting anyone to hear. "Lorie, I probably shouldn't tell you this because I don't want to make matters worse, but to tell you the truth, Gail does not like you. The reason I say that is because when she does make any remarks about you, I always get the impression that she is just plain jealous of you."

Lorie's mouth fell open in surprise. "Why on earth would she be jealous of me?"

Mary Lou continued, "Well, for one thing, you are real pretty, and the boys all like you. Plus, you have a dad and a nice family. Gail's mom is broke and doesn't do anything about it, and her brother is useless, to hear her tell it. Do you need more reasons than that?"

Suddenly, the bell rang, and everyone moved swiftly to their seats. Lorie sat there for a few moments, trying to ingest everything that Mary Lou told her. *Maybe I should talk to Mom again before asking Gail over*, she thought.

After school, on the long walk home, Lorie tried to talk to Emma about it. "Oh, for goodness sakes, Lorie, anybody can see that she is jealous of you. But Mom seems to think that if she is invited over and we play some games and have a good dinner, it would make things better for both of you. Mom is the type that accepts everyone, and she just naturally does it with kindness. That seems to work for her." Lorie added, "I guess she hasn't met anyone like Gail yet." Reluctantly, both girls agreed.

A feeling of doom crept into the pit of Lorie's stomach as her mom called from the bottom of the stairs. "Lorie, come on now. It's time to pick up Gail." Lorie couldn't understand why Gail's mom didn't drive and hoped that her mom wouldn't be the one to constantly have to pick Gail up for everything under the sun. *Why should my mom have to play taxi for them?*

Lorie looked over at her mom while she was driving. *Mom is so pretty*, she thought, *not only on the outside but on the inside as well. She has such a kind heart.*

Theresa Richards was a lovely woman with her natural blond hair, piercing blue eyes, and, of course, her heart of gold. Lorie felt lucky to have such a nice mom and was glad that she inherited her mom's good features. Although her mom would always say, "It's not what's on the outside that counts but what's on the inside," sometimes Lorie thought that her mom might be an angel in disguise.

As they drove on, Theresa said, "Now, Lorie, I want you to understand that some people have a hard road to travel through life. When things are difficult, they might not act very nice all the time. That does not mean that they are bad people but just that they are unable to deal with all the problems that life throws at them. When we are kind to those people, we are bringing a little bit of Jesus into their difficult situations. And remember, Jesus is the master healer."

Lorie listened attentively, for she knew that her mother was very wise, and she really wanted to do the right thing. But as her mom continued to talk and tell her of the plan for the day, Lorie felt rebellion creep in, almost to the boiling point.

"Lorie, we are going to play a game today. It's something I made up. We are going to have a contest. Last night, I boiled a dozen eggs. So today, you, Emma, and Gail will color them and do whatever artwork you girls want to do to decorate the eggs. Now you know that I would always like yours and Emma's eggs the best, but because Gail will be our guest and because she needs to have something nice to happen in her life, I am going to pick her as the winner and give her a little gift. I've already told Emma about this, and it's okay with her."

Lorie didn't know what to say. She thought, *No, it's not okay with me. Why would you ask me such a thing?*

Theresa could tell that Lorie was not happy with that idea, and actually, Emma was not happy with it either, but she finally agreed. Theresa was waiting for an answer. "Lorie, don't let me down now. We want to show love and kindness today."

Lorie looked at her mom in disbelief. Even though she hated the idea, she didn't have the heart to argue with her mom. *I know she means well*, she thought. Then she softly said, "Okay."

Theresa smiled. "That's my girl!"

Theresa and Mrs. Zeller seemed to get along nicely as they chatted for a bit while Gail was getting ready. Lorie sat in silence, looking around at the humble lodging. *Gee, they really don't have much at all. Maybe Mom is right about being kind to people who are going through a rough time.* When they were ready to leave, Gail kissed her mom goodbye and seemed to be happy to be going to Lorie's place for the day.

While Lorie and Emma showed Gail their rooms and all their dolls, Gail seemed to be enjoying herself. Lorie let her pick whatever she wanted to play with. Theresa then fixed the girls a very nice lunch consisting of tomato soup, turkey club sandwiches, homemade sugar cookies, and milk. After lunch, Theresa told the girls about the hard-boiled eggs and that she wanted them to decorate the eggs with their best artwork. "Whoever is the most creative will get a prize. I'll stay out of the room until you are finished. So call me when you are ready." Theresa already knew what kind of artwork her daughters would usually do when coloring and decorating eggs. So staying out of the room was just for Gail's benefit. Gail seemed to like the idea. Lorie and Emma only pretended to like it but tried their best to go along with it for their mom's sake.

Gail smiled the whole time she was decorating her eggs. Lorie thought, *Maybe Mom was right. Maybe all Gail needed was for someone to be really kind to her and show her a good time.*

After the girls finished with the eggs, they called Theresa back into the room. Theresa looked over all the eggs very carefully. "Gee, this is a big decision," she said. "You all did such a wonderful job on decorating these eggs. They are equally beautiful. But since I must pick one group of eggs, I will pick this group here, but the other two groups are equally in second place."

Gail was so happy that her eggs were picked. She said, "Of course, you would pick my eggs because they are the best."

Lorie and Emma stood there and bit their tongues. At that point, Lorie wanted so much to tell Gail exactly why her eggs were picked, but glancing over at her mom, she decided to say nothing. Theresa was also taken aback by that remark. She knew Gail would be happy about being the winner, but she thought her comment was a bit arrogant, to say the least.

For a moment, Theresa was lost for words. Then she said, "Gail, in God's eyes, we are all the same. He thinks all our works are good. When something good happens to us here on earth, the first thing that we should do is to thank God for his kindness and also to remember to be a good sport when either winning or losing. Always show appreciation but do it in a humble way. And remember, the hand of God is behind all good things."

Gail thought, *Well, I guess she didn't like what I said, but since I'm the winner, who cares!* Then she smiled and said, "What's my prize?"

Theresa wondered if Gail had comprehended anything she said but decided not to make a big deal of it. "Okay," Theresa said. She reached for a small box that was sitting on top of the refrigerator and handed it to Gail. It was wrapped so beautifully that it caught Gail by surprise. "Gee, it's almost too pretty to open," she said with a smile but continued to unwrap it. Lorie and Emma's eyes met with much disapproval regarding the proceedings, but they tried not to show their feelings to Gail or their mom.

Gail was pleased to see what was in the box. There was a little heart-shaped bottle of Blue Waltz perfume and some pretty barrettes for her hair. She looked at Theresa with a sincere smile. "Gee, Mrs. Richards, this is so nice. Thank you."

Theresa was pleased that she liked her prize. "You're welcome, Gail. Now you girls go play but don't go far. When Mr. Richards gets home from work, we'll have supper."

The girls headed outside. Gail found some Indian dolls earlier while looking through the toys and wanted to play Indian village with them outside. While they were playing out back, Theresa happened to look out the window. *Yes, they seem to be getting along okay,* she thought.

Before long, Mr. Richards arrived home from work. Theresa filled him in on the happenings of the day. "Fred, Gail and her family are having a rough time. Gail's father has passed away, and her mom doesn't have much. She has a brother, but from what Lorie has told me, he's a difficult guy who gives his mother a lot of grief. Gail has not been very friendly to Lorie. I thought if we showed her some kindness by inviting her over to spend the day with the girls, maybe things would be better for her. Maybe if she had a friend in Lorie, she would learn to be kind as well."

Fred shook his head and said, "I can't claim to understand women, but I do know that you have a heart of gold, Theresa. I also know that some people cannot be changed no matter how hard you try. Maybe it would be better if you let the girls work things out for themselves. Sometimes when we try to push our opinions on others, we just wind up making things worse."

Theresa nodded in agreement. "Okay, after dinner, I'll take Gail home and have a talk with Lorie. I know that she was not pleased with my ideas, and I certainly don't want to alienate her." With that, Fred gave her a little kiss and went to wash up for dinner.

When the girls came in, Gail asked if she could spend the night. Theresa was surprised as she didn't think Lorie or Emma would want that. Not knowing how to answer that question, she looked at Lorie.

Lorie said, "It's okay with me, Mom."

Theresa said, "Well, you would have to call your mom and check with her. As for pajamas, you can borrow a pair from Lorie."

Gail seemed to be thrilled with that answer and ran to call her mom. With everyone in agreement, the girls seemed to be happy. They did want to play Ghost Tag before going to bed. So Theresa gave them an old sheet, and they wore themselves out before turning in for the night.

The next day, Sunday, they got up, and while getting ready for church, Gail proceeded to tell Lorie about a dream that she had. Lorie was surprised that Gail would tell her about such a dream since it was very negative and almost hateful regarding Lorie.

Fred and Theresa's room was close to the girls' room, and Fred happened to hear Gail talk about her dream to Lorie. He went to the kitchen where he found Theresa busily making breakfast for everyone. "Theresa, I just don't like that Gail. I don't want her coming here anymore."

Theresa was taken aback by that comment. "Fred, why are you saying that?"

Fred proceeded to tell her how Gail was talking to Lorie about her dream. "It was almost like she was happy about having a hateful dream about Lorie. There is something about that girl. I don't want her here anymore."

Theresa remarked, "Fred, it was only a dream. Some dreams are bad, but that doesn't mean that the person is bad. Still, if you feel that strongly about it, we won't ask her to come back. But if I were you, I would give that a little more thought."

Fred shook his head and said, "I've thought about it, and the answer is still the same."

That evening, Theresa sat down with the girls. "Girls," she said, "we have to talk."

Lorie could see the concern in her mother's eyes. "Mom, what's wrong?"

Theresa patted Lorie on the shoulder. "Lorie, your father overheard Gail telling you about a bad dream that she had of you. He said she sounded rather hateful while telling you about that dream and almost happy that she had it. He has a bad feeling about her and does not want her to come over here anymore. I hope that having her here this weekend will not cause you more problems. You know, we all tried to give her the benefit of the doubt. Abraham Lincoln once said, 'I destroy my enemies when I make them my friends.' And Jesus said 'to pray for those who hate you and pray for those who spitefully use you and persecute you that you may be sons and daughters of your Father in heaven.' But sometimes when we encounter difficult people in our lives, we will need to set limits. So we must pray for Gail and her family, and when we see her, we must show consideration and kindness. But if she wants to come here anymore, you will have to tell her that you will have to get the okay from your dad and just leave it at that for now. If you have a problem with her, your dad will go to speak to her mother."

Lorie was relieved to hear that her mom was not going to push her to be friends with Gail any longer. She knew that her mom meant well, but Gail was a difficult person. It seemed that her personality could change from one minute to the next, which would throw Lorie off guard and would ultimately cause hurtful feelings. Lorie was uncomfortable being around people like that but was thankful that she had caring parents who looked out for her and tried to protect her from a sometimes cruel world.

Time went by rather quickly. Lorie soon found herself in high school. The years were kind to her as she had grown into a very beautiful and popular girl. She didn't have many classes with Gail while in high school, so she had little reason to say much to her. But she was always kind and polite when she would see her. On the other hand, Gail's looks did not improve much over the years. She was still rather homely with a vindictive personality that seemed to get worse each year. She secretly hated Lorie and was extremely jealous of her.

During their senior year, with the prom approaching, many guys were asking Lorie to be their date for the prom. This became the talk in the gym locker room. The girls were constantly discussing the prom and the guys. Gail was not excited about the prom, for no one had asked her. She started to fantasize how she could destroy Lorie's night at the prom but was afraid that if she got in trouble, she might not be able to graduate with the class. So she thought and thought as to what she could do. "Yes," she said to herself. "I have a plan."

Mark was a kid who didn't have much going for him. He was not what you would call handsome but not particularly ugly either. He usually got in trouble for dumb stuff, like pulling pranks on his classmates or putting gum on a teacher's chair. Gail knew that he came from a poor family, and she also knew that he would do anything for money. She felt sure that if she would pay him, he would go to the prom with her, if for no other reason but for the money. *Okay,* she thought. *Now where do I get the money? First, I have to talk to him. Maybe we can come up with some kind of deal.*

Later that day, she slipped him a note stating that it was important for them to talk, and she mentioned a time and place. She wasn't sure that he would show up but hoped that his curiosity would be the driving factor in this case. She got to the appointed place before him. Looking at her watch, she started to get nervous. Pacing back and forth, she looked at her watch again. *Okay,* she thought. *He's not going to show.*

Suddenly, he appeared. With a smirk on his face, he said, "What's this all about?"

Startled, Gail felt like saying, "Forget it," and run away. But she knew it was now or never, so she made her pitch.

With a deep breath, she began. "Look, Mark, I have a problem, and I think you are the one who can help me solve it."

He laughed and said, "So why would I want to help you? What's in it for me?"

Gail thought that if she could make Lorie out to be a real witch or bitch, maybe she could make Mark feel sorry for her and go along with her scheme. "Well, to begin with, I am being mocked and taunted continuously by one of our classmate, Lorie Richards. She constantly makes fun of my looks and always puts me down in front of her friends. I've even heard her say rather hateful things about you already. Now she is bragging about so many guys asking her to the prom, and she doesn't know which one to choose. Then she made a hateful remark about me not being able to get a date. So this is my plan. If you don't have a date for the prom, I will pay you to go with me. That way, Lorie won't be able to make fun of me for not having a date for the prom."

Now Mark was really laughing. He knew Lorie for many years, and he never heard her say anything bad or even slightly negative about anyone. On the contrary, she was always kind to everyone. He could see that Gail was so jealous that even her green eyes looked greener as she was spinning her tale. But on the other hand, he really needed the money. *I guess it wouldn't hurt to see how much I can get out of her*, he thought. "Okay, cut the crap," he said while trying to control his laughter. "So how much are you willing to pay me?"

Gail thought for a moment. "Well," she said, "how much would you want?"

He knew that Gail didn't have a dad and that her mom was old and not doing all that well. He also knew her brother was usually in trouble and didn't help out much, even when he was working part-time. And he could tell by the clothes Gail wore that she didn't have much money to spend like the other girls. So what figure could he possibly come up with? "Okay," he said, "I'll have to rent a tux, so I'll need money for that. But you will have to take care of your own transportation and whatever. I'll meet you at the prom."

Gail was pleased that he was going along with her scheme and tried to hold back a smile. But she still didn't know what it was going to cost her. "Well, how much do you want?"

Mark scratched his head while giving it some thought. "Let me find out what the tux will cost. It will be the cost of the tux plus my time. Like I said before, you will have to take care of everything else. We'll talk tomorrow."

Before he left, Gail said, "Now this is between you and me. Do not mention this to anyone. If you do, you will make a fool out of both of us, and we already have enough problems as it is."

As he walked away, he mumbled, "Speak for yourself. Chill out! 'Mums' is the word!"

Walking home, Mark gave her proposition some serious thought, *Well, let's see. The guys would probably poke fun at me showing up with Gail at the prom. But on the other hand, money speaks louder than words. I certainly could use the extra bucks. I guess I'll just lay it on the line with her—pay up and I'll show up.*

Lorie held her breath as she looked in the mirror. She felt like a princess and radiated with a special glow.

Theresa and Fred walked into her room. "My, my," Theresa said, "you are absolutely beautiful."

Fred added, "That's our girl! You'll be the prettiest girl at the prom."

Lorie was so grateful to have such wonderful and caring parents. "Thank you both for this lovely dress. This means more to me than you could ever know." With a warm hug to each parent, she ventured downstairs just as her date arrived.

Jake stood at the doorway, holding a beautiful corsage. He looked stunning in his tux. Fiddling with the camera, Theresa and Fred insisted on taking a dozen pictures.

Lorie could see that Jake was starting to feel a little uncomfortable. "Mom," Lorie snapped, "we don't need any more pictures. They will be taking a picture of us at the prom."

Theresa realized that she may have come across a little overbearing. So wishing them a good time and making them promise to drive carefully, she walked them to the door. Tears filled her eyes as she watched them leave. "Oh, to be young again," she said softly.

Fred put his arm around her and lightly kissed her forehead. "We've had our turn. Now it's their turn," he said as he gently closed the door.

Arriving at the school, Lorie was in awe when viewing all the handsome couples and fantastic decorations. Compliments on her gown were constant, and the evening was like a dream. When it was time to pick the king and queen of the prom, Lorie had no idea that she would be considered. She had many friends whom she thought highly of and was actually hoping one of them would be picked. When she and Jake received the crowns, she thought to herself, *No way! This has to be a dream.* And of course, like all dreams, it came to an abrupt end all too soon.

Later that evening, feeling like she had enough, Gail started to bad-mouth Lorie. She began making up things that Lorie had said to her and about others. At that point, Mark distanced himself from her and just hung around the punch bowl.

Lorie's best friend, Mary Lou, overheard some of the remarks. She knew that Gail was jealous of Lorie but couldn't believe that she would try to ruin the prom for everyone by making such hateful remarks. She didn't know if this was the time or place but felt like Lorie should be aware of what was happening. "Lorie, you won't believe this. Well, maybe you will. Anyway, Gail is saying some really awful things about you. She's actually making up stories. I can't believe anyone would believe anything she has to say. But she puts on this really good act, and I think she may have some people fooled."

Lorie felt sick in her stomach at this news. "Mary Lou, I don't want to cause a scene, but this has got to stop. She has been a pain in my side for years. Maybe it's time to confront her."

Mary Lou looked over at the doorway. "Well, if you're going to say anything, you better catch her before she leaves."

Lorie's eyes met Jake's. He could see that she needed moral support. "Hey, I don't like what she is doing to you either, Lorie. So whatever you decide to do, count me in."

Lorie, Jake, and Mary Lou headed quickly for the door. Just outside the door, Lorie spotted Gail talking to a few people. Walking up to her, she said, "I heard you've been spinning some pretty wild yarns this evening. Would you mind repeating them in front of me?"

Gail's face turned pale white. The others who were standing with her quickly departed. Lorie looked her square in the eye and said, "I asked you a question. Do you want me to repeat it?"

Gail stammered, "I ... I don't know what you are talking about."

Lorie let in on her. "Look, Gail, for years, you have been a pain in my side. I have always gone to great lengths to be your friend, even though I have never gotten any cooperation from you. All you ever seem to do is to make negative remarks behind my back and make up stupid stories about me. Well, let me tell you something. No one believes half the stuff you say, and to top it off, you are making a fool out of yourself. I want this to stop, and I want this to stop here and now. Do I make myself clear?"

With that, Gail hissed back at her as she quickly walked away, "No one talks to me like that. You'll be sorry."

Lorie awoke to the sounds of a ringing phone. She heard her mother answer it and started to drift off to sleep again when her mom appeared in her room. "Lorie, Mrs. Zeller would like to speak to you."

Lorie opened her sleepy eyes and tried to focus. She noticed the confused look on her mom's face. "Oh, Mom," Lorie said as she started to remember confronting Gail the night before. "As you know, Gail has been impossible for years now. Finally, I just got fed up with her talking negatively behind my back all the time. I just wanted it to stop."

Theresa knew what Lorie had gone through over the years with Gail. It wasn't always easy to turn the other cheek. In spite of the difficulties, she admired Lorie for her perseverance. "Lorie, I can't tell you what to do, but maybe it would be good if you would talk to Mrs. Zeller. Let her hear your side. That might help her be able to deal with Gail in an appropriate manner."

Lorie felt like running away, but she knew that was not an option. Noticing the kind smile on her mother's face, Lorie said, "Okay, I'll speak to her."

"Good morning, Mrs. Zeller," Lorie said in a soft voice.

"Lorie, what is going on between you and Gail? She came home last night crying and said that you embarrassed her by talking hateful to her in front of her friends. Why would you do that?"

Lorie was shocked at Mrs. Zeller's description as to what happened. "Mrs. Zeller, that was not what happened. First of all, for years, I have been kind to Gail and tried to be her friend. But she has always been so jealous of me, talking behind my back and making up untrue stories about me. She was at it again last night. All I did was to tell her to stop. I'm sorry if by doing that, it got you upset. I don't have anything against you. I just got fed up with Gail's lies. That's all I have to say now. Do you want to talk to my mom?"

There was a silent pause for a few moments. Then Mrs. Zeller said, "No," and hung up.

Theresa bit her lower lip before speaking, "Lorie, stating that Gail is jealous of you might have been a bit harsh."

Lorie leaned back against the wall as if she was exhausted. "Oh, Mom, it's the truth, and I'm just so tired of it. Why can't people just accept themselves for what they are? Everyone has some kind of talent. Gail could have a good life if she would just focus on the things that she is good at and stop worrying about other people. Maybe I should have said something like that to Mrs. Zeller."

Theresa looked tenderly at Lorie. "Come here, baby. You need a big hug."

Lorie was thankful that her mom was a compassionate and understanding person.

Theresa added, "Don't worry, in a few days, I'll give Mrs. Zeller a call, and we'll have a nice chat. It will be okay. I promise. Lorie, life is a learning experience. When you get out in the workforce, you will again run into these same kinds of problems. Because you have had this experience with Gail, hopefully you will be better able to deal with these kinds of situations when they arise in the future."

Lorie listened attentively to her mom. Once again, she thought, *Mom is so wise.* Looking defiant, Lorie said, "Mom, when I get out in the business world, I am not going to let anyone get to me the way Gail did. I am going to stand firm in my convictions and deal with everything in a very factual and businesslike manner."

Theresa laughed and gave Lorie another hug, saying, "That's my girl! That's the spirit!"

CHAPTER 1

"Ashes to ashes, dust to dust."

The words seemed distant and faintly audible as she sat in the flickering sunlight streaming through the stained glass windows. Lorie hated the thought of being alone after so many years of marriage. She wondered what she would do now. She'd been fortunate, a happily married woman with a wonderful husband, and now ... this. She felt utterly lost and alone.

Jake had always taken care of everything—finances, household repairs, and even the details of their many sailing trips. Their love of the sea had grown with each adventurous jaunt, a mutual pleasure now evaporating.

Her body felt numb due to the stress and concerns of the past few days, and she found it hard to focus. Her head spun with empty details as she sat in the church. Her mind drifted back to when she met Jake so many years ago. She remembered the camping trip and all the things they'd shared together during that time—long walks, gazing at the dappled sunlight filtering through the trees, cascading waterfalls, and the quiet, peaceful nights. A smile crossed her face as she thought of roasting marshmallows at campfires while telling amusing stories. *So long ago.* She knew those memories would stay forever young in her mind.

The funeral Mass dragged on. Father O'Malley's voice faded as Lorie's thoughts again carried her back to happier times. She could almost smell the gentle ocean breeze and feel the warm sun against her skin as she leaned back on the deck of their sloop, her long blond hair flowing in the wind.

Lorie enjoyed watching Jake when they were out at sea. He was a handsome, powerfully built man with dark eyes that frequently reflected the childlike happiness he felt. He had an instinctive intelligence when it came to sailing, and it had been a breeze for him to obtain his captain's license. He'd worked hard to perfect his craft.

Lorie, however, wasn't interested in the techniques or the mechanics of how to sail. She just enjoyed being out at sea on their sloop, *Sunrise*. At times, Jake would try to explain the technical aspects of sailing to her, but it was over her head. Still, she would smile and listen intently, never imagining that she too would someday master the art of sailing.

"Lorie, the sextant works on the same 'split-image' principle as a camera range finder," Jake had explained. "But by using mirrors, two separate objects are brought together in the eyepiece; one is fixed, and one is adjustable. The double-reflecting principle permits great accuracy and is the basis for how the measurements are recorded."

"I think I'll leave the calculations up to you," she said, applying suntan lotion to her sleek bronze toned legs. She'd treasured the hours they'd spent at sea, the two of them alone in a world of waves and swells.

Father O'Malley's voice brought her back to the present. Lorie studied the stained glass window near her. *So intricate*, she thought. *Just like the facets of our lives.* Her eyes swept the inside of the church, tears staining her cheeks. Jake's voice filled her head: *Spring reflects hope, even on this most gloomy day.*

For weeks, Lorie lived in a world of memories, a life that no longer existed, and her despair became unbearable. As the days trickled by, the Bible became her constant companion. Friends and neighbors checked on her often, but she didn't feel like talking to anyone. She sat alone each evening, reading her Bible and hoping to find some answers.

Through her grief, memories materialized, floating through her consciousness like wraiths. She remembered a teacher she'd had in grade school, a nun who always put the Lord first in every aspect of her life. Sister Odilia was getting up in years, but the sparkle in her eyes reflected the love in her heart. She loved working with the children and would often quote scripture to them, especially when she thought they needed it. "We know that all things work for good for those who love God, who are called according to His purpose" (Romans 8:28).

Lorie smiled at the memory, thumbing through her Bible and searching for the passage she sought. Suddenly, a verse caught her eye: "A faithful friend is a sturdy shelter; he who finds one finds a treasure" (Sirach 6:14). The verse echoed in her mind and brought her thoughts to her best friends, Kate and Bob, and how she had been avoiding them lately. It was time to move on with her life. That night, with many unanswered questions still swirling in her head, Lorie prayed, "Thank you, God, for my life. Please help me to bear my troubles." Finding the strength she needed, she was determined and hopeful she would be able to handle the many difficult situations that lie ahead.

Rising early, Lorie peered out her window, watching the chirping birds. It's time to get back to her job and get on with her life. She shuffled downstairs for her morning coffee.

Pondering a plan of action, she found herself dialing Father O'Malley's number and asked him if she could stop over to chat.

When she arrived at the rectory, Lorie saw Father O'Malley standing in the opened doorway, a tall, heavyset man with ruddy dark hair and a kind face.

"Good morning, Lorie." A smile lit up his face.

"Good morning, Father." Lorie held out her hand to him. They walked side by side to his office.

"I was wondering how you were doing but wanted to give you time to grieve." Father O'Malley sat silently for a few moments, waiting for Lorie to respond.

"Father, I'm so confused. I feel that I want to talk about things, but truthfully, I don't know where to start."

"Lorie, changes beyond your control are likely to be more stressful than those you direct. Jake's untimely death is perhaps the most difficult type of stress. You should not rush the grieving process. You must take small steps to fill that void in your life. There are many ways you can do that. Stay active with work, sports, hobbies; all these things will help. It's important for you to have faith in yourself and to put your life, both present and past, in perspective. You have moved from one stage of life to another. Right now, you see this as a negative, but as time heals and you move on with your life, something positive will come from this situation. It's hard to cope at first, but by developing strategies for dealing with these transitions, we can learn how to build on our strengths and even grow in the process."

"Father, your wisdom is enlightening. I guess the main thing I'm worried about right now is that there will be times when events will be out of my control. I'm afraid I'll make a wrong decision. As you can imagine, I'm feeling a little overwhelmed with everything that has happened lately."

Father O'Malley smiled at her kindly. "Sometimes you're better off making a choice even if it turns out to be the wrong one. If it doesn't work out, don't keep blaming yourself. Life is a learning process. We must learn from our mistakes and then move on. Remember, there comes a point when worrying becomes counterproductive and stressful. Think things through carefully before making any decisions. If you need to discuss anything, please feel free to call on me anytime. After all, I'm a good listener." His hearty laugh filled the air.

"Thank you for the meeting today, Father." Lorie stood to leave.

O'Malley also stood. He blessed her with the sign of a cross. "May God watch over and strengthen you more and more each day."

He then handed her a holy card. Thanking him once again, Lorie left with the promise to keep the Lord in her heart and to have faith in herself.

Arriving home, Lorie looked at the holy card. She read the inscription: "Yet the Lord is my stronghold, and my God the rock of my refuge" (Psalm 94:22). Lorie felt better now that she had talked to Father O'Malley. She put the holy card on her refrigerator, a small magnet holding it in place. Seeing this everyday might help her. Now that she decided it was time to go back to work, thoughts of Jake and feeling sorry for herself had to be put on the back burner. It was time to get down to business.

Going back to work was much harder than she anticipated. She tried to take her duties seriously, although she felt a little detached and indifferent at times. She was a good secretary and always enjoyed her work in the past. Now with Jake gone, her world seemed to lack the joy that it once held. She sat back in her chair, staring out the window in silent prayer. A deep emptiness occupied her whole being. Suddenly, tears filled her eyes. "Jake, oh, Jake," she muttered to herself. Thoughts of their sailing trips together entered her mind. The sea was an intimate part of their lives, a cherished escape. She remembered the eager smile on Jake's face as he mastered celestial navigation, and the use of tables required to establish the boat's position, and how he plotted his charts intensely.

"Ursa Major, or the Big Dipper as it is called, is the most important polar constellation in the Northern Hemisphere," he said with enthusiasm.

So many lessons, so many memories. Her thoughts drifted back to one evening in particular. Moving lazily along on a calm sea, she marveled at the beauty of the night sky.

"Jake, isn't it amazing! The stars seem so close. Why, you could almost reach up and touch them!" Lorie exclaimed.

"As you know, our galaxy is the Milky Way and is but one of thousands, perhaps millions, which make up the universe," Jake replied. "No artist could do it justice."

Lorie was amused by his observation. He was right, the wondrous works of God. Looking back down at her desk, she returned to reality. Realizing that it was no use getting sentimental again, she forced herself to think about the projects at hand.

While Lorie had been on bereavement leave, a new CEO was hired at the Glendale Company. Lorie felt like this could not have happened at a worse time. Trying to deal with a new boss only added to her confusion. Every day, James Lowden walked into the office full of pomp, his briefcase under his arm, his steely gray eyes flashing wickedness. There was an air of precariousness about him. A sandy-haired man with a hard look on his face. Lorie felt that he expressed supreme indifference toward her. Was it her imagination? She didn't have anything concrete to base these underlying feelings on. Still, even when he would smile at her, she noticed that his eyes did not smile. She tried to measure him without bias but felt strongly that he was a player, and inscrutability was a minimum requirement. Yet Lorie had a strong sense of duty and tried to make the best of the situation. She noticed that James seemed to be intent on changing things from procedures to staff and was slowly starting to work in corrupted little schemes. She saw him as both clever and pretentious, putting on pleasantries for the board of directors yet having a dual personality.

James's wife, Anna, was lovely and gracious with long dark hair that was soft and glowing and with delicate, flawless features. She wore a large deep green emerald ring on her left hand that Lorie was tempted to praise, but she didn't want to sound overly impressed. Lorie noticed how James looked at Anna disapprovingly whenever she had a question or comment while giving her a tour of the company. Lorie thought that James was domineering and inconsiderate toward his wife. After politely meeting many of the board members, James escorted her out the entrance.

As they were leaving, Lorie overheard James address Anna in a low, breathy voice, "With the formalities over, there is no further need for you to come to the office. From now on, it will be business as usual."

James proceeded to walk her to the car. A disturbing sensation filtered through Lorie; the Lowdens' life appeared to be full of uncertainties, like a paradox. What made James so arrogant and intransigent? Deep in thought, she searched for answers. Grimly, she concluded that James reasoned that his business life was his own, and a wife had her place. Lorie detected a little artificial warmth and wondered if he really loved Anna. She found James's attitude to be inexcusable since there were many social events that went along with the position of CEO. She truly felt sorry for Anna. James apparently provided well as far as material possessions go, but where was the love? Even though it was none of Lorie's business where James's personal life was concerned, this incident made him appear more objectionable in her eyes.

Lorie could not believe how things had changed since she first started working for Glendale fifteen years ago. People had always come and gone, but it seemed like the ones who were left were people she didn't particularly like. They were okay at times but, on the whole, seemed to be cutthroat and backstabbing. She wondered how long she would survive in this environment.

It wasn't always this way.

She remembered when she had interviewed with Sandra Freedman, then the director of Glendale. Sandra was a plain-looking woman, considerate, but somewhat mediocre and a bit disorganized. But Lorie instantly liked her and was pleased when the position as secretary was offered. Sandra assured Lorie that a good career starts with a giving spirit.

"Life gives to the giver. If you continually serve this company well and perform your duties to the best of your abilities, you will work out well here," Sandra told Lorie.

Right from the start, Lorie began to feel at home and was able to balance her home life with her new career.

Lorie enjoyed going to work each day. She worked closely with a girl about her own age, Diane Holden, in the marketing department. Diane was a thin, petite girl with honey blond hair and a huge smile. Diane believed in positive thinking.

"We are the only ones who can put limits on ourselves," she'd say. Diane preferred to think outside the box, giving Lorie more confidence in the daily challenges that were part of her job description. Diane and Lorie quickly became friends and worked on many projects together.

She remembered the annual Christmas party and fund-raiser and how they had to work on it months in advance. Lorie was told that she would be instrumental in organizing the event. This seemed to be a big deal, but Diane convinced her that it would be a snap. She showed Lorie how to start, handing her a long list of area businesses. They had to call everyone on this list and ask for a donation of either a dessert or an item to be donated for the silent auction. Glendale was well-known in the community, and the area businesses supported the company's traditions. Lorie didn't know if she could handle the task, but Diane assured her that she would quickly get the knack of it. "Just butter them up, sugarcoat the request. You'll be surprised how quickly the donations will add up."

Lorie soon discovered that she was a natural when it came to requesting donations. Soon, the lists were completed.

The next step included scheduling employees and volunteers to pick up donations. Again, Lorie was hesitant, unsure if she could persuade employees to help out since some of them didn't seem to be cooperative. Diane again assured her that she could handle the assignment.

"Remember, sugarcoat," Diane said as she handed Lorie the long lists of employees and volunteers.

Lorie started with the volunteer list. The volunteers that she had met since working for Glendale all seemed very friendly whenever anything was needed. The head of the volunteer group was run by an energetic gray-haired lady with an endearing smile. Esther was both efficient and effective. Being a retired widow, she looked forward to working on the many fund-raisers for local organizations. Lorie pulled the volunteer file and quickly found Esther's number.

"Hello, Esther. This is Lorie from Glendale."

"Well, hello, Lorie. What can I do for you today?"

"I would like to meet with you sometime this week, at your convenience, to discuss our upcoming Christmas fund-raiser. Would you be interested in helping with this event?"

"Of course, I would, my dear," Esther responded. "I can stop by the office tomorrow morning, if that's okay."

Cheerfully, Lorie thanked Esther, grateful for the assistance. With Esther's help, Lorie was able to get most everything scheduled for pick-up but found this assignment to be harder than the last one. There were still a half-dozen items that she couldn't pawn off on anyone else. She decided to do the extra work on her lunch break. Lorie didn't mind donating some of her personal time to the company. After all, she liked her job. She also knew that Jake wouldn't mind since he was somewhat of a workaholic himself.

As the event grew close, Diane had one last project for Lorie. "Lorie, you have done such a great job in helping with this fund-raiser. I would like you to come up with a Christmas centerpiece for the front side table in the hall. Just keep a record of your expenses for the materials you need to buy and turn it in when completed."

Lorie looked at Diane in amazement. "You want me to create a centerpiece?"

Diane smiled. "Yes, use your imagination."

Driving home, Lorie thought about what she would make for the centerpiece. Stopping at a craft shop on the way home, ideas began to fill her head. She bought a piece of cotton batting, four red candles, half a dozen large pine cones, artificial snow, and a few tiny figures of carol singers. Enthusiastically, she worked on it all evening. When finished, she sought Jake's approval. "Jake, I needed something special in the way of a table decoration for the Christmas party and was told to use my imagination. What do you think?"

Jake examined it studiously, and Lorie noticed the look of scrutiny on his face. She thought he didn't like it. But then he smiled and said, "It's striking. You're an artist."

Lorie was pleased but also realized that he just might be a little prejudiced. "Thank you, Jake. I just hope Diane and Sandra have the same opinion."

Jake put his arm around her and said, "If they don't like it, they have no taste." They both laughed then headed upstairs for the night.

The next morning, Lorie carefully brought in the centerpiece and placed it on the hall table. As she was arranging it, Diane arrived. "My goodness, Lorie!" she exclaimed. "That is beautiful. Did you do that yourself?"

"Of course, I did," Lorie said. "You told me to use my imagination."

"Wait until Sandra sees this. She'll love it."

Lorie smiled. "Well, if she doesn't like it, I'll just have to tell her my Saint Nicholas story. That always gets a laugh."

Diane looked puzzled. "Okay," she said. "Tell me the story."

"Well, Jake thinks this is so funny, but it's supposed to be true. Anyway, back in those days, according to tradition, a father was to provide dowries for his daughters so that they could enter into a respectable marriage. People looked down on anyone who did not do this and considered it to be unthinkable. Well, there was a poor man who had three daughters. He was a good person and tried his best to live by all the rules. He loved his family and realized that he needed to get the money for his daughters' dowries. But try as he could, it just wasn't happening. It is said that Saint Nicholas heard about this man's predicament, but not wanting to embarrass him by giving him charity, he tossed a bag of gold through the man's window. Saint Nicholas did this on three different occasions so the daughters could enter into a respectable marriage. And that is how eventually gift giving came to be."

Diane shook her head. "You made that up."

Lorie was laughing but insisted that it was a true story. "Hey, Jake laughed so hard when I told him that story. The bag of gold flying through the window every time a daughter wanted to get married really tickled him."

They were still laughing about the story while looking over their lists for the event when Sandra came in. "Who brought that lovely centerpiece in?" she asked.

Diane looked at Lorie and said, "See, I told you she would love it."

"It's really beautiful," Sandra said, patting Lorie on the shoulder. "Thank you so much. Lorie, you seem to be a girl of many talents. I'd like to have your opinion on the menu for this year's party. The girls on that committee have come up with several menus, but we have to make a definite decision today."

Lorie was pleased that she was asked her opinion. "I'll do my best, Sandra," she said happily.

Later that day, Lorie came to Sandra with her evaluation regarding the menus that the committee had put together. "Sandra, I looked over the menus liked you asked, but instead of picking one of them, I took a few things from each menu and put together a new one. This is what I've decided. For the appetizer, frosted pear melba; the salad, endive, watercress, and tomato combination; the entrée, standing rib roast of beef; vegetables, duchess potatoes, green beans with mushrooms and baked acorn squash; for dessert, a date and nut torte with whipped cream and, of course, coffee and tea."

Lorie waited for Sandra's response.

"This sounds great, Lorie," Sandra said, looking over the list. "Have you also thought about the hors d'oeuvres?"

"Yes," Lorie said, pulling another list from her folder, "but I was thinking that maybe someone else would like to create that one."

Sandra held out her hand. "Let me see what you recommend."

Lorie handed her list to Sandra. "Let's see now," she said thoughtfully. "We have salted nuts, stuffed celery, olives, radishes, carrot curls, sugared almonds, chocolate mint sticks, and eggnog."

Sandra shook her head. "No, this would be great if our dinner was a casual affair, but for a formal dinner, we need something more appropriate like assorted tea sandwiches, things like that. Do you think you could come up with some good ideas by tomorrow morning? I will need all lists to be completed and presented to the board at that time."

"I do have many cookbooks at home," Lorie said. "I'm sure I could come up with something suitable."

"Okay, I'll see you in the morning. Be sure to come in early. I'll need some help in setting up for the meeting."

That evening, Lorie spent hours going through her cookbooks, trying to come up with the perfect hors d'oeuvres for the event. When Jake walked into the kitchen and asked if she was coming to bed, she demurred.

"Jake, this is important. I don't want to let Sandra down. She is depending on me to provide the perfect list of hors d'oeuvres for the Christmas event."

"Okay, let me look over what you have so far," Jake said. "I'm a pretty good judge when it comes to food. I know what guys like."

"Jake, remember it's not just guys," said Lorie, laughing. "There will be many influential people at the event, and half of them will be women."

"Yes, you're right, as usual, but let me give you my opinion anyway." Lorie handed him the list, and he looked impressed. "Yes, this does look good. Caviar eggs, escargot, stuffed mushrooms, bite-sized soufflés, sweet and sour meatballs, liver pate, peach-glazed ham cubes, and apricot steak bits. A meal fit for a king, I presume."

"And that is just for starters," Lorie said, again laughing. "Wait until you see what else we are having."

Jake gave Lorie a big hug, kissing her on the forehead. "You are such a dedicated employee. They are lucky to have you. Now you have to get some sleep."

Lorie and Diane were discussing table placements when Sandra returned from the meeting.

"Girls, the meeting went well. Lorie, the board was particularly impressed by the menu. They told me to be sure and thank the committee for doing such a great job. I told them that although everyone was working hard for the event, you were mainly responsible for putting together the menu."

Lorie was pleased.

"Thank you, Sandra. I hope the event will be successful."

Lorie tried not to disturb Jake as she got ready for the big day. He turned over in bed as she was about ready to leave.

"Hey, where are you going so darn early on a Saturday morning?" he asked.

"Jake, sorry, I didn't want to wake you. I have to go in super early this morning to set up for tonight. I'll be back to get dressed for the evening. Don't forget to wear your good suit tonight." She gave him a little kiss. "See you later."

Sandra and Diane were already going over last-minute details when Lorie arrived.

"Lorie, I'm glad you're here," Sandra said. "You can start by helping Diane supervise the table settings. I'll be back shortly."

"I don't know what's going on, but Sandra and the chairman, Bill Green, have not been getting along very well lately," Diane said when she left. "They had another disagreement this morning. I've tried to find out what the problem is, but all Sandra says is that it's a power play, whatever that means."

Lorie was surprised. How could anyone not like Sandra? There was not an ounce of prejudice in her. She was a good businesswoman, kind and fair to all. She did occasionally hear some of her phone conversations. She didn't realize then what that was all about, but now things were starting to become clearer. "Well, maybe it's not serious.

They will probably work out their differences after all the stress of this fund-raiser is over. Sometimes everyone wants to do things their own way instead of realizing that this is supposed to be a team effort."

"I hope you're right, Lorie," Diane said, a worried look on her face. "But you know what they say about gut feelings."

The girls worked with the volunteers for hours, arranging the artistic table settings of fine china, smooth textured linens, and crystal glassware. Low floral arrangements were placed on each table. When everything was in place, they returned home to get ready for the evening.

The evening came and went without a hitch. It was tastefully marked by ingenuity and grace and a lovely end to a rather hectic year. The Christmas party and fund-raiser was always an elegant affair with everyone expressing their usual appreciation and compliments. Lorie and Diane were especially pleased when several of the board members personally thanked them for a job well done.

The New Year brought some rather unexpected changes to Glendale. Sandra Freedman and Bill Green were in constant disagreement, and it soon became apparent that there were major problems between them. Lorie didn't know what to make of Bill Green. With his narrow eyes, sleazy smile, and sophisticated attitude, he seemed to radiate cynicism and impatience. Lorie felt that it would be in her best interest to stay on his good side and was determined not to get involved to the point of playing favorites. Lorie kept telling herself to keep a low profile. She didn't want to jeopardize her job in any way.

The snow softly fell as Lorie awoke to her menacing alarm clock. Yawning, she whispered to Jake to get up. She stared at the ornate snowflakes striking the window. While getting ready for work, she wondered if there would be another battle today between Sandra and Bill Green. Hoping for the best for all concerned, she headed downstairs for breakfast.

"Jake, breakfast is ready!" she shouted while setting the table and wishing the back porch was heated. The snow glazed the landscape so beautifully, and the porch would have been a wonderful place to relax and enjoy the morning.

Jake lazily strolled into the kitchen and shuffled over to the coffeepot. "I can never figure out why you are so darn happy in the morning," he said with a grin.

"Baby, it's a new day! Each day that we are given is a blessing. At least, that is what the nuns always told us in grade school."

"You are my blessing," he said, hugging Lorie. Holding her close to him, he gently kissed her soft smiling lips.

The weeks turned into months, and things continued to worsen between Sandra and Bill Green. Lorie's desk was just outside of Sandra's office. Lorie felt uncomfortable when overhearing phone conversations between Sandra and Bill and wished herself to be somewhere else as calls in Sandra's office would often erupt in arguments. Sandra normally exercised her authority in a direct and businesslike manner, projecting a restrained influence in most situations. But Bill Green seemed to unleash an overwhelming force within her. Lorie sensed that he was backing Sandra into a corner and feared their conflict would eventually turn into an explosive situation.

Arriving at the office early one morning a few weeks later, Lorie was stunned as Sandra ran past her out of the door, shouting, "I quit!" Lorie froze in amazement, unable to speak. She really didn't know what to say. Sandra was quite angry and seemed to be unapproachable. Diane also arrived just as Sandra was leaving the building. She tried to find out what was going on, but Sandra was in no mood to explain.

"I've had it," she said, storming out of the building. "I'm not going to put up with this torment any longer."

The girls stood there for a moment, immobile and confused as they watched Sandra speeding out of the parking lot.

Each day, Diane and Lorie worked diligently in order to keep things status quo while trying to make some sense out of the current situation, arranging files that were strewn about the huge office.

"Sandra certainly had her own system as to where things should be filed," Diane said jokingly. "It may take a long time before we can get things in order so that we can find them."

Lorie agreed wholeheartedly. She paused and looked out the window. The sky was so blue, and spring had arrived; the flowers by the window's edge seemed so graceful. She missed Sandra and was hoping that somehow things would work out and that she would return. Suddenly, she spotted a Rolls-Royce pulling slowly into the driveway.

"It's Bill Green," she whispered. "Boy, this should be interesting."

The girls casually went on with their work as he strolled into the office. Lorie looked up and politely smiled as Diane stood up to greet him.

After the usual small talk, Bill Green stated that since Sandra was no longer with the company, a new director would be hired shortly. "Girls, I want to commend you on handling this situation in a methodical manner. I assure you that the current situation has not imperiled your employment in any way. A new director will be hired within a few weeks. Until then, direct all pertinent calls to my office."

Diane and Lorie looked at each other in astonishment. Looking up at Bill, Diane asked, "So what you're saying is that there is no chance Sandra will be back?"

Bill proceeded to pull a paper out of his briefcase. "According to the bylaws, it expressly authorizes removal without cause. The power to remove an officer rests with the person or persons authorized to elect or appoint him or her. Generally, this power is given to the board of directors. And as you may remember, it was Sandra who walked out on us, leaving no alternative for removal."

With a rather shifty smirk on his face, he calmly walked out the door. Diane and Lorie stared at each other in disbelief.

"I guess we will never find out what really happened between Sandra and Bill," Diane said. "I tried to call Sandra on several occasions, but she is not taking any calls."

"Maybe it's better if we don't know too much," Lorie replied as she reluctantly resumed her tedious task.

It was a typical morning at Glendale, phones ringing, piles of paperwork on each desk, and the smell of coffee lingering throughout the office. A well-dressed middle-aged man casually strolled into the office. Lorie looked up from the stack of papers she was thumbing through. "May I help you, sir," she said.

He stood there for a few moments before speaking, "I was told to come in today for an interview," he said, adding he was looking for one of the board members.

"Please be seated, sir," Lorie replied, and off she went to find out if Diane knew what time the interview was to take place. When she returned, she noticed that the gentleman was already talking with a board member, Sam Davis, who has been with the company since its inception.

Later that day, the girls were told that they had a new boss, Mr. Harry Watson. Mr. Watson was an organized man with a good sense of humor, and he knew the business world thoroughly. He seemed to be good for the company and appeared to get along well with board members. Lorie and Diane worked closely with Harry. There were many programs and projects that were completed satisfactorily under Mr. Watson's leadership. But as time went by, both girls noticed tension brewing between Harry and Bill Green.

Harry learned what had happened to Sandra. Sandra was a free spirit and knew what she wanted to accomplish but wanted to do things her way and in her time frame. Bill Green despised the fact that Sandra would not accept any of his ideas no matter how insistent he was. Bill's dislike for Sandra turned into contempt, causing turmoil between them. Harry didn't personally know Sandra but did feel the administrative control that Bill Green wielded. Harry was determined not to let Bill get the upper hand on him and that he was not going to be forced to leave the company. Harry scheduled casual meetings with board members, usually at a golf course or bar. He was bent on convincing them that there should be a limited time frame in which a board member could serve as chairman. He expressed his concerns regarding the economic development of the company and discussed the benefits of new ideas. Finally, at the next official board meeting, he set forth a formal proposal. After much deliberation, it was decided that board members could only serve as chairman for five years. A vote was taken and the motion seconded. Bill Green suddenly realized that he was losing control. Indignant, he said that the vote was unjust and walked out. Harry had prevailed.

After a new chairman was elected, things were going well, and in due course, even Bill Green accepted the new conditions. But it wasn't long before rumors started about Harry's personal life and how he was always on the town with a different woman. Despite never being a problem at work, Harry's reputation worsened. The situation became explosive when Harry was seen by a few board members having a cozy dinner at the Hilton with the attractive secretary of a state senator. Life at the office became very uncomfortable for Lorie and Diane when several board members asked if they were being sexually harassed in any way.

"Mr. Watson has always been a perfect gentleman," Lorie replied. Diane agreed. Harry was always respectful to the girls in the office, but with all the rumors, they knew that Harry was in hot water.

One afternoon as the girls were leaving the office, Diane said, "Lorie, I just can't take it anymore. I feel like my job is being threatened because I repeated some of the rumors that I've heard. So I'm going to throw in the towel. I've had another job offer, and I'm going to take it."

Lorie was surprised and saddened by this development. She didn't know that Diane was planning to leave, and her confidence slipped away with the news. "Diane, please don't make this decision hastily," Lorie said. "Just think long and hard before you make such a major move. You have worked so long for this company and have always been a dedicated employee. I'm afraid that you will really miss this place if you leave."

"I'm sorry, Lorie," Diane replied, "but I've made my decision already. I'm going to give two weeks' notice tomorrow."

Harry was surprised when Diane calmly gave her notice. She seemed very cold toward him, and he felt a chill down his spine as she spoke. Harry suspected the real reason she was leaving was because she had been responsible for some of the rumors about him. At this point, he suspected everyone, including Lorie. His suspicions got worse after Diane left. Harry became surprisingly cold toward Lorie and more businesslike than usual.

Lorie thought she would be offered Diane's position since they had worked so closely together for a few years, but Harry had other plans. He hired June Chrisner, a woman who was somewhat stern and severe. Lorie felt ashamed by the thoughts that went through her mind regarding this woman. *Lord, forgive me*, she would think as she tried to help the woman get acclimated to the new position. But June seemed to have little experience with office work, and Lorie wondered how June had qualified for the job. Lorie had to do all the letter writing, proofreading, and just about everything else while June treated her like a second-class citizen, collecting a darn good salary to boot. Lorie soon became depressed and discouraged.

After a few weeks, Diane called Lorie one evening at home.

"Say girl, how would you like to meet for lunch one day this week?" Diane said. "I have so much to tell you about my new job."

"Well, maybe we could get together one day next week," Lorie said, hesitating.

Feeling Lorie's reluctance, Diane asked, "By the way, how is the new marketing manager working out?"

"Oh, Diane, I really don't know where to start," Lorie said, almost bursting into tears. "The woman is a real Dr. Jekyll/Mr. Hyde. I'm not kidding. I never know which one she will be when she walks into the office each day. One minute, she can be as nice as ever, and the next minute, she is ready to crucify me even if I'm not responsible for whatever it is that she is mad about. I'm sorry, I shouldn't talk like this, but the woman is making my life miserable."

"Oh, Lorie, I'm so terribly sorry to hear that," Diane said. "I was really hoping that everything would work out okay for you, but with things being what they were to begin with, I really had my doubts that you would be happy there."

Lorie felt like she wanted to tell Diane another rumor that she had heard but was reluctant since the outcome was not certain as yet. Diane sensed that Lorie wanted to tell her something else and kept prodding her on.

"Okay," Lorie replied. "I heard that we are going to get a new director and that the title will be changed to CEO."

Diane didn't seem surprised at the news. "Somehow, I figured this would happen," she said.

Not wanting to continue the conversation, Lorie promised to keep Diane posted. Softly hanging up the phone, she sensed that her life would become more difficult in the coming weeks. The only thing keeping her sane was Jake, who took things in stride and insisted that she not think about work when at home. "Put all that out of your mind," he'd say each evening as he poured her a glass of cabernet.

One by one, the board members entered the conference room where Lorie had made sure everything was set up nicely. Lorie tallied up items in her head that were needed, such as coffee, cups, sugar, cream, and pencils. Everything was perfect, as usual.

Heading back to her office, she thought of Harry and how she felt he was somehow being forced to resign because of the rumors about him. But he enjoyed his work and was good at it. Still, there had been some corruption in the eyes of the board, and they felt that Harry had too many irons in the fire.

"All those ladies … it really was inexcusable." She wondered if his wife, Alice, had heard any of the rumors or if she would believe them. Alice was an attractive woman with an aristocratic air about her. She seemed to live in a world of her own. As long as she had wealth and could travel whenever and wherever she desired, she was happy. "Maybe Alice really didn't care what Harry did so long as she had what she wanted." Lorie wondered if she would have a new boss soon and if Harry would exit the same way Sandra did.

"Here we go again," Lorie sighed as she made her way back to her desk.

The days passed quickly. Lorie continued to carry on her duties at the office and continued to try to please June, something that she was beginning to think was an impracticable task. June was impossible to work with. Lorie tried not to become resentful as she needed her job, but in the back of her mind, she wondered how long she would be able to put up with the stress associated with this monster of a woman. Slamming a group of files down on Lorie's desk, June flashed an arrogant look toward her as she walked away.

Gee, that hair, Lorie thought. *She looks just like the bride of Frankenstein today.* Lorie felt bad for thinking unkindly of her and thought, *Must be stress bringing out the worst in me.*

Lord, help me to get through this day. Please, please help me, Lorie prayed as she continued to work as quickly as she could while secretly counting the minutes before closing time. She took comfort that she and Jake were going out to dinner and would at least have a pleasant evening.

Before Lorie left for the day, she remembered leaving her sweater in the lunchroom. Heading back down the hall, she heard muffled voices in a room. Not wanting to be noticed, she quietly peeked into the room. June seemed to be arguing with a tall dark-haired man who was rather good-looking. Lorie did not want to pry, but the conversation appeared to be somewhat stimulating. She felt that there would be no harm in listening for just a few moments. June seemed rather anxious about something. Suddenly, Lorie realized that the man was June's husband. She found it hard to believe that June would have a husband to begin with, wondering how anyone would want to be married to someone like her. Even though she knew it was none of her business, she wondered what they were so upset about. Something was terribly wrong with this picture. Realizing that Jake would be waiting for her, she quietly exited the premises.

The sunset was pleasing and the shadows mystifying as they made their way to the Village Restaurant. Lorie touched Jake's arm gently.

"What a lovely evening to go out to dinner. Thank you, Jake, for being so considerate," Lorie said.

"You seem to be under so much pressure at work anymore," Jake said. "You need to relax more, baby. You just have to do what I do. When I'm away from work, I put all the problems of the day out of my mind. Enjoy the evening. Tomorrow is soon enough to have to deal with it all over again."

"Yes, you're right. Let's just enjoy the evening."

Jake wanted the dinner to be especially nice for Lorie, trying to get her mind off work. With his recommendation, they decided to splurge. Dinner was elegantly served, starting out with a grape sherry cup and ending with baked Alaska.

"Jake, that meal was absolutely fantastic," Lorie stated. "Thanks so much for a wonderful evening."

"Your quite welcome, my dear," Jake said with a whimsical smile. "How was your fillet?"

"Oh, it was perfect. The whole evening is perfect."

There was a sweet fragrance in the night air as they were leaving for home. Lorie closed her eyes for a few seconds. She was thinking how very fortunate she was to have a husband like Jake.

The next morning, whispers of the approaching dawn swept over Lorie. Awake, she rolled over to reach for Jake and was surprised that he was not in bed. She sleepily ventured downstairs. Finding him relaxed in his favorite chair, reading the *Nautical Almanac*, Lorie felt confused.

"What on earth are you doing up so early?" Lorie said with a yawn.

"I've been thinking about a vacation. We both could use some time away from the smorgasbord of dilemmas that we face each day. Sometimes you just have to get away and chill for a bit. What do you say?"

"Yes, I think that is a great idea, Jake," Lorie said, enthusiasm replacing her drowsiness. "You certainly don't have to twist my arm. Let's try to synchronize our schedules this week."

"It's a deal," Jake replied.

Lorie glided toward Jake and sat on his lap, her arms enveloping him. Their lips met in an ardent embrace as the *Nautical Almanac* fell silently to the floor.

CHAPTER 2

In the dimly lit room, José Tamayo leaned heavily against the wall, smoking one of his favorite cigars that seemed to never leave his lips. His large shoulders and thick eyebrows gave his face an air of decadence. José was Spanish-American, born in the United States, but with strong Colombian ties.

"Do you realize what these drugs would bring on the black market?" he said hoarsely.

June stared at him intensely with a solemn expression. The tone of his voice reflected impetuousness and violence. There were times when she regretted being in love with him.

"I'm not going to let anything stand in my way," he stated. "Working for Glendale would be a great cover for our operation."

"Okay," June replied. "Since I've landed the marketing job here, I do have some input on things in general. So let me see if I could get you hired in the maintenance department. There happens to be an opening right now."

"Don't worry," he said, smiling at her with strangely gleaming eyes. "No one will ever suspect anything. Everyone will think we are just a hardworking couple trying to make a living, working for a reputable company."

June smiled back at him, but inwardly, she had her doubts as to how this would all work out. But she was smart enough not to disagree with him when he had his mind set. Although June loved José, she felt that he could easily dismiss her from his life without a second thought. She hated those feelings and tried desperately to be agreeable.

"See you later," he muttered, walking out of her office.

June sat still for a moment. The weight of her body sunk into the chair. Her mind drifted back to the time she spent in prison long ago. She considered herself fortunate, and she really didn't need José. She'd had her share of female partners in the past and wouldn't mind having a few of them around right now, if they weren't still in jail. She loved José but could go either way. A stealthy smile crept across her lips as she remembered her lustful, ruthless days at the prison. When she told José she was bisexual, he laughed. It did seem to turn him on, but June wondered if he believed her. Better not to say anything else about it now. José was hers, and she wasn't about to share him with a two-bit hooker or anyone else. If he tried to leave, it would be the last thing he'd do. June was determined to please José even if there was a possibility that going along with his underhanded schemes would throw them back into the abyss of past psychological forces. But she thought it was going to work out. She'd make sure of it.

A pale glimmer of dawn was starting to light up the sky. Awakening, Lorie remained silent for a while, closing her eyes and listening to distant sounds through the window. She thought about the birds and how their songs always seemed so happy. She looked over at Jake, sleeping peacefully. She took comfort that "at least he had a good night," even as she had been restless. The conversation she overheard between June and José made her toss and turn. A sick feeling welled up and engulfed her completely. Something was amiss at the office, and she was determined to find out what was going on.

When she arrived at the office, several board members were standing around, looking rather bewildered. Through the grapevine, she learned that the early morning meeting did not go well, and the board felt somewhat put out by Harry's sudden disdainful and impatient exit. Lorie thought it was very odd that both the bosses she had while employed at Glendale left the company in the same way. Manners, in the corporate world of social conduct, were not always applied.

After Harry left the company, the workdays started to drag. June seemed to take over and became more demanding and unreasonable. Lorie tried to squelch hateful thoughts, reminding herself it wasn't productive to think that way. But she couldn't help think that June had qualities fit for a KGB agent. Respectability was apparently something that she had never learned, and Lorie wondered what June's childhood was like. Were her parents responsible people?

Lorie couldn't be cruel about the situation. She felt that revenge is not the key, nor was self-pity.

June Chrisner was born in a poor city neighborhood where children were mostly ignored or used. The first unfavorable influence in her life was her father, who was usually in an alcoholic stupor. The police regularly picked him up at their apartment for disturbing the peace. Instead of hating the police, June became bitter toward her father, Ed. When not in jail or drunk, Ed seemed melancholy and depressed. June was determined that once she was able to leave home, she would never again return. June didn't understand why her mother, who worked for a laundry and dry-cleaning service, stayed with Ed. June hated the vulgarity and self-destructiveness of her home life. She became street-smart at an early age and found solace in unorthodox drug use. Vice was never merely a pleasure for June but a form of liberation. June ended up in prison. While incarcerated, she learned of her mother's death, causing her to develop a violent dislike for Ed. June knew her mother had worked herself to death. She didn't want to wind up like her mother. June needed to get out of prison and get on with her life. But she had no illusions about the hardships awaiting her on the outside. Still, something deep inside her whispered, "You're going to make it, girl. You're going to make it."

When June was released from prison, she'd been scarred. Prison life had been brutal and left her cynical. Because she didn't really have any scruples, June was not ashamed about being in prison. But now she was determined to find work, and she wasn't too particular about what kind of work. Anything would do.

But June's past followed her, and her prison record kept her from getting a respectable position. Finally, a sweet little old man gave her the break she needed. Jack Riley, a retired state government employee, hired her to be his housekeeper. Riley worked with the probation and parole board many years ago and felt sorry for June and the predicament that she found herself in. He told her he'd pay a fair wage for a fair day's work and that, if she proved trustworthy and a hard worker, a good reference would follow. June was thankful, but Riley told her not to let him down. June showed up on time each day to clean, cook, and do laundry, developing a system to quickly finish her chores.

One day, while Mr. Riley was out, June decided to go to the stables to see the horses. She didn't think it would hurt to just take a peek every once in a while as she really admired their beauty. June was surprised to see that they were thoroughbreds. While feelings of wonder occupied her at the sight of these graceful and elegant creatures, June suddenly realized that she was not alone. Abruptly turning around, she saw a dark handsome man staring at her.

"Sorry, I didn't mean to startle you," he said in a soft voice. "My name is José, and I take care of these horses for Mr. Riley."

June extended her hand. "Hi, I'm June, and I take care of the house for Mr. Riley."

They both laughed. After that meeting, June and José saw each other just about every day, if only for a few minutes. Their friendship became strong and binding. Finally, June felt like she could really put the past behind her. Now that she had enticed José to ask her to marry him, and with Mr. Riley's good work reference, she could proceed in a no-nonsense, straightforward way toward a life that she felt she deserved but was, until now, out of reach.

It wasn't long after Harry's departure that James Lowden suddenly appeared on the scene. As a friend of one of the board members, he had the connections necessary to get his foot in the door. When Lorie first returned from funeral leave, she hoped the new boss would help her cope with the situation she faced each day with June. But those hopes were almost immediately squelched as James seemed only concerned with his own well-being and his ability to exercise power and control. He looked upon June's repugnant personality as one of her strengths. In his mind, nice people finished last.

Lorie glanced up at the clock. Almost time for lunch break. Suddenly, José strolled into the office and made his way to the coffeepot. Lorie looked at him disapprovingly. His presence always caused her some concern. Was it because she suspected him of some illicit action, his attitude, or just the sheer weight of his eyes when he looked at her? Regardless, she always felt uncomfortable when he was close. Lorie managed a slight smile, just to make things more agreeable, but continued to look busy so as to avoid conversation. He stepped in June's office and shut the door behind him. Lorie heard the faint sounds of a rather intense discussion. She was tempted to listen but instead headed out to lunch, thinking it was none of her business.

Returning from lunch, she found James standing at her desk, looking through a file. For a well-born heel, it seemed as though he employed every conventional virtue to make himself look more acceptable. Of course, it was only an act. He might have the board fooled, but Lorie saw right through him.

"Lorie, could you come into my office for a few minutes? I would like to go over a project with you before I go out of town."

Lorie followed James and sat down across from his desk. He was standing a few feet away from her while speaking but slowly moved closer and got behind her. Before she knew it, he was massaging her neck and shoulders. Lorie was shocked by this maneuver.

"Mr. Lowden, really!" she shouted, standing up.

James realized that he was out of line and hurriedly apologized.

"Sorry, I didn't mean to offend you. Actually, I must go out for a bit. We can discuss the project later," he said and left abruptly.

Later that afternoon, as Lorie headed over to the water cooler, she passed two women talking in the hall. Since they were from another department, Lorie just smiled quickly and proceeded to get a drink of water. Even though the women were talking quietly, Lorie distinctly heard one of them complaining about James's roaming hands. Lorie didn't know the women well enough to jump into the conversation and acted like she wasn't listening. The women walked back to their offices.

Lorie stood there for a few minutes feeling completely dumbfounded. It appeared that James had a real problem. Lorie did not want to make waves and possibly lose her job by speaking up but wondered what she would do if he tried anything again. She found herself hoping that one of the other women would eventually say something. That way, it would get rid of a depraved boss, and she could still keep her job.

Lorie kept her eyes and ears open at all times. She didn't trust James, José, or June. Her suspicions grew as she kept close watch at the office. She wondered why June had never taken José's last name when they married. Smiling to herself, she thought, *It must be a women's lib thing.*

But soon she began to see a pattern, noticing that James and José were having many closed-door meetings. Lorie was perplexed by what seemed to be a thriving relationship between the two. She knew something was going on, but what? James's attitude had changed over the past few months. He seemed more distant and preoccupied. At first, Lorie liked it that way because he didn't bother her with any more of his obnoxious advances. But as time went on, she sensed that something sinister was brewing between James and José. Lorie had never approved of snooping, but the detective within her wanted the truth. She found herself listening to more conversations at the office and taking mental notes. When James was away, she would look for clues in his office. She found things that she didn't understand but was determined to find out what James and José were up to.

Each time James went out of town, June became more insufferable toward Lorie. Lorie began to feel that June had some sort of personal vendetta against her. On many occasions, June would get highly irritated by the way José would stare at Lorie. Maybe June thought that her husband might be interested in an attractive widow. Was it jealousy that was turning this mentally unsound woman into a monster? Lorie wasn't sure how to handle this predicament. She couldn't confront June regarding this matter even though she desperately wanted to tell her that she thought José was a creep and would not want to be with him even if he were the last man on earth. Comments like that would only fuel the fire. Lorie thought the only thing to do at this point was to stay calm and try her best to get along. Confrontation wasn't her style, but she wondered what would happen if she was provoked long enough.

While working at her desk one dreary afternoon, Lorie sensed someone standing in front of her. She looked at the person quizzically because there were no appointments scheduled for that afternoon. The woman looked at Lorie with dark narrow eyes. Her face seemed hard with thin lips and short dark hair.

"May I help you?"

"I'm here to see James Lowden," the woman replied.

"Do you have an appointment?"

"No, but he told me to stop by sometime today, whenever I got a chance, so here I am," the woman snapped. "I'm a friend of his," she added.

"If you give me your name, I'll tell him that you are here," Lorie replied.

"Monica Goller," she said in a rather nasal voice.

Lorie rang James's office to announce Monica. In a few seconds, James came out to greet her. He gave her a slight hug and ushered her into his office, closing the door behind him. Lorie noticed that the woman wore an extremely short skirt and posh cutout wedge shoes. Lorie thought she looked like a hooker but quickly censured her thoughts. After all, she didn't even know the woman. Still, she wondered what this was all about.

Later that afternoon, James emerged from his office with Monica by his side. He told Lorie to ring June's office and have her come over. While they were waiting for June, James informed Lorie that he had hired Monica to be his assistant. "She'll be sharing this office with you, Lorie. I'm having a desk brought in for her. Please see that she is informed on all the projects that we are currently working on."

A sick feeling rose within Lorie. There seemed to be something ominous about this woman. Lorie tried to smile and extended her hand, but a piercing voice inside her head rang loud and clear, *Here we go again!*

That evening, Lorie called Diane.

"Hi, kiddo," Diane said in a happy tone. "I was just thinking about you today. How are things going with the bride of Frankenstein?"

Diane laughed, but the silence on the other end of the phone gave her sufficient grounds for concern. Diane continued in a low voice, "Hey, Lorie, are you okay?"

"Yes, but maybe just a little down today," Lorie said quietly. "I just felt like I needed to talk to a friend, someone who would really understand, and you popped into my mind."

"Hey, girl, I'm always ready to lend an ear. What's up?"

Lorie began to relate the day's events to Diane. When she finished, both girls sighed. Diane didn't know what to make of the situation and was grasping for some words of comfort to give Lorie. She could find none. Without thinking, she blurted out, "And another monster to contend with!" Lorie knew that Diane really wasn't trying to be funny. She was always there when Lorie needed to talk. Lorie didn't expect anyone to have answers, but it always helped to talk about things rather than to keep it locked up inside. Diane was Lorie's shoulder to cry on whenever things got difficult or impossible at the office. The girls ended by agreeing to have lunch together the following week. Hanging up the phone, Lorie headed upstairs, thinking, *I'll just take things one day at a time. Yes, one day at a time.*

Lorie's thoughts wandered back to the last vacation she and Jake had together. Flying to the Bahamas, they landed on a perfect sunny day at the Nassau International Airport. By three o'clock in the afternoon, they met their captain and crew of a sixty-five-foot catamaran and got on board with ten other people. Everyone was in a good mood. It was a six-day trip out at sea, stopping off to visit a few islands. Lorie remembered how the captain made them laugh with stories of *Blackbeard* and pirates treasure. She remembered the two educational trips to see the Bahamian lizards and the Cays Land and Sea Park, the oldest national park in the Bahamas. The catamaran then headed for park headquarters on Warderick Wells. There, they hiked to the highest point on the island and viewed a magnificent turquoise bay accentuated by a crescent of pure white sand. The days were sunny and the water crystal clear. She remembered all the wonderful sights while snorkeling with Jake—lavender vase sponges, colorful coral and queen angels, yellow goatfish, sergeant majors, and, her favorite, the queen trigger fish.

"Well, baby, this is it, the last evening of our trip. Did you have a good time?" Jake asked with a twinkle in his eye.

"Oh, Jake, I can't remember having such a relaxing time," Lorie said. "The weather was splendid, and the people are great. It's just been a perfect vacation."

Jake smiled, pondering thoughts of their next trip. "The bartender whipped up a batch of margaritas," he said. "Let's join the others. Who knows, maybe we might get to hear another *Blackbeard* story."

Lorie laughed as Jake hugged her. Yes, golden memories tucked away in the hidden recesses of her mind.

The next morning, Lorie arrived slightly earlier at the office. Today was Monica's first day at work, and Lorie wanted to get things organized before her new co-worker arrived. She had just started when Monica strutted into the office. Looking over her shoulder, Lorie did a double take. She couldn't believe what she saw. Monica looked like something out of *MAD* magazine. She wore a short jumper, sky-high Louboutin boots, and a hairdo that reminded her of a porcupine.

"Good morning, Monica," Lorie said methodically.

"Yeah," Monica replied as she proceeded slowly to her desk.

Lorie noticed the beads and several gold chains hanging on Monica's neck. She wondered if those chains had come from James. Mentally scolding herself again for thinking such thoughts, she started to instruct Monica about her duties as James's assistant. She wasn't surprised to see how little Monica knew of office procedures. This was a rerun of what she had to contend with when instructing June. Lorie wondered how these people got hired and became anxious for quitting time. She couldn't wait to tell Diane about this undesirable situation.

"Diane, I've been trying to call you all evening. You won't believe today's events at the office. It's just mind-boggling, to say the least."

"Hey, slow down, girl," Diane said, noting the agitation in Lorie's voice. "Sounds like you had an eventful day. I'm almost afraid to ask what happened."

Lorie proceeded to give Diane all the sordid details of the day. Diane's thoughts mimicked Lorie's completely as she said aloud, "How do these people get hired? Surely, there is more to this than meets the eye."

"Yes, of course," Lorie replied. "Like this afternoon when James went out for a smoke break, Monica went out for her smoke break too. Now I wasn't trying to spy, but I did happen to look out the window to where they were sitting, and you won't believe this, but Monica was rolling her own cigarettes. Now I'm wondering if maybe it wasn't just regular tobacco."

There was a bewildering tone in Lorie's voice. Diane was baffled by these unusual developments. Not knowing what to say, Diane reassured Lorie that eventually everything would work out one way or the other.

"Just hang in there for now, girl," Diane added. "Remember, nothing lasts forever. Don't worry about the office when you're at home and do what we both have always agreed on. Just take things one day at a time. It's all you can do."

Lorie agreed and felt somewhat at peace with herself that evening. After all, she was doing her best each day to try and get along at the office, even though she did not understand the nature or character of her co-workers. That night, Lorie prayed for strength and tried to believe in her heart that tomorrow would be a better day.

As the weeks went by, Lorie got the impression that James was conducting business as usual during the day, but later in the evening, an unlawful or unauthorized operation kicked in. Judging from invoices she found, Lorie figured that he was somehow moving ill-gotten funds into the company. It involved a series of complex financial transactions. Then the illegal funds were accounted for by adjusting a legitimate transaction. She didn't understand how he was skimming money for himself, but she was pretty sure that this was something that he and José were doing together. Afraid to say anything for fear of reprisal, she decided to wait until she had more evidence.

"I turned the money over to my broker," José said. "He will purchase the goods for us. Proceeds will be good, minus his commission, of course."

James intently stared at the invoices on his desk while speaking in a whisper, "This will all be done below government radar, of course."

"As usual," José replied.

"We can't get careless now. The money must always be broken up into smaller, less suspicious amounts. We don't want the banks to report any large transactions to the government."

"James, you forget, I know my business. Trust me." José flashed a malicious smile as he leaned against the wall.

"Well, as long as we use various financial transactions, bank-to-bank transfers or wire transfers, and continually vary the amount of money in the accounts, it will be difficult for the feds to follow," James said. "We've got to make the dirty money as hard to trace as possible. Then make it appear to come from a legal transaction."

José leaned forward, his smile taking on a serious hue. "Ah, today's generation of drug traffickers have become much more sophisticated than in the past. They don't want to antagonize their own government or, for that matter, Washington, DC. Yes, technology is the key and, of course, our trusted human couriers."

"You seem to know your stuff."

"Time increases knowledge, James."

"Incidentally, the pot you smoked back in the sixties and seventies carries a more powerful punch nowadays. The THC content has been rising. Yeah, what can I say, genetic modifications and improvements in cultivation. That's what did it."

James looked over his shoulder at José. His tired face showed no skepticism or cynicism. He felt he could rely on him.

"José, I need you to meet with the supplier and make the necessary arrangements with him so that a deposit can be made into my foreign bank account."

"I'll take care of it," José said, then walked slowly out of the office.

José was born in a poverty-stricken area of Brooklyn. The neighborhood was rife with hoods and gang members. His mother was a loving person who tried to steer her son in the right direction, but his father's alcoholism and drug use caused José to feel alienated and rebellious. He started smoking pot at a young age and dropped out of school. Before he realized it, he was involved with a local gang and started to deal drugs. The money was good. He had a natural con man's charm and thought he had found his niche in life. But he started to screw up and wound up in prison. While incarcerated, he realized that an early parole was possible for good behavior, even if he had to fake it. Since he was determined to get out as soon as possible, he took courses that helped him to get his diploma. That looked good on his record, and the parole was granted.

While reading books, José became fascinated with horses and was determined to find a job working with the animals. He figured that would keep him out of trouble and out of prison. The prison set up an interview for him with Jack Riley, a former probation and parole officer. Jack had several thoroughbreds and was looking to hire another stable hand. During the interview, Jack thought that José was "a victim of circumstances, born on the wrong side of the tracks." He admired how much José had learned in prison regarding the care and training of racehorses. He decided to take a chance on him.

"You've got the job, José, but let me down once, and you're out. Is that clear?"

José was elated. He was determined that nothing would prevent him from excelling at this job. This was the chance he was waiting for. But as time went on, drugs and money tempted him more. Before long, his past became part of his present.

James was left deep in thought. He knew they had to make it impossible for authorities to trace the dirty money while it was cleaned. José understood the peso exchange and worked well with the peso brokers. His financial consultant oversaw the foreign investments, deals made for tax exemptions, and drug money being laundered through his connections. That resulted in a kickback on the laundered money. James pulled out his checkbook. Looking over his expenses, he figured that if he cut down on the amount of cash that he took from his paycheck, he could use the laundered money to make up the difference. He thought that as long as he took some cash from his paychecks, the government would have a hard time proving he was doing anything inappropriate. James knew he was in too deep to back out. He slowly turned out the lights and left the office.

Morning came all too soon for James. The dark gray fog seemed to swallow his car as he tried desperately to see the road. James always put on a good front for the board, and he wasn't about to let bad weather keep him from making the monthly board meeting on time. James forced a smile at Lorie as he entered the office. Then he motioned for Monica to come with him. Lorie found it hard to believe that James would actually take Monica into the board meeting.

Lorie thought it wouldn't be so bad if she looked professional. She wondered what the board members thought of Monica. Today she wore a suit, but it was way too short and way too tight. The stiletto platform pumps only magnified her appearance.

"Good morning, gentlemen," James said.

Taking a seat, he proceeded to open his briefcase. Monica greeted everyone and offered beverages to the members. Then she sat silently with pen and notebook in hand, ready to take the minutes. Although she pretended to know shorthand, there was a concealed tape recorder as her secret weapon. James tried to appear optimistic during the meeting but had trouble concentrating. He hoped the meeting would be short today. Listening to everyone's comments, he tried to think of a way to end the meeting.

"Yes, stimulating the economic development in the region is important," James said, "and we have already maintained many successful partnerships with government agencies and corporations in the regions. Your ideas for future development are insightful and require further discussion. We can continue this topic at our next meeting. Please have your reports ready by then. Also, at our last meeting, we discussed having a fund-raiser. Have you given any thought as to what kind of event would be appropriate?" James eyed each committee member as he waited for suggestions.

Finally, a voice from the back of the room announced, "Let's have a tennis tournament." Al Chambers, a longtime board member, had arrived later than the others. Not wanting to disturb the meeting, he sat inconspicuously in the hazy sunlit room.

Becoming aware of Al's presence, James smiled sardonically and said a bit testily, "Glad you could make the meeting, Al."

Al was a slim willowy man with an infectious smile. James wasn't one to openly give credit where credit was due, but he did think the idea was good.

"Okay, do we have any other thoughts or opinions to present before taking a vote regarding the tennis tournament?" Everyone seemed to be in agreement. A formal proposal was suggested. A vote was taken and the motion seconded.

"Gentlemen, we've gotten much accomplished today. We'll discuss the details at our next meeting. Thank you and have a good day."

James was relieved when the meeting finally came to an end. Board meetings were a waste of time and too political. Casting a devilish look toward Monica, he nodded, and she followed him to his office. She sat across the desk from James, and he stared at her crossed legs, noticing the lace of her panties peeking out from under her short skirt. He smiled derisively as he picked up the phone.

"Anna, don't wait on dinner for me tonight. I'll be working late this evening. Our next fund-raiser was discussed at the board meeting today, and I'm in the middle of making some arrangements for that event."

Monica looked at James with eyes of pure steel. She sensed an aura of invincibility about him.

"Well, that was easy," she said as they left for her apartment.

That evening, James stood by the window, staring out into the night.

"What are you thinking?" Monica asked.

He got back into bed and pressed her body against his. "I want you to play in the tennis tournament."

Monica gasped as she pulled away. "I'm afraid I would make a mockery of the game, James. I haven't played in years."

"You know what they say about riding a bike," James said, laughing. "It will all come back to you. Don't worry; you'll have months to practice. After all, it's not the US Open. It's just a fundraiser, and you're in."

Shopping for something appropriate to wear for the tournament, Monica found a hot little outfit. Hurrying home, she ran upstairs to try it on again. Looking in the mirror, her hands glided over the detailed stitching of sequins and seed beads that bedecked her white sleeveless top. This wasn't an ordinary tennis outfit, but if she was going to play, she wanted to look damn good doing it.

Even though Monica had always liked the sport, being pushed into a tournament at this point in time left her with mixed feelings. She wanted to please James, but she was afraid that she would wind up making a fool of herself on the courts. She glanced down at her flattering white shorts with the crossover V waistband that hit just below the navel. Remembering the tennis videos and private lessons that James had arranged for her, she thought she would be ready for the challenge.

James sat in brooding silence at his desk, deep in thought. He always thought that money, power, and success were the most important things in life. Now he had the power and ability to seize the moment. It might be a double-edged sword, but he was confident he could deal with it.

The ringing phone interrupted his thoughts. James answered and said a bit irritably, "What is it?"

"You have a call on line two, James," Lorie said.

"It better be important. Who is it?"

Lorie wanted to say, "Forget it," and just walk out of the building. Instead, she reminded herself to be businesslike and not take anything personally. "It's Al Chambers."

"Okay, put him through."

"How are things going with the tournament, James?"

"Good, they're going good, Al," James replied. Al's sunny disposition created a vision of a giant smile in James's mind. James stifled a laugh. "I've talked Monica into being one of the participants. She spends all her free time practicing."

"Excellent!" Al said. "If there is anything I can do to help out, just give me a buzz."

"I'll keep you in mind, Al. Thanks for calling."

Lorie noticed how James's personality would change when he had to deal with a board member. It was as if he had an ulterior motive for working at Glendale. Even though she would not tell anyone, she knew that James and Monica were having an affair. She also suspected something else was going on behind the scenes. She knew in time she would learn the truth and that everything would become clear.

Monica was watching a tennis video when her phone rang.

"Hey, baby, it's me," James said. "How's it going? Learning anything new?"

"Well, yes, I did, actually. Each player is allowed three challenges per set plus one additional challenge during a tiebreak. The player keeps all existing challenges if a challenge is successful. If the challenge is unsuccessful and the original ruling is upheld, the player loses a challenge. Does that make sense to you?"

James couldn't help but smile. He knew that she was just trying to be cute in her own way.

"Hey, you're the expert," he shot back. "I've arranged some practice sessions on the courts tomorrow, so be there at nine o'clock in the morning sharp."

"Yeah, okay, nine sharp. I'll be there. Is that it?"

James laughed. "Yes, that's it for now. Try and get a good night's sleep tonight. I'll see you in the morning."

The next day, James and Al watched as Monica practiced with a pro from the local club.

"She's amazing," James said.

"Remarkable, she makes it look easy," Al replied.

Monica stood at the net, waiting. When the pro hit a shot deep to the baseline, she took off in full flight. While still running, she flicked her wrist and whipped a shot across the net, surprising herself. *Gee, I hope that wasn't just a fluke. Maybe I'm really getting the hang of this.*

As the tournament approached, June was glad that Monica was out of the office more often to practice. It was apparent that they didn't like each other. Lorie often overheard June making unkind remarks about Monica. José seemed to find it amusing and would really irritate June, saying "catfight," and bursting into laughter.

Lorie, weary from the office tension, felt like she needed a break. She decided to call her old friends, Kate and Bob. It had been a long time since she'd seen them. Before Jake passed away, they would often get together.

"Hi, Kate, this is Lorie. Remember me?"

"My god, girl, how could I ever forget one of my best friends? Bob and I were just talking about you yesterday, and we were thinking that maybe you would be interested in double-dating with us next Saturday, but we didn't want to offend you if you thought it was too soon. What do you think?"

"Golly, Kate, things have been so hectic and unbelievable at the office that I haven't even given that a thought as yet. It seems like each day I go into survival mode just to get through the day."

"It's that bad?"

"Yes, I'm afraid so," Lorie sighed.

"Well, that answers my question," Kate said. "It's time for you to have a little fun. You know what they say about all work and no play. So it's settled. We'll pick you up on Saturday at seven o'clock in the evening. Be ready for a fun evening: dinner, show, and dancing afterward."

Kate would not take no for an answer. Lorie was almost sorry that she called. She didn't know if she was ready to go on a date but decided to give it a try since she trusted Kate.

Lorie was nervously waiting for Saturday evening to arrive. When Kate, Bob, and their friend Rich arrived, they made quick introductions and left for dinner. Before leaving the restaurant, Kate and Lorie went to freshen up.

"What do you think, kiddo?" Kate looked deeply into Lorie's eyes, hoping to see some kind of approval.

"I don't know, Kate. I'm sure Rich is a nice person, but he's really not my type. This whole evening is making me feel very awkward."

"Hey, give him a chance, why don't you?" Kate said. "You feel strange right now because you lost your husband, but you can't sit at home and cry for the rest of your life. Remember, life is for the living. It's important to make the best of each day. It's time to move on, Lorie."

Lorie felt trapped. As much as she always enjoyed time spent with Kate and Bob, she didn't particularly like Rich or really have anything in common with him. Maybe she still missed Jake too much. Maybe in her mind, no one would ever be able to replace what they had together. Only time would tell. But one thing she was sure of, Rich would never be a person that she would want to date. She didn't want to hurt Kate and Bob, and she knew they were worried about her being alone. They meant well. But she wanted to end this charade without hurting anyone's feelings. She did her best to get through the evening graciously but made no promises to Rich to see him again.

Lorie dreaded going to the office on such a dreary Monday morning. As she picked up her car keys and headed out the door, she wished she could call in sick today and actually get away with it. Approaching the office, loud voices echoed in the hallway. It sounded like a heated discussion. Hesitantly, she walked in. James, June, Monica, and Al suddenly stopped talking and looked toward the doorway.

"Good morning," Lorie said meekly, not knowing what was going on. Suddenly, she felt like maybe she had done something wrong.

"Lorie, you're just the person we want to see," James said.

Lorie felt a lump in her throat and swallowed. James told her the woman who was to be Monica's opponent in the tennis tournament was unable to play. She had slipped going down her basement steps and fractured an arm. After much deliberation and because of the time constraints, they were not able to get anyone else to take her place. Since all the flyers and advertisements had gone out, nothing could be cancelled at this point.

"Lorie, we have taken a vote and made a decision regarding Monica's new opponent. You will be filling in for us."

Lorie's mouth fell open. She was speechless for a few moments. "James, I couldn't possibly play in the tournament. It's been a long while since I've played, and I would need a lot of practice before I would be able to even attempt something like that. I'm afraid I will have to decline."

"No, no, no, my dear Lorie, you don't understand," James said sternly. "I'm not asking you to do this. I'm telling you. You have a few weeks to practice. I will have someone work with you for a few days after work and go over the rules of the game. Now if you'll excuse me, I have to leave for a meeting."

James defiantly walked out of the office. Al followed him, looking somewhat bewildered. Monica and June stood there smirking, as if to say, "You are going to look like a fool on the courts." They headed back to their workstations.

Lorie felt sick in her stomach all day. She knew it was just nerves. How in the world could she accomplish such a task? She tried to remember everything she had learned taking tennis lessons long ago. She certainly needed to practice. Monica was given time off to practice, but Lorie had to do her work plus Monica's work, so her practice time was limited.

When she arrived home that evening, she heard the phone ringing even before she opened the door. Thinking it was Diane or Kate, she rushed to pick it up. "Hello."

"Hi, Lorie, this is Rich."

Lorie almost felt like crying. Besides having a terrible day at the office and having to deal with the tournament, now a man she didn't particularly like but had to be nice to was on the line. All she could muster was a big sigh.

"Lorie, are you okay?"

"Yes, I'm sorry. I just had a bad day at work today, and I'm very tired."

"Well, I won't keep you, but I just wanted to know if you would like to have dinner with me Saturday night."

Lorie was glad that she had a legitimate excuse for not going out with him.

"Rich, my boss informed me today that I have to play in our tennis tournament. It's a fund-raiser that we are participating in this year. I'm afraid I will have to decline your invitation, but thank you for asking." Lorie hoped that information would end the call.

"Lorie, that's wonderful. I'll come to watch you play. How do I get a ticket?"

Lorie thought it couldn't get any worse. Then she decided to level with him.

"To tell you the truth, Rich, the girl who was supposed to play had an accident. I was pushed into this at the last minute, and I'm not near ready for anything like this. I haven't played in a long time. My boss is a complete ass, excuse my French. So I don't think you would enjoy the fund-raiser. Save your money."

Lorie felt like hanging up the phone but didn't want to be rude.

"Lorie, I play tennis, and I'm not trying to brag, but I'm not bad at it. I could work with you this week a little, if that's okay with you."

Lorie was surprised by this suggestion but decided to decline the invitation. "Thank you for offering, but I don't think anything will help at this point."

"Hey, I don't charge." Rich laughed. "Let's get together tomorrow evening. What have you got to lose?"

Lorie thought for a moment, *He was right. I had nothing to lose. It can't possibly get any worse.* Reluctantly, she agreed.

The weeks seemed to be flying by, and Lorie was thankful for the help from Rich. Things started to come back to her as she practiced more. She was so focused on the tournament that she developed a one-track mind. She didn't realize that Rich was becoming more attracted to her as they spent long hours together practicing.

"Well, tomorrow is the big day, Lorie," he said. "How do you feel about it now?"

"I feel nervous and numb at the same time," Lorie said. "Does that make any sense? I'll be glad when it's all over."

Rich smiled. "Hey, I would really like to see you play. Would it be okay if I showed up? I promise I won't be disruptive and make you laugh."

At this point, Lorie didn't care who was there. She sort of felt like jumping off a cliff anyway. Lorie tried to ignore his question, thinking she'd give it her best shot. If James wanted to fire her afterward, so be it. She started to get her things together.

"I'm going to turn in early tonight," she said. "Thank you so much for all your help, Rich. You have been so kind, and I really appreciate it."

"Hey, no problem," Rich said, putting his arm around her. "Why don't we get something to eat before it gets too late?"

Lorie nonchalantly maneuvered out of his embrace.

"I'll have to pass this evening. Tomorrow is a big day, and I still have things that I want to take care of tonight, but thank you once again for all your help," Lorie said, quickly heading for her car.

Rich stood there, watching as she drove off. "In the best of my dreams, there you are."

Lorie glanced in the mirror before leaving the house. She thought she looked physically fit in her white shorts and shirt. Even though her sneakers were very comfortable, she bought thick woolen socks to cushion her feet. Speed was important, and she didn't want her feet to start hurting and slow her down.

When Lorie took the court, everything around her seemed like a blur. She tried to focus, scolding herself for being nervous, and kept telling herself it was only a game and for the fund-raiser. She'd do her best and go home. She tried to keep these thoughts in her mind, but then she saw Kate, Bob, and Rich. She was hoping to play without her friends watching.

The game started. Lorie spotted Monica. She reminded herself to focus as she gripped the handle of her racket. Monica stood behind the baseline on the right side of the court. She threw the ball straight up into the air, and as it started coming down, she hit it hard with her racket. The ball hit the net. Monica was surprised. The second serve was also no good. Monica had double-faulted and lost the point. As the game progressed, Monica's ball sometimes went into the net or out of bounds, earning Lorie the points.

Monica must be as nervous as I am today, Lorie thought. Strangely enough, this made her feel more relaxed. As the game continued, Lorie started to attack. In the following game, she hit a few aces and was able to adjust to each situation. She was glad that Rich had worked on her topspin and flexibility. Monica's spirits were sinking. Even though she felt completely lost in her first set, she was determined that she was not going to leave the game disillusioned and slowly started to fight her way out of the quandary. She never thought of Lorie as a worthy opponent and wondered how much effort it would take to get back into the match. Although she had played well during her practice sessions, she realized that it wasn't always easy to play your best tennis in the first set.

Finally, Monica was up a break point in the second set. The crowd cheered, giving her more confidence. Monica slammed an ace to save a match point. "Time to start using my sublime backhand more often," she whispered to herself, smiling.

The game continued to ebb and flow. Lorie was consistently good returning serves, taking advantage of Monica's lack of steadiness and timing. She slowly inched toward victory, converting a second match point with a forehand winner and serving an ace to wrap up the win.

The victory was a complete surprise to James. He looked frustrated and thought that Monica must have hit the bottle before the game. "Why couldn't she have waited until afterward? Dames," he said under his breath in disgust as he headed to the bar. "Next thing you know, they will probably be giving Lorie the Newcomer of the Year award."

With the tournament over, Lorie was surrounded by co-workers and board members. She basked in their congratulations and good wishes and felt like a celebrity.

But when Lorie saw Monica walking off the court, she noticed the severe look she gave James as she walked away. James returned the stare with glassy cold eyes until he noticed board members congratulating Lorie for her win. He walked down to greet them, his demeanor changing.

Lorie was packing up her gear when a man with a notebook approached. "Lorie, I'm Matt Phillips, a columnist from the *Evening Post*. I need to get a few quotes about your terrific game today."

"Hi, Matt," Lorie smiled as she turned to greet him. "I don't know what I could say about the match. Actually, I believe it was luck. I was ready for a tough match. There were some things that weren't good in my game, but I tried to keep a positive attitude. So I really kept fighting to the end. Monica was a good opponent but didn't seem quite consistent today. I believe we both had a case of the nerves. There was a lot of tension out there. But hey, it was for a good cause and really a lot of fun."

Monica approached Lorie and Matt. "I didn't shake your hand," Monica said as she extended her hand to Lorie. Lorie was surprised by Monica's sudden change of disposition and thought it was probably just an act. Still, Lorie was pleased that Monica was trying to act properly, if for no other reason than the sake of the company and their fund-raiser.

Matt turned to Monica and asked how she felt about the game.

"It's not really the way I wanted it to end," Monica said with a crafty smile. "But I'm okay, and I was happy to be able to help with the fund-raiser. It was a lot of fun."

With a wave of her hand, she was gone. Matt watched her as she walked away.

"Glendale is very fortunate to have such loyal employees such as Monica and yourself, Lorie. I'll have some positive remarks regarding this event. Be sure and read my column." He shook her hand again before leaving.

"Thank you, Matt," Lorie beamed.

"Lorie, Lorie, Lorie!" Kate shouted as she, Bob, and Rich ran over to greet her. "What a terrific game, girl! You looked like a real pro out there. What drama!"

"Hey," Lorie replied. "You have to thank Rich for all his meticulous help and persistent practice sessions."

"I know quality when I see it," he said, touching her arm while looking into Lorie's eyes.

An uneasy sensation filled Lorie as she saw the longing in his eyes. She wondered how she could get rid of Rich now. Did he think she owed him something, like being his girlfriend?

Lorie quickly tried to change the subject. "Hey, they have tons of good food here today. Please, guys, don't waste any time now. Hope you are hungry." Lorie turned around abruptly. Someone again was calling her name. Diane came running over to her.

"Hey, girl, way to go," she said as she gave Lorie a little hug. Lorie was so relieved to see her. Now she had an excuse to get away from Rich.

"Guys, this is a very good friend of mine and a past co-worker, Diane Holden. Diane, please meet Kate, Bob, and Rich, my good friends from the yacht club."

After the introductions, Lorie casually managed to slip away with Diane for a bit. "Diane, I am so glad that you showed up when you did. I wanted to get away from Rich but didn't know how."

Diane looked surprised. "I thought they were your friends, Lorie. What gives?"

Lorie knew that it was only right to give some sort of an explanation, even though her feelings were unsettled. "Diane, I really like Kate and Bob. They were friends for a long time with Jake and me. They seemed to be worried about me being alone and set up a blind date with Rich a few weeks ago. I'm sure Rich is a nice guy, but he's really not my type, and I don't know how to handle this without hurting him. I think he has gotten the impression that we will be going together, and sometimes he comes on strong. Not in a bad way, of course, but I can see the yearning in his eyes, and it makes me feel very uncomfortable."

Diane was surprised and laughed at Lorie's predicament. "Why, you old Mata Hari!"

"Diane, I'm serious. Rich is also in my yacht club, a relatively new member, but has been friends with Kate and Bob for a good while. He seems like the type who would try to get even if I don't date him. I hope I'm wrong, but I feel he has that kind of personality."

"Gee, Lorie, I'm sure it will all work out somehow. Just be yourself. The one person you have to be true to is yourself. You can't go through life trying to please everyone because no matter how hard you try, there will always be someone who isn't pleased. You just have to do what you feel is best for you. After all, if you don't take care of yourself, who will?"

Lorie looked bewildered but knew what Diane was trying to say. "You're right, of course, Diane, but sometimes things are easier said than done."

Diane patted Lorie on the shoulder, and they walked over to join the others.

"What a day," Lorie said to herself as she glided into her house and flopped down on the sofa. The phone rang. Lorie was almost too tired to answer it. She reached over to pick it up without moving from her spot. "Hello," she mumbled.

"Lorie, are you all right?"

Lorie was relieved when she heard Diane's voice. "Yes, I'm fine, just very tired."

"That's understandable, of course. I won't keep you. I couldn't really talk at the fund-raiser, but my goodness, I was so surprised to see what Monica was wearing for the tournament. I was just wondering what you thought."

"Diane, what can I say," Lorie said, laughing. "Monica is Monica! You should see how she shows up for work most days. It's unbelievable."

"What do you suppose James thinks about this?" Diane said, giggling.

Lorie hesitated for a moment before speaking. "Diane, I don't like to gossip. For one thing, I need my job. So if you can promise that you will never ever repeat what I'm about to tell you, I'll let you in on what I've discovered."

"Lorie, I promise. What in the world is going on?"

Lorie was sorry she said anything but blurted out, "James and Monica are having an affair."

"No way!" Diane shrieked.

Again, Lorie wished that she hadn't mentioned it but continued, "I'm afraid it's true. Actually, as much as James is a real rat, I feel sorry for his wife. Anna is a beautiful woman, and she impresses me as being a very nice person. Frankly, I don't see what James sees in Monica with her unconventional use of language, spiked hair, and sluttish wardrobe. What can I say? They say love is blind, and in James's case, it seems to be true."

Diane took a deep breath. "I'm speechless! You know, Lorie, to be perfectly honest, I was watching James and Monica at the fundraiser for a bit, and I sort of got that impression before you ever said anything about it. Now I'm wondering if other people see it too. What do you think?"

Lorie thought for a moment. Suddenly, she burst out laughing. Diane was puzzled.

"Lorie, what on earth is so funny?"

"Diane, I'm not trying to change the subject, but I have to tell you something funny about Monica. You see, she really doesn't have much, if any, office experience. She was hired because she was James's friend. My assignment was to teach her everything I know, and let me tell you, she's not real swift most of the time. Anyway, to get back to what I was laughing about, since Monica is James's personal assistant, she attends the board meetings each month. She is supposed to take notes and type the minutes afterward. But I've observed her on different occasions when she is supposed to be taking shorthand. God, this is a hoot!"

Lorie started laughing again. Then calming herself down somewhat, she continued her story, "She sits there scribbling and trying to look professional, if that's possible, but all the while, she has this little concealed tape recorder going."

"Goodness! Is that legal?" Diane gasped.

"All I know is that I do all the work," Lorie signed, "but James tries to make Monica look good in every situation. Sometimes I feel like the company rug, something for him to wipe his feet on." Lorie looked at the clock. "Gee, I didn't realize it was so late. We'll have to continue this discussion some other time. Please remember not to repeat any of this."

"Lorie, don't worry. My lips are sealed. I learned my lesson when Harry was our boss."

Lorie was almost too tired to make a comment but added, "I would take Harry any day over James. Believe me, there is more going on than what meets the eye at Glendale."

CHAPTER 3

Monday morning already, Lorie thought as she hurriedly got ready for work. She wondered what James, Monica, or anyone would say to her about the tennis tournament. She knew that James was very annoyed by Monica's failure and was hoping that he wouldn't take out his frustrations on her. Arriving at work, she tried to hide her fears.

"Good morning, James," she said in a friendly voice.

"Morning," he said in a dry tone of voice, barely looking at her as he walked into his office, closing the door behind him.

Monica showed up a few minutes later. She didn't seem to be in a good mood either. Lorie hesitated before saying, "Good morning."

Monica glared at her for a second but said nothing. She walked over to her desk, sat down, and fiddled with the contents of her purse.

Lorie thought, *If looks could kill, I would have been dead in an instant. What's with these people? Just because I won the tennis tournament?* Lorie knew that this was going to be one of those days when the phrase "walking on eggshells" would be a reality. To make matters worse, June walked into the office and slapped a group of folders down on Lorie's desk with a list of what she wanted done for the day. Lorie was used to this treatment from June, so she silently started the tasks at hand. Looking up, she noticed that June was just standing there instead of walking away as she usually did. "Is there something else you needed, June?" Lorie said.

"It would have been nice if you had asked me that during the fund-raiser on Saturday. I could have used some help then, but no, you had to run all around the place with your friends after the tennis tournament. James didn't appreciate that either. I'm sure he'll say something to you about it."

Lorie was shocked. She stood up and stared June in the eye. "June, if you remember, I was playing in the tennis tournament. It was a struggle just to be playing that long. I was exhausted afterward."

"Oh boo-hoo," June said as she walked away. "Just don't let it happen again!"

Lorie was perplexed. She looked toward Monica's desk and was not surprised to see her co-worker harboring a pernicious smile. A hopeless feeling welled up in Lorie. Had she fallen into the devil's den?

James sunk down in his chair, closing his eyes and holding his head between his hands. At this point, Monica was the least of his worries. Throughout everything, one worry remained: keeping up the charade. Laundering drug profits became more complex as time went on. With his legitimate front and José's reliable connections, what could go wrong? But the insanity of it all had been building. The ethical principles that he previously held, if ever there had been any, were now an unrecognizable maelstrom. His thoughts traveled back to a time long ago when life was simpler. Thoughts of his father briefly entered his mind. George Lowden, a stocky, round-faced, and balding man, was a barber and worked long hours to provide for his family. James recalled his dad reprimanding him on many occasions, telling him to buckle down and get serious. "Put first things first," he used to say. But as time went on, James became rebellious. Flashbacks of his college years flooded his mind: a room filled with books, empty glasses, and half-empty beer bottles, weekend parties, and girls, girls, girls. Back then, he was full of enthusiasm and idealistic dreams.

Dreams are cheap, he thought as his mind drifted to the present. *Now it will take guts.* "Monica, could you come to my office and bring your notebook," James squawked over the intercom.

Monica strutted into his office, a conceited smile across her face.

"Now, now, James," she cooed, "why so uptight? The board was really pleased with the fund-raiser. Sorry I wasn't your shining star, but hey, nobody's perfect."

James disregarded her remarks. "The board meeting is coming up. Make sure Lorie has everything ready and in order and make sure you're there on time. That's it." James resumed looking at the papers on his desk.

Monica stood there for a moment, her expression one of pure ice. She hastily left his office, slamming the door behind her. "You don't shut me out just like that," she whispered under her breath.

Lorie looked up, startled by the strikingly loud noise, thinking there was trouble in paradise.

James greeted the board members as they slowly trickled in on a dreary morning. "It's great to see you all here. And glad you could make it before the end of the meeting, Al," he said with a wry smile. A ripple of laughter filled the room.

"Wouldn't miss it for the world," Al responded. A huge smile filled his face as he added, "If you're going to make this organization go places, then you can count on me."

"Thanks Al," James replied. "I guess you are referring to the successful fund-raiser that we had on Saturday. Monica, would you please pass out the agenda and reports and read the minutes from our last meeting."

Monica's voice sounded a little scratchy. James wondered if she had coffee or breakfast yet. She was not a morning person, and getting ready for the early board meetings was a trial for her. When she finished, a motion was made to approve the minutes, then seconded.

James reported that the results from this year's fund-raiser far exceeded those of prior years, both in attendance and monies raised.

Curtis Thompson, chairman of the board, slowly stood up as he interrupted. "James, in the past, we've had the holiday party fund-raiser and then again had one in late spring or early summer. Since this one was such a success, I would like to get everyone's opinion about having another one in the fall this year."

"You're not talking about having another tennis tournament?" James gasped.

"No, no, no, although the girls did a wonderful job," Curtis said, chuckling. He glanced over at Monica and nodded. "I was thinking of a golf tournament."

James looked at Curtis, a heavyset man, and wondered whether he was indeed a golfer. Curtis caught the expression of anxiety on James's face.

"Now, now James," Curtis continued. "I know that fund-raisers are a lot of work and very demanding, but you have a wonderful staff and a group of volunteers that is second to none. If anyone could pull this off, I'm confident that it's you."

James took the compliment to heart. *If that's what the old boy wanted, then that's what he was going to get.* He exchanged smiles with Curtis.

"Okay, do we have a motion to proceed with a golf tournament in the fall?" Al raised his hand first, and the motion was seconded.

"On motion duly made and seconded, this resolution is unanimously adopted," James said in a crisp voice.

The meeting rambled on with all reports duly noted and placed on file. Finally, after much discussion, James tried to hasten the progress without looking too impatient. "Gentlemen, I believe we have covered all pertinent material," he said. "Do I have a motion for adjournment? On motion duly made and seconded, the meeting is adjourned."

Heading back to his office with Monica, James whispered, "How's your golf game?" Monica glared at him for a few seconds, then hurriedly walked back to her desk.

"She'll come around," James sighed. "There's no doubt about it."

Lorie was surprised to learn about the golf tournament and was hoping that James would not include her in any of the activities. As she continued to go about the tasks at hand, June's shrill voice echoed over the intercom. "Lorie, come to my office, now!"

Lorie felt her skin crawl. *This couldn't be good.* She was barely in the office when June shouted, "Didn't I ask you yesterday to bring me the flyers on past events for this project I'm working on? Well, where are they? Were you too lazy to go into the closet down the hall to get them?"

As usual, Lorie was stunned by this ridiculous accusation. "June, I couldn't reach them. The box in front of what you needed was too heavy, and I couldn't even reach it standing on a chair. So I asked the custodian to get them for me. I was waiting until he had time to do it."

"When I tell you to do something, you don't go running to the custodian," June said, her face beet red. "That is not his job."

James heard all the shouting and came into the office. "What's going on in here?" he sounded irritated and gave June a cold, piercing stare. June repeated what she had told Lorie. James dismissed Lorie coldly. Heading back to her desk, she wondered what James was going to say, so she quietly snuck back toward June's closed office door and listened intently. Lorie was surprised to hear James reprimand June.

"June, what has gotten into you? I was walking down the hall when I saw Phil up on a stepladder fidgeting with old boxes. I asked him what he was doing, and he told me that he was getting flyers for Lorie because she couldn't reach them and almost fell off a chair, trying to get those heavy boxes out of the closet for you. My question to you is this: Who gave you the authority to change Lorie's job description? She is not a custodian. She needs to help Monica with the many projects that are going on here and can't very well do that if she's in the hospital with a broken leg collecting workman's compensation. Is that understood?"

June wanted to just get up and strangle him but didn't want to do or say anything that would jeopardize her job or, for that matter,

José's. She knew José would throw an angry fit if she made waves, and getting slapped around was something she went out of her way to avoid.

"Sorry, James, I didn't realize those boxes were heavy and on the upper shelves. I just thought Lorie was being lazy again. I don't believe in wasting time, so I try to keep after her."

James didn't buy it for a moment. He knew how June treated Lorie, but he didn't care. He needed Lorie to do most of the work for June and Monica and didn't want to see her injured playing custodian. Once again, with a stern voice he said, "Are we clear?"

June nodded in submission as James departed.

June sat in her office, stewing. *He'll not talk to me like that and get away with it. No way! Now all I have to do is to think of something that will get Lorie in trouble, big-time. Then we'll see how kindly he talks to her. Yes, that will make my day.*

At that moment, José walked into the room. He could tell that she was upset. "What's going on?" he said.

"José, you won't believe how James just spoke to me. He was actually yelling at me for no reason."

"Come on now, June. What did you do to piss him off?"

José's comments seemed more like yelling than asking. This infuriated her that much more. "Look, you yourself have noticed that James seems to be getting a little unhinged on occasion!" she shouted. "We have a lot going on here, and I don't want him screwing up things for us. I don't want to wind up in jail again because of his inability to cope with things. Test him out, José. See if we can really trust him with our current operation. If not, he'll have to be cut off." June leaned back in her chair. A look of exhaustion settled over her face.

"June, get hold of yourself. We have a good operation going here. I don't need a wife who is going to blow everything by acting irrationally. I will deal with James when I see fit, not before. Now get that look off your face and get back to work."

José walked out of the room, slamming the door behind him. June sat there for a moment, almost paralyzed. Finally, she got up and slowly walked over to the window. Looking out over the distant hills, she thought about how to get back at Lorie. It was her fault that James yelled at her. She couldn't let Lorie get away with that. *Okay, Lorie, get ready for some fireworks.* June smiled to herself as she started thinking up a plan.

Lorie was diligently working when the daily mail arrived. She went through the stack meticulously as always. She knew how fussy James was about his personal mail and was careful not to open anything that would upset him. She set everything that she considered personal in his inbox before dealing with the usual "menagerie," as she called it. As Lorie continued to work on the mail, Monica walked over to her desk.

"Hey, I need you to look at something I'm working on for James. It will only take a minute."

Lorie knew that whenever Monica needed something, she was supposed to stop whatever she was doing to help her. If she didn't, she would pay a price when Monica told James. She quickly walked over to Monica's desk with her. While she was distracted by Monica, June walked to Lorie's desk, pulled out a personal piece of mail from James's inbox, slit it open, and put it back into his inbox. She left the room quickly, unnoticed. Lorie was soon back at her desk, completing her morning duties before lunch.

After lunch, Lorie barely had a chance to sit down when James's angry voice came over the intercom, calling her into his office. She glanced at her watch. She wasn't late getting back from lunch. Opening the door slowly, she stepped into his office. Not saying a word, she stood there until James looked at her. He threw the opened envelope at her.

"What do you have to say about this?"

Lorie looked confused. She picked up the envelope and looked at it. It was a personal piece of mail that she remembered placing into James's inbox earlier but couldn't understand what point he was trying to make.

"Well, Lorie, I'm waiting for an answer!" he shouted.

"James, I don't know what you want me to say. This is a piece of mail that I put in your inbox earlier today."

"So tell me why you thought it was your business to open it before putting it in my inbox?" James's face was bright red.

"James, when I put that piece of mail in your inbox, it was sealed. I never open any of your personal mail, and I don't know how that happened."

Lorie figured she was being framed by June or Monica but was not about to suggest that to James, as that would only magnify his rage. She stood there waiting for him to fire her but was surprised when he sat back down and dismissed her coldly.

"Get back to work and don't let it happen again."

James looked back down at his desk and continued going through his mail as if she was already out of the room and not worth worrying about.

Lorie walked out and shut the door quietly behind her. She noticed June standing by Monica's desk. The two girls smirked at her as she walked back to her desk.

It's obvious what happened, Lorie thought. From now on, when she was away from her desk, she'd put the mail in a plastic bag and take it with her. Lorie felt her spirits sinking. After a short prayer for strength to get through the day, she labored on but felt that her efforts were unrewarding and pointless.

The phone was ringing even before Lorie got into her house that evening. She hurriedly ran over and picked it up.

"Hi, Lorie, did you just get home?" It was Rich.

Oh God, she thought. *Why did I pick up the phone? After a day like today, I'm in no mood to try to be nice or kind to Rich.* Sounding disappointed, she said, "Oh, hi, Rich."

"Hey, sounds like you had a rough day," Rich said, noting the tone in her voice. "Bet you're too tired to cook. Would you like to go out to dinner tonight?"

Lorie was tempted to say, "God, no!" Instead, she told Rich she had a rough day at work and was just too tired to be good company tonight. Maybe another time would be better. She tried to get him off the phone as quickly as possible but in a gentle and considerate way. She always tried to treat people like she would want to be treated, in a respectful manner.

After hanging up the phone, she said to herself, *Doesn't he ever give up? What can I say or do to make him realize that I'm not interested? I don't want to hurt his feelings, but at some point, that is exactly what is going to happen in order for me to get my point across. Oh, I do dread that moment, but it's inevitable.*

The phone rang again, and she prayed it wasn't Rich calling back. Lorie picked up the phone slowly. She was relieved to hear Kate's voice on the other end.

"Hey, Lorie, Rich called and invited all of us to dinner Saturday evening. He's doing the cooking, and let me tell you, he is a good cook. He had us over for dinner before. Bob and I can be over to pick you up around seven? What do you say?"

There was a long silence on the other end of the phone, and Kate wondered if Lorie was still on the line. "Lorie, are you there?"

"Kate, I think I mentioned this to you in the past. I'm sure that Rich is a nice person, and I know that you and Bob have been friends with him for many years, but truthfully, he just isn't my type. I don't want to hurt his feelings, but I don't want to do anything that he would consider to be encouragement either."

"Lorie, it's just dinner for goodness sakes," Kate said. "You can go with us and leave with us, no strings attached. Besides, give him a chance. He's the type of person that sort of grows on you."

Kate laughed, but Lorie didn't think it was funny.

"Can I get back to you on this?"

Kate was still laughing. "Lorie, you're just too serious. I'm not taking no for an answer. See you on Saturday."

As the phone call ended, a hopeless feeling crept through Lorie. She really liked Kate and didn't want to ruin their friendship but wondered why she was trying to push her into a relationship with someone she wasn't attracted to. Maybe she didn't realize the harm this could cause in the long run. What could she do to make her understand? Confused and bewildered by the situation, Lorie decided to try and put everything out of her mind. After fixing dinner and relaxing with a hot bath and a glass of wine, Lorie turned to her only comfort when she was alone. Picking up her Bible and cuddling up on the sofa in her favorite blanket, she proceeded to find a peaceful end to a traumatic day.

A dream sailed through Lorie's mind that night. Through a mist, Jake's face came into focus. They were on vacation. Jake was smiling as they ran along the shore and played in the surf. The warmth of the sun and the wind felt invigorating against the coolness of the water. Lorie glanced up at the palm trees as they swayed gently in the breeze. The mist began to get deeper and deeper. Suddenly, Lorie was awake.

"No, no," she cried. "Don't go, Jake! Don't go!" Almost immediately, she fell into a dark-hued somber sleep.

Lorie sat at her desk, thinking about her dream the night before. It was a happy dream but ended too soon. Bittersweet feelings overwhelmed her. She knew that she couldn't sit there and cry and tried to put the dream out of her mind as she watched Monica and James head out for a smoke break. Even though she thought James was arrogant, egotistical, and self-centered, she couldn't understand why he was attracted to Monica. She figured that Monica probably saw money signs when she was with James. Or maybe it was the power she felt being the boss's girlfriend. But what did he see in her? With her crazy spiked hair and her generally punk style, how could anyone possibly be turned on by that?

The ringing phone caused Lorie to spring back to reality. "Glendale Corporation! This is Lorie. How may I help you?"

"Hello, Lorie. This is Anna," she said in a soft, soothing voice. "How are you doing?"

Lorie liked Anna, but this was puzzling. She was such a beautiful person, in body and spirit. How could she let James treat her so badly? She seemed intelligent. Couldn't she see through him? And if she could, why did she put up with it? If there was an answer, it was beyond Lorie's realm of comprehension.

"Lorie, since James is going out of town tonight and won't be back until late tomorrow, I was wondering if I could drop something off at the office for him to sign. I'm calling to see if he already left, or if I could still catch him."

Lorie was confused. She always knew when James went out of town because she made the arrangements. She was about to tell Anna that he was not scheduled to go out of town but hesitated.

"Lorie, are you still there?"

Lorie suddenly felt like she was between a rock and a hard place. She knew the repercussions would be bad if she didn't say what James wanted, but what was she supposed to do? They never had personal conversations. She was told what to do each day and nothing more. "Sorry, Anna. I was just trying to find that schedule. It's not at my desk right now. Can I call you back in a few minutes?" Lorie was bewildered but tried to hide her confusion.

"Sure, Lorie, but I do want to catch him before he leaves. Maybe I should just take my chances and come out."

A panic button went off in Lorie's head. She didn't know how to handle this. Voices in the hall were getting closer. James and Monica were coming back from their smoke break.

"Anna, could you hold on for just a minute?" she said as James and Monica walked into the room. "I'll be right back."

"James, Anna is on line one. She wants to bring something to the office for you to sign."

Lorie saw the annoyed look on James's face, but he took the call.

"Yes, Anna, what is it?" James sounded perturbed. "No, it doesn't have to go out this week. Don't worry about it. I'll take care of it when I get home. I'll be back tomorrow night, late, so don't wait up for me."

Before he hung up, Lorie heard him say, "Yeah, me too." Then he and Monica left for the day. Lorie wondered about the "yeah, me too." She figured that Anna must have said, "I love you," before they hung up, but James couldn't say it back to her. All he said was "yeah, me too." How sad and unfortunate for Anna. Lorie was in the habit of saying little prayers each day just to get through the day. Now she sat in silence, bowed her head, and said a little prayer for Anna.

Lorie was relieved when the workday was over and hurried out of the building. The day had been stressful and left her feeling exhausted.

She knew she needed a good night's sleep. Even though she felt too tired to eat, she needed to keep up her strength and looked for something for dinner. Leftover spaghetti, breadsticks, and spinach salad. "A meal fit for a queen," she said, chuckling to herself as she warmed up the spaghetti.

After dinner, she was startled by the ringing phone. "Hi, Lorie. How's my favorite girl today?" Lorie was irritated by the sound of Rich's voice and even more annoyed by what he said. Why would he say something that stupid? She didn't want to be his favorite girl. Still, she tried to be kind.

"Hi, Rich, I'm fine, just very tired. I had a rough day at work again today, and I'm getting ready to turn in for tonight."

"That's okay," Rich replied. "I won't keep you. I just wanted to call to invite you to my place for dinner Saturday night, and I would be honored if you would do me the pleasure by accepting. I might add I'm a really good cook," he said as he laughed jovially. Lorie felt sick to her stomach. She knew where this was going and didn't want to go there. She wondered if she could get out of this.

"Rich, can I get back to you on this?"

Lorie could feel the concern in his voice as he asked, "Is there a problem? I've also invited Kate and Bob, and Kate mentioned that they could pick you up."

Lorie was lost for words. "Rich, I'm just exhausted right now and need to sleep. I'll call you back tomorrow." After a quick goodbye, she hung up the phone. Angry feelings toward Kate welled up in Lorie for having set the date with Rich in the first place. How in the world was she supposed to get rid of him? She was beginning to feel like there was a leech clinging to her and that she was smothered.

Tomorrow would be another hopefully better day, she thought as she headed up the stairs. Her head rested softly on the pillow. Sleep loomed over her like a comforting blanket.

Lorie was up early the next morning, refreshed from a good night's sleep. While she sat in her kitchen with her usual cup of coffee, she thought of last night's conversation with Rich. She still didn't know what she was going to say to Rich about Saturday. She had to focus on work. She'd call Kate and ask her how to get out of this mess. She knew Kate and Bob thought the world of Rich, and it wasn't going to be easy. But she needed to do something.

Lorie's mind was racing as she drove to work. *So many decisions to make and no real guidance.* Pulling into her parking space she prayed, *Lord, please help me get through yet another day.* Surrounding herself with an invisible shield of prayer, she solemnly marched into the office.

The phones started to ring before Lorie got settled at her desk. Since she was not supposed to start work until nine o'clock in the morning, she was reluctant to answer them too soon. Hearing heavy footsteps from the hallway, Lorie looked up. June came stomping into the office with a wrathful look on her face. Lorie felt like she was caught in a snare. She always thought of June as a Dr. Jekyll/ Mr.

Hyde personality and never knew which character would emerge any morning.

June looked at Lorie with vehement indignation as she shouted, "Are you goofing off today, or are you going to answer the damn phones?"

Lorie tried to answer in a calm voice without trembling. "June, it's eight forty in the morning, and I just got here. I'm not supposed to start working until nine o'clock in the morning, but I do answer the phones as soon as I get in and get settled even if it's before nine. I was just about to pick up the phone before you walked in."

"Pick up the damn phone now. As soon as you're through, come to my office." June stomped out of the office.

Lorie quickly picked up the phone. After taking care of the calls, Lorie headed to June's office with low spirits and diminished vitality. She knocked softly on June's door before opening it. As soon as she stepped into the office, June commanded her to sit down. Lorie could not understand why June was so upset and apparently mad at her. She had done nothing wrong but realized June always felt better after lecturing someone. June had to feel like she was in control of everything and everyone at all times. Lorie knew this session would not be good but hoped that it would be over quickly so she could get back to work.

"I'm doing my annual performance report on all employees under me," June said. "I'm told that the general purpose of this report is to be as mutually helpful as possible but at the same time to prevent wasting time on a person who is not likely to prove satisfactory. After I present my reports to James, he will have a personal conference with each employee. Then he will decide whether or not the employee will work out here in the long run. I might add that James values my opinion but also will take into consideration how the employee tries to clean up their act and measure up to what is expected of them at Glendale. Are we clear on this?"

Lorie noted the hostile behavior and wished that she could write a report on June. "Yes," Lorie said dryly.

"Okay, now that we are clear on that point, let me go over some of the things that I have written in your report. There are three columns: good, fair, and poor. Here are the categories: instructions, following instructions, initiative, industry, accuracy, clearness, speed, and general cooperative spirit. I believe that you fall into the 'poor' category in each of these classifications, and that is what I am submitting in my report. If you can make a sincere effort to improve, maybe James will be lenient. That's all for now."

June continued to go through papers on her desk without looking up and, with a wave of her hand, dismissed her. Lorie knew that it was useless to try and have a meaningful conversation with June. Walking back to her desk, Lorie realized she was the one who trained June and Monica. Neither of them knew much about office work to begin with, and Lorie seemed to be doing all the work that they were supposed to do. It was crazy. She was working with a bunch of uncanny people. Years ago, Glendale was such a great place to work. How could a situation this bizarre develop? Lorie knew she had to make things right. It might take time, but eventually, she'd find out what is really going on around here.

James sat quietly at his desk, recounting the details of the past few months, enumerating all the possible pitfalls. A soft knock on the door interrupted his train of thought. James looked up as José slowly walked into the room. "Everything under control?" James said, trying to be casual.

José nodded.

"We just made a big score, pot and heroin. As payment to myself, I kept a couple of kilos."

James looked like he had seen a ghost, his eyes angry and piercing. "What are you trying to do, open the proverbial Pandora's box? If we are caught with any of this stuff, it's all over. You know that."

"Hey, the way I have stuff stashed, no one would ever find it," José said. "Christ, they would literally have to tear down my walls. Why are you so uptight, James? Relax, everything's cool. Trust me." José smiled stealthily as he relaxed in the chair by the widow.

"Look, José. So far, our timing has been impeccable," James said. "Just don't go getting careless on me now."

James began working through the papers on his desk. With the conversation abruptly ending, José got up and slowly walked out, closing the door behind him. James felt sick to his stomach. His mind flashed back to his fearless college days when he could be consumed by an unmanageable obstinacy. His rebelliousness now edged more toward an attitude of defensiveness.

I could use a shot of bourbon right now, he thought. With that in mind, he spoke into the intercom, "Monica, could you please come to my office."

Monica casually strolled in, softly closing the door behind her. A sultry smile crossed her face as she moved slowly toward him. His thoughts swirled uncontrollably as he took her in his arms. Remembering that they were in his office, he stepped back. "I need a drink. How about you?"

Monica nodded. Heading over to the cabinet where he kept his liquor, he quickly poured them each a glass of bourbon.

"James, you seem so uptight. Is everything all right?"

James took another sip of bourbon. "Sure, everything is fine. Now that you're here, let's talk about the upcoming golf tournament."

Monica knew that James was trying to change the subject since she had seen José leave his office just a few minutes before. She was sure that they had a disagreement but didn't know why James was not confiding in her.

"Okay, James, cut the crap," Monica hissed. "I saw José leave your office. He didn't look happy. What's going on?"

"I should have never gotten you involved with any of this, Monica," James said, a dull ache of remorse in his voice. "Actually, everything is fine right now, but there are times when I feel that José is getting a little careless. If the bottom drops out, just play dumb. You don't know anything, got it?"

"Hey, James," Monica replied, "José is a pro. He knows what he's doing. He has good connections. Yes, he's a real casual person on the outside, but he has all his trumps in place on the inside. You worry too much. Relax!"

Her silk dress seemed to float over her body as she moved closer to him and glided into his arms. Caressing the fine woven material, his mood softened. His tension eased, and for the moment, life was simple again.

Lorie glanced at up at the clock across the room. This was her favorite time of day, and being able to leave the office somehow made her feel victorious. Today, however, was different. She had another problem to deal with as soon as she got home. Lorie tried to conceive a plan before she walked in the door that evening. She had to put a stop to this matchmaking. *Kate means well, but it had gone far enough.*

Entering her house, Lorie headed straight for the phone. She wasn't sure how to resolve this but felt that it was Kate's responsibility to help her get out of this current situation with Rich since it was Kate and Bob who created it. Lorie took a deep breath when Kate answered the phone.

"Hello!" Kate shouted breathlessly.

"Hi, Kate, I'm glad you're home now. I really need to talk to you about something."

Kate sensed an urgency in Lorie's voice. "Yeah, I just got in the door, but hey, what's up?"

"It's about the dinner Saturday night at Rich's place," Lorie replied.

"He told me that we were all invited, but Bob's mom is having a dinner at her place for his brother's birthday, so it doesn't look like we will be going. But I told Rich that we can pick you up and drop you off at his place. Then he can take you home later that evening."

Lorie was almost speechless. She couldn't believe that Kate would make all these arrangements without consulting her first.

"Lorie, are you there?"

Lorie felt her temperature rise but didn't want to say anything that she would regret later.

"Yes, I'm here. I'm just surprised that you would make all these plans without talking to me first."

"Well, I didn't know what Bob's mother had planned for Saturday," Kate explained. "When I found out, I called Rich right away because I didn't want him to plan a big meal and buy all that extra food. Actually, I think he likes the idea of having a romantic dinner for the two of you."

Lorie felt defeated and was lost for words. How could she make Kate understand she wanted no part of this? Honesty seemed to be her only option. "Kate, you are my friend, and I know that you mean well. I also realize that Rich is a good friend to both you and Bob, but like I tried to tell you before, he is just not my type. I don't want to hurt him or cause a problem for you, but please try to understand where I'm coming from. I don't want to date Rich. I know that he is a nice guy, but truthfully, I'm starting to feel smothered. You know how stressful my job is. When I go home at night, I want to feel like I can relax. I can't have someone demanding my free time. He seems to think that I am his girlfriend, and that has got to stop right now."

Lorie took a deep breath. Now Kate was lost for words. She felt the anguish in Lorie's voice. She hadn't realized that she had caused any problems. Her only intent was to help Lorie get through the bereavement period.

"God, Lorie, I am so sorry. I didn't realize ..." Kate could not finish her sentence. Tears filled her eyes as she began to see the predicament as Lorie saw it. "What can I do to help?" she said meekly.

"Kate, can you come over tomorrow evening after work? Let's try and figure out how to deal with this situation. The longer we put it off, the worse it will get. I know Rich will not be happy at first, but if we explain the situation in a nice way, maybe we can all still remain friends."

Kate agreed with Lorie's logic, but as they ended their conversation, unsettled feelings abounded, and Lorie knew that sleep would not come easy.

The next day, Lorie hurried home after work. She hoped that Kate would get there early enough to have ample time to figure out a plan. The more she thought about it, the more complicated it became. Perplexed and deep in thought, the doorbell quickly brought her back to reality.

"Kate, I'm so glad you could come over tonight. I hate to make waves, but I truly hope you can understand where I'm coming from."

"Lorie, I owe you an apology," Kate said, almost in tears. "I never meant to cause you any problems. Bob and I have been friends with you and Jake for so many years. When Jake passed away, we worried about your well-being. We didn't want you to feel alone or that you should quit the club just because your sailing partner was gone. We also felt that you would need help with the upkeep on your boat. I'm really sorry now, but at the time, we thought Rich would be a good companion for you."

"Kate, you don't need to apologize for anything," Lorie said, hugging her friend. "I know your intentions were good. Maybe it's not Rich that's the problem. Maybe it's me. Maybe it's just too soon for me to jump into another relationship. With my job being so utterly crazy and me still missing Jake, I just can't take any more pressure right now. They say time heals. Just give me some time."

The girls hugged again.

"Lorie, I do understand where you are coming from, and I don't want you to get stressed out about this situation. Heaven knows, you have enough on your plate already. Bob and I have known Rich for many years. I'm sure he will understand. I don't think he is the kind of person who holds grudges. Now put some coffee on, and let's figure out the best way to handle this."

A soft drizzling rain filled the morning sky. Tired from the long hours spent talking with Kate, Lorie almost felt like calling in sick for work. But she thought it best to go in and that June would be more hateful toward her if she called off sick. What she really needed was a vacation away from everyone and everything.

As soon as she got to work, James called her into his office.

"Have a seat, Lorie. I want to go over your yearly performance report.

Oh, God, I'm really not in the mood for this nonsense right now. Please, God, help me get through this.

"Now let's see," James continued. "It looks like you have rather low grades on every aspect of this report. Would you like to comment on this?"

"Yes, I would," Lorie said, taking a deep breath. "I believe I have been resourceful in many ways. I trained both June and Monica for their positions, and I am cooperative and helpful to them whenever they need anything. I get to work on time each day, and I get my work done efficiently. I would also like to add that the success of a business, in my opinion, depends to a large extent on the wisdom of management, not on one individual."

"So I gather that you don't feel that this report is accurate," James said, glaring at her. "Well, well, well, let's see now. For starters, you will need to improve the quality and quantity of your work. You will also have to take the initiative to try and develop more responsibility. In other words, try to take more interest in the company and your work. Also, you will need to become more flexible when changes occur. If this is acceptable to you, then I think we can find some common ground."

Lorie felt her blood boil. Nothing he said made any sense to her or even applied to her. She was a good employee who always went out of her way to please everyone, plus get the work done. What was he talking about? Once again, Lorie was lost for words. Trying to have a conversation with James was almost as worthless as trying to have one with June. *How did these people ever get the positions they held?*

"I'm lost for words, James. I've always given this company one hundred percent and followed a logical sequence for any assignment that I've been given with standards for speed and accuracy."

James wanted to end the meeting just as much as Lorie did. He was aware that she carried much of the workload for the other girls and really didn't want to push her into quitting. Abruptly, he changed the subject. "We have a fund-raiser coming up in the near future. It's the golf tournament that we talked about previously. In your spare time, start practicing. We'll talk more about this later. I have to leave to go to a meeting now."

James picked up his briefcase and started pushing papers into it. Confused, Lorie hastened out of his office, closing the door sternly behind her. Walking back to her desk, she noticed June leaning against a doorway. After staring coldly at Lorie for a few seconds, she turned and walked away. *If looks could kill.*

As soon as Lorie got back to her desk, she saw Monica approaching with an arm full of folders. *What was this about?*

"Lorie, James wants us to start working on the upcoming fund-raiser," she said as she plunked the folders down on Lorie's desk. "So go to it, girl. Check with me as soon as you have completed this part of the assignment."

Without waiting for a reply, she turned and walked back to her desk. Lorie watched in amazement as she noticed how Monica's hips swayed provocatively from side to side. Lorie shook her head. She thought there was no doubt that Monica was a streetwalker. Looking upward, she paused and prayed from the heart, *Lord, forgive me for thinking such a thing and please help me get through the day.* Then she buckled down and got busy immediately, working as quickly as possible.

The end of a workday never seemed to come fast enough for Lorie. Looking up at the clock, a sigh of relief came over her. She hurried out of the building as fast as she could. While driving home, many thoughts ran through her mind. Why was she rushing home? All that waited for her were more problems. Kate seemed sure Rich would understand her reluctance to date him, but Lorie didn't share that certainty. She had a feeling that this wasn't going to be resolved for a long time.

Lorie could not relax enough to enjoy supper but forced herself to eat a little. She wanted to put off her plans for the evening, but after talking to Kate about the situation, they both agreed that the sooner things were dealt with, the better. It was time to deal with Rich. Taking a deep breath, Lorie picked up the phone. Rich sounded delighted that she called, making her feel even worse. "Rich, I really need to talk to you about something. Would it be possible for you to come by this evening?"

"I'll be right over," he said.

Feeling sick to her stomach, she wanted to call Kate and also have her come over. But she couldn't call because they agreed Lorie would talk to Rich alone. Afterward, Kate and Bob would talk to him and try to smooth things out if he was still upset. Lorie poured a glass of wine and tried to calm down before Rich arrived. Before long, the doorbell rang. She moved slowly toward the door, dreading to answer it. Rich was standing there with a big smile on his face, flowers in one hand, and a bottle of wine in the other. *Oh dear God, this even makes it harder.* It took every effort she could muster to force a smile. "Come in, Rich, and please sit down. You really shouldn't have brought anything, but thank you."

Lorie took the flowers and put them in water. Rich started to open the wine when Lorie stopped him. "Please, Rich, this really isn't a social call," she said. "I need to talk to you about something. Could you please sit down and let me try to explain something to you?"

"What's wrong, Lorie?" said Rich, a puzzled look on his face. "Whatever it is, you know I'll help you."

Lorie hesitated for a few moments, trying to find the courage to speak. "Rich, as you know, Kate and Bob were friends with Jake and me for years, just like they have always been your friends," she said. "When Jake passed away, they were very worried about me being alone. That is why they played matchmaker. It was because of their concern for me. They think the world of you. As far as they are concerned, we should be a couple. Without realizing what harm can be done to people's feelings when playing matchmaker, they have tried to push us into a relationship that I am not ready for. I don't want to be anyone's girlfriend at this point in time. I'm still mourning. I know Kate and Bob meant well, and I understand why they did what they did, but I do feel bad that all of this has caused you to get the wrong idea as to where our relationship is heading. I'm sorry."

Lorie didn't know what else to say. She tried to be as kind and truthful as possible. But Rich was angry. He got up, walked quickly to the door, and slammed it hard as he left. Lorie was stunned. She hoped he wouldn't do anything drastic, despite Kate's insistence Rich would not react in a violent manner. Lorie quickly ran to the phone and called Kate, who seemed to be waiting for her call.

"Kate, Rich just left. I tried to be as kind and truthful as possible, but he became very angry. He slammed my door so hard when leaving that I actually checked to make sure nothing was broken. I can't believe that he got so angry. It's not like we were really going together as a couple. We never even kissed. I can't believe he is taking this so hard. He's acting like we actually had a serious relationship, and now I'm dropping him. This is really freaking me out."

"Calm down, Lorie," Kate said. "I'm sure that after he cools down, he will realize that he was way out of line and will offer an apology. Meanwhile, Bob and I will check on him. I'm really surprised that he would take it so hard. Like you said, you were just casual friends and not in a serious relationship. I guess in his mind he was expecting that you would become a couple. But hey, it's not the end of the world. Life goes on, right? Lorie, don't worry now. I promise you that we will make it right."

Kate felt bad and seemed sincere that she would fix the rift. Lorie knew that Kate's intentions were good.

"I never doubted your friendship, Kate," Lorie said. "Sometimes things just don't turn out the way we want. I guess we all feel pretty bad tonight, but tomorrow is another day. All we can do is hope for the best."

The conversation ended on a friendly note. Feeling exhausted, Lorie headed upstairs, her Bible in one hand, aspirin in the other.

The next morning at the office, Lorie was confronted by James as soon as she got to her desk.

"I've scheduled a special board meeting for tomorrow regarding our upcoming fund-raiser. Monica will need help with this. Make sure she has everything she needs as soon as possible." James walked to his office, closing the door behind him.

Another good morning, Lorie thought sarcastically. Just as Lorie started working on the new assignment, the sound of clicking high heels caused her to look up. "Little Miss Hot Stuff" approached. But as soon as the thought entered her mind, she reprimanded herself. *Stop it now. Try to be kind.*

Even though it was a struggle, she managed a little smile and said, "Good morning, Monica."

Monica looked perturbed and replied, "Yeah." She handed several folders and lists to Lorie. "I take it you already know about the board meeting for tomorrow. Some of the things listed here are rather extensive, so if I were you, I would get on it right away."

She turned and walked away. Lorie stared at Monica's shoes and noticed she actually was wearing shoes with rhinestone-accented ankle straps. She tried to hold back a laugh. *That certainly was not typical office attire.*

Before she left the office for the day, Diane called.

"I'm glad I caught you before you left. Want to stop off for a drink and maybe some dinner on your way home?"

Lorie was glad for the invitation. She needed to be around normal people at least once a week. This helped her to be able to put up with the nut cases that she had to deal with each day. People like Diane were an outlet for her and helped put things in perspective.

When Lorie arrived at the Holiday Inn, Diane was there waiting, a couple of drinks already on the table. Diane asked her if she wanted to splurge and dine there. Lorie thought for a moment. She glanced over at the big beautiful piano bar.

"Oh heck, why not," Lorie said. "Let's eat here."

A smiling waiter brought more drinks to their table. Diane had ordered Cointreau cocktails. Lorie smiled as she took a sip.

"This is good," Lorie said. "You remembered that I used to like this drink, and still do, but it's been a while since I had one."

"We really need to do this more often. Seems like we get bogged down with all the problems that each day brings and just don't spend enough time relaxing."

"Yes, things are certainly crazy at work. Plus, now I have another problem. Remember Rich, the one I introduced to you at the tennis tournament?" Diane nodded. "Well, I'm just not ready for another relationship yet. Anyway, I tried to explain this to him in a nice way, but he is so upset, and now I really feel bad."

Diane knew that Lorie was pushed into that situation by some well-meaning friends. "Lorie, I know what your problem is: you are just too nice to people in general. That is why you let yourself be talked into dating someone who is not your type, and that is also why some people at work treat you so badly. You have got to stop turning the other cheek all the time. You have to learn how to say no."

Lorie knew Diane was right, but that's how she was raised since childhood.

"Diane, my parents were very religious," Lorie said, tears filling her eyes. "I truly believe my mom was a saint. She always taught me to be kind and polite to everyone and to turn the other cheek. She always said that it was better to say nothing at all than to say something that you would be sorry for later. She always said to have a smile on your face. She thought of it as a little gift of hope to others who may need that smile."

"Your mom sounds like she was a great lady, Lorie," Diane said. "It's too bad that so many others were not as fortunate to have a mom with so much wisdom."

"Would you ladies like another drink before dinner?" the waiter asked.

"No, thank you. Just give us another minute, and we'll place our order," Diane replied. "So, Lorie, what sounds good to you today?"

"Well now, let me see. For the appetizer, I think I'll start out with the fruit cup. For the entrée, I'll have the chicken breasts flambé Barbarossa, the orange-glazed carrots, and the cranberries and almonds relish. For dessert, I will probably have the stuffed baked apples and amaretto with coffee."

"You must be hungry. That sounds like a meal fit for a king. Actually, it sounds so good that I think I will order the same thing, if you don't mind."

"I don't know if I'll be able to eat all of it," Lorie said with a laugh, "but I can always have leftovers tomorrow night."

The dinner was top line, and the evening was good therapy for Lorie. She always felt as if the imaginary weight on her shoulders was somehow lifted after talking shop with Diane.

"Well, I guess we had better call it a night," Lorie said with a little yawn. "Morning comes all too soon."

"I know what you mean. I think that eating this much makes me feel sleepy too." Diane stretched as she stood up. "Any more I just can't sit real long without getting stiff. It must be old age catching up with me."

With a little hug and a promise to get together real soon, they parted and headed home for the evening.

CHAPTER 4

Remembering the early board meeting, Lorie arrived ahead of the others. She hurriedly accumulated the reports and information to be presented at the meeting. Following the order of business from the agenda and checking for accuracy, she paused when she noticed the golf tournament fund-raiser listed under new business. She still could not believe that she was scheduled to play in the golf tournament. But if she refused, she feared she'd lose her job. Of course, with the way things were going at the company, that wouldn't necessarily be a bad thing.

Hearing footsteps, her thoughts suddenly came to a halt. She turned to see James quickly approaching.

"Is everything ready for this morning's meeting, Lorie?"

"Good morning, James," Lorie said, forcing a smile. "Yes, everything is ready."

"Did all the board members respond as to whether they will attend?"

Lorie looked at her list. "Yes, you will have a quorum today."

Before Lorie had a chance to comment on the golf tournament, the piercing sound of high heels drew their attention to the open doorway. Monica pompously stood there with a conceited smile on her face.

"Monica, come to my office," James said. "I need to go over some things with you before the board meeting this morning."

"Sure thing," she replied.

Lorie watched as they walked away. Monica's short cheetah print dress and two-inch heel T-strap sandals just didn't seem appropriate to wear to a board meeting. *Unbelievable*, Lorie thought, shaking her head.

Returning to her office, she saw June. A stony look was plastered on June's face as she stood with her hands on her hips. "Well, I shouldn't have to remind you, but make sure the coffee service is set up properly for the board meeting and that there are enough copies of the reports for everyone."

Without waiting for a reply, she abruptly departed. Lorie stood there for a moment in amazement. *How could anyone be so darn hateful?* she thought. As she walked down the long hall, she prayed, *Lord, I feel that these people are pushing me into a corner. Please help me get through yet another day.*

Taking some last-minute documents up to the meeting room, Lorie was greeted by Al Chambers.

"Good morning, Lorie," Al said with his usual big smile.

"Well, good morning to you, Mr. Chambers," Lorie replied.

"So how is the hardest-working secretary doing these days?"

Lorie didn't know how to take that remark. She knew that James never had anything good to say about her and wanted the board to think that Monica handled everything. But maybe some of the board members could see through that.

"Mr. Chambers, you know that we all work hard here at Glendale," Lorie said.

They both chuckled at that smart retort.

As members began to congregate in the meeting room, Lorie wisely departed. Monica greeted the board members, served coffee, and waited for James to call the meeting to order. James announced that a quorum of the directors was present and that the meeting, having been duly convened, was ready to proceed with its business. James then had Monica read the minutes of the previous meeting for approval, followed by various reports of officers. Discussion of the upcoming golf tournament fund-raiser followed. Al Chambers asked if the selection of players had been confirmed.

"If I may make a comment, I'm glad to see that you have Monica and Lorie listed here to play in the golf tournament as well," Al said. "They did a splendid job with the tennis tournament and played one heck of a game."

Monica stood up, smiled, and took a bow, causing mild amusement with the group.

"The girls are pretty active, of course," James added, "and are always willing to contribute their time for the good of the company and the community."

James concluded by stating, "On motion duly made and seconded, the golf tournament fund-raiser details are unanimously resolved. Now if there is no other new business, do I have a motion to adjourn the meeting?"

The motion was duly made, seconded, and adjourned.

Lorie was busily working at her desk when Monica returned to the office. As she passed Lorie's desk, she said, "You better start practicing. This is going to be one hell of a game, and unlike the tennis tournament, I'm going to beat the shit out of you."

Lorie was speechless once again as she watched Monica wander over to her desk. *What was with her?* The fund-raiser was for the good of the community. It should be considered fun and not a hateful competition between two people. But since she made that remark, Lorie was determined to practice hard. When she got home that evening, Lorie collapsed onto her sofa, glad the day was over. She was too tired to fix supper. Suddenly, the ringing phone interrupted her thoughts. It was Kate.

"Boy, you sound tired, like you had a rough day at work today," Kate said.

"Just the usual," Lorie said softly.

"I'm just calling to remind you of the yacht club meeting tomorrow. Bob and I can pick you up. It's at seven o'clock in the evening."

"I don't know, Kate," Lorie said, the idea of the meeting making her uncomfortable. "Belonging to the yacht club was Jake's thing, and now that he is gone, it's just not the same."

"Hey, we're your friends too, and we want you to keep active with the club. Remember all the good times we've had together?"

Lorie hesitated for a moment. "Kate, what about Rich? How can I deal with someone who is so angry with me because I don't want to be his girlfriend? Going to the meeting right now might not be such a good idea."

"Hey, I'm going to tell you something," Kate said, laughing. "Bob and I almost died laughing about this. But first, I need you to promise me that you won't repeat any of this because we do like everyone in the club. Of course, we realize that sometimes some of the club members do some strange things, but basically, they're a good bunch of people."

Lorie was confused. "Kate, what are you talking about?"

"Well, I don't think you need to worry about Rich anymore," Kate said. "Sometimes Rich goes to a strip club with his single friends. He's never made a habit of going often, but you know how men are. Sometimes they just go for kicks or whatever. Well, other than the usual flirting that they do with the girls, he's never actually wanted to date anyone that worked there. Now that you apparently broke his heart, he is actually dating one of those girls."

"Good, I'm glad he's found someone," Lorie said. "Maybe now we can be friends again without any strings attached."

Kate laughed again as she tried to speak.

"Kate, what in the world is so funny?"

"Well, I'm sure this relationship won't last. Let me describe this girl to you. Now I'm not trying to cut her down, but she reminds me of a cartoon character. I kid you not. She has huge silicone boobs, gigantic lips that she paints bright red, bleach blond hair with black roots, and mile long fingernails, also bright red. Her name is Candy. She's a little older than the other girls that work there and has a big butt. I think she may be an ex-striper. Bob said that all she does is hang around the bar, drink, and tell dirty jokes. I asked him how he knew that, and he said that it was common knowledge, just things he's heard from some of the other guys when they found out that Rich was actually dating her. All I can say is that Rich must have really liked you to go to such an extreme to try and get even with you in such a bizarre manner."

"Oh my, Kate, it can't be that bad."

"Oh yes, it is." The girls laughed harder.

"Please, Kate, stop it. The important thing here is that Rich is happy. Maybe it won't last forever; nothing does. But at least if he's content he won't be so angry and hateful to me anymore."

Kate tried to compose herself as she said, "So does that mean that you'll continue to come to the meetings and maybe even go on a little trip with us?"

"Trip? What trip?" Lorie didn't understand.

"I hadn't planned on talking to you about this tonight, but since you missed the last meeting, I'll fill you in. Our group is planning a trip to the Chesapeake Bay area. Most everyone is taking their boats. Once we get there, we plan on having a sailing race. Before you say no, let me say that Betty would be glad to be your partner. I've already mentioned this to her, and she said that if you decide to go, she will pick up half the cost. What do you think?"

Lorie was starting to get perturbed with Kate again. *Why was she always trying to fix her up with someone? Didn't she learn her lesson yet?* Once again, Lorie knew that Kate meant well. "Kate, I really wished you hadn't said anything to Betty," Lorie said. "Like you, I don't like to talk about members of our club and agree that they are basically a good bunch of people. That being said, I feel that there is something you should know about Betty. Right after Jake passed away, remember the trip I took with the club to Florida?"

"Yes, what about it?"

"Well, remember that Betty was my roommate and we were supposed to go half on all expenses? I'm not trying to count pennies here, but you won't believe how she took me on everything. First of all, we ate at the resort's restaurant for convenience, and the food was good. Each time though, we would ask for separate checks, and each time, the waitress put everything on one bill. Betty refused to sign any of the receipts, so I signed them because the waitress said that she couldn't redo the bills, and one of us had to sign the receipt. The waitress said that when we pay our final bill for the resort, they could divide the dinners at that time. Yes, I know this sounds weird, but Betty said that was fine with her, so I went along with it. Of course, when it was time to check out, Betty ran down and checked out, then brought me my bill. I couldn't believe they actually told her to give me my bill. My guess was that she didn't want to pay for any of her dinners, so she paid her bill and then told them that she would deliver my bill to me since we were roommates. In essence, she got several free meals off me, and I might add that they were not inexpensive meals. But even when she would occasionally pay for a meal, many times she would ask me to leave the tip because, as usual, she would say that she was running a little short on money. And any time we were gearing up to go anywhere, she always expected me to supply bottled drinking water. Do you really think it would hurt her to supply her own water once in a while? Also, we originally agreed to split the parking fee at the airport. Well, wouldn't you know it? When it was time to pay, she said, 'Could you pay the parking right now? I'm a little short. When we get to my house, I will write you a check.' The parking fee was sixty dollars. So when we got to her house, I helped her with her luggage. Afterward, I sat down at the dining room table thinking that she was going to write me a check. Then she says, 'I have things put away right now, and I don't want to keep you waiting. It would be easier for me if I could just send you a check in the mail.' I had my suspicions at that point, but I was tired, so I agreed. Well, wouldn't you know it? She never sent me that check. Once, sometime afterward, when I thought that maybe it just slipped her mind, I reminded her about it. Do you know what her answer was? She said, 'I don't owe you any money!' She acted like I insulted her by asking about it. There were other times when she tried to borrow money from me, but since I know she will never pay it back, I'm very leery about giving her more. On another sailing trip, we both had identical waterproof Harken sack packs, but hers was a bit more worn than mine. I also had my initials on my bag with pen, but very small. After that trip, when I went to put things away, I noticed that the sack pack was not mine, but the strange thing about it was that all my items were in the bag. Apparently, sometime during the trip, she had switched bags with me. Because of the type of pen I used for my initials, it would have been easy for her to scratch it off by now. If I say anything about this to her, she will not only deny it but will act like I am accusing her unjustly."

Kate was surprised. "Gee, Lorie, I'm sorry. I didn't know she did all those awful things to you. But to tell you the truth, she's tried to pull a few things over on me in the past also, but I guess I'm just too tight with my money. I know this is not a laughing matter," Kate added. "The woman apparently has a problem."

"Kate, the amazing thing to me is that her husband left her so much money when he died," Lorie said. "She also had a large inheritance from her parents since she was an only child. She is set for life. My husband didn't believe in having a huge amount of life insurance, and I don't have much money at all. It seems ironic that she has so much but yet expects everyone else to pay her way for everything."

"Do you think it would help if you talk to her about it and try to explain your financial situation?"

"No, my financial situation is none of her business. Plus, I don't think she would care even if I was starving to death. The only thing she seems to care about is trying to get something out of me every chance she can. Just like when we shared a locker down at the dock at the resort. She said that we could go half on paying for the lock that we had to buy. So I said that I would pay for the lock and just keep it afterward since I could use it back home. Well, when it was time to get our things out of the locker, she said that she would go down later to get hers. So I got my things out and locked it again to keep her things safe. Later, she went down to get her things. Before we left the resort, I asked for the lock since I had paid for it. Take a guess as to what she said. 'I don't have the lock. Didn't you get it?' Now how could I get it when she had to go down and unlock the locker to get her things out? Kate, does any of this make any sense to you?"

Kate didn't know what to say and hesitated before speaking, "Lorie, I can't believe that she would steal an inexpensive lock. It couldn't have cost that much."

"No, Kate, it didn't cost much. It's not the money that bothers me in this instance. It's the fact that she finds it so important to get something out of me every chance she can. It's the principle of it all. I just can't deal with her anymore."

"Lorie, I understand how you feel. That is really lowdown on her part."

Lorie was tired and wanted to end the conversation. "Kate, I don't like confrontation. I'm a peacemaker at heart. I was brought up to be kind to everyone and always turn the other cheek. So please do not say anything to Betty about this conversation. She would probably deny everything and maybe even become hateful. Heaven knows, there is enough hate at work to have to deal with each day. I wouldn't want to add her to the list also."

"You're right, Lorie," Kate said. "Saying anything to her would only make matters worse. It does sound like she could use some counseling though."

"Yes, but how can you tell someone that they need counseling when they think they are normal? Trying to use people to get money or things out of them may seem normal to her."

"Kate, I'm very tired tonight," Lorie said. "I doubt that I will attend the meeting tomorrow, but please call and fill me in. I promise I'll go next time."

"You know what they say about all work and no play, Lorie," Kate said. "Don't get in that rut."

"Yes, Kate, I know," Lorie said, realizing her friend was concerned about her well-being. "I'm going to fix myself something to eat right now and then go to bed. Thanks for listening tonight and understanding. Keep me posted."

After hanging up, Lorie sat by the phone for a few minutes, wondering if maybe she told Kate too much. She didn't like talking about anyone in the club, but on the other hand, she felt that Kate should be aware of what she had gone through with Betty. Although Lorie was kind to everyone, she didn't like when people would use that to take advantage of her. She also was hoping that Kate would learn her lesson and stop trying to fix her up with people. Kate assumed that because Betty and Lorie were both widows, they would be good companions and roommates on trips. Since Kate already spoke to Betty regarding the next trip, Lorie felt she didn't have a choice but to tell Kate about the way Betty had taken advantage of her. Finally, deciding that she made the right decision, she got up and headed for the kitchen. Now she had to start thinking about the golf tournament.

When Lorie strolled into the office the next morning, she was surprised to see that Monica was already there. Monica didn't look up as Lorie walked into the office. She was busy reading something. Lorie nonchalantly walked past Monica's desk, pretending to need something from the supply closet. Glancing over her shoulder, she noticed Monica was reading a golf manual.

Gee, she's at it already, Lorie thought. *I guess that's all she'll be doing now for the next few months while loading me up with all her work.* Feeling a little perturbed, Lorie decided not to say anything. She returned to her desk and began working on her daily assignments.

As soon as James arrived, Lorie noticed that he motioned to Monica to come into his office. Since he did not shut the door, Lorie once again visited the supply closet, which was close to James's office. She stood there very quietly, trying to listen to what James had to say.

"Monica, I have arranged to have a golf pro work with you several times a week until the tournament. Make sure you are available for the lessons each week. That's it for now. I'll talk to you later."

Lorie pulled out some supplies from the closet and headed back to her desk. Sarcastically, she wanted to ask James when she could schedule private golf lessons at the company's expense. The idea of James paying for expensive lessons for Monica agitated Lorie to the point that she only spoke when absolutely necessary for the rest of the day. When June abruptly placed a pile of folders on Lorie's deck, she didn't even bother to look up. Totally disgusted, she just felt like saying, "Screw it!" On second thought, biting her tongue, she realized she didn't want to say anything she'd be sorry for later.

When finally she looked up, June was standing there.

"Have this report done by the end of the day," June said, slapping her hand hard on the pile of folders she placed on Lorie's desk.

Not waiting for Lorie to reply, she walked out of the office. Lorie noticed Monica watching the scene with a devilish smile on her face. Lorie thought that June and Monica would be friends, not combatants. Trying to put the incident aside, she focused on her work.

That evening, Lorie decided to call Diane.

"How goes it with the office monsters?" Diane laughed, but Lorie was silent for a few moments.

"Same old, same old."

"I'm sorry, Lorie," Diane said, knowing by the sound of Lorie's voice that all was not well at the office. "I know it's not a laughing matter. Personally, I don't see how you can stand it there anymore. If I were you, I would look for another job."

"Diane, I know you're right on one hand," Lorie said, "but I'm not ready to throw in the towel just yet. I need to find out some things first. If what I suspect is true, there may be a light at the end of the tunnel."

"Lorie, what are you talking about?" Diane said, confused.

"Diane, I don't want to talk about that right now. I'm calling tonight to see if you could possibly help me out with something,"

Lorie said, not ready to confide her suspicions to anyone until she had more proof. "It's regarding the upcoming fund-raiser, the golf tournament. I need some help since James insists that I be one of the players. I did play golf years ago, but after Jake and I joined the yacht club, I didn't play anymore. I remembered that you told me about your golf game some time ago and wondered if you could help me practice and maybe give me a few pointers."

"You know, Lorie, I'm not that good at golf myself," Diane said. "I don't think I would be much help, but I do know someone that is pretty good. I'll give him a call and see if maybe he can help you. He does owe me a favor anyway, so maybe I could get him to agree. Even if it was just for two or three lessons, I'm sure you would find it helpful. He's really good."

"Thanks, Diane," Lorie said, relieved. "If you could arrange that, I would deeply appreciate it."

Feeling she had accomplished a goal for the evening, sleep came a little easier that night.

Early Saturday morning, Lorie waited at the Silver Lake Golf Course. Seeing Diane's car pull in, Lorie walked over. Then she noticed a rather handsome man also getting out of the car.

"Lorie, I'd like you to meet my favorite cousin, Dave," Diane said.

Lorie smiled and extended her hand. "I'm very pleased to meet you. I've heard that you are excellent at golf, but I suppose Diane is somewhat prejudiced."

"Like everyone, I have my good days and bad days," Dave said with a laugh.

"I haven't seen any of his bad days," Diane said.

Lorie was amused. She instantly liked Dave.

"I usually don't tell anyone that we are related," Diane continued. "That way, when anyone needs golf tips, they won't bug me to have Dave come and help them."

"Gee, I guess I'll be one of those who will bug the heck out of you until the fund-raiser is over," Lorie said. "It's been years since I played golf, and I really don't want to participate in this event, but I have a boss who will not listen to reason. He just gives me one assignment after the other, and if I don't know how to do something, he expects me to hurry up and find out."

Seeing the discouragement in her face, Dave said, "Hey, cheer up. If you have played golf in the past, with a little refresher course, it shouldn't take that long for you to feel confident again. So let's get started."

"Okay, now that we have that settled, I'm going to head out," Diane said. "I have some errands to take care of today. Good luck with your golf game, Lorie. Thanks once again for helping out, Dave. See you all later." She waved goodbye and left.

Lorie studied Dave as he talked to her about the game. He was rather good-looking with naturally curly dark hair and a little mustache. He seemed to be sincere and knowledgeable. *Maybe he can help me*, she thought. Lorie remembered that in the past, she had a tendency to be a slow player. She remembered that Jake would always tell her to speed it up so that they would be able to make it around the course in a timely manner. Jake used to get so upset with her at times. Previous games flooded her mind, making concentration almost impossible. Dave could see that she was upset.

"Lorie, the only thing I want you to try and do today is to relax," Dave said. "Remember, golf is supposed to be enjoyable."

"I know, but I feel that I was pushed into something that I'm really not ready for," Lorie said, smiling. "That makes me nervous."

"Hey, I will help you get ready for the tournament," Dave said, patting her on the shoulder. "I have confidence in you already. Now you have to start having some confidence in yourself."

Lorie tried to relax. She knew Dave was right, but that would be easier said than done. Smiling, she picked up her club and gave it a shot. "Oh dear," she said softly. "That is not what I expected."

"Now, don't worry," Dave said, trying to follow the ball as it headed straight for the woods. "We'll see if we can find the ball. Maybe it would be good practice to hit it from where it lies. Remember,

Lorie, we are just practicing today. It will take you a few practice sessions just to get the feel of it again, but it will come. I guarantee it."

Lorie thought that if anyone could help her, Dave would be the one. As the day went on, practicing her golf swing left Lorie feeling exhausted. Dave could see that she was getting tired.

"Lorie, let's call it a day. You need to get some rest. If you like, we can practice again tomorrow."

Lorie was surprised to hear him say that. "I would think that after today, you would feel like you had enough," Lorie said in amazement.

"I told you that I would help you, and I meant it. Actually, you did pretty well today, taking into consideration that it's been a while since you played."

"Flattery will get you nowhere," Lorie said as Dave laughed. "I don't want to impose on your time."

"Golf is never an imposition for me," Dave said. "I love the game, and I don't mind giving helpful hints to others. I'll see you here tomorrow morning, if you don't have any other plans."

"Dave, you are so kind," Lorie said, smiling. "I'll be here tomorrow morning." With that, they parted for the evening.

When Lorie got home, she immediately called Diane. "Diane, why didn't you ever mention that you had such a wonderful cousin?"

"So I take it you like him?"

"Diane, he was so kind and patient. I thought I played horribly, but he said that I did well, considering that I haven't played for a while, and wants to get together again tomorrow morning for another practice session."

"Sounds like you two really hit it off," said Diane, pleased. "He's a nice guy, but he's not a glutton for punishment. He must really like you."

Lorie was taken aback by that remark. "Diane, I'm not looking for a boyfriend. I'm just trying to survive at work. I'll take all the help I can get. But yes, he does seem like a guardian angel. If I were looking for a boyfriend, I would want it to be someone like Dave."

"Believe me, the feeling is mutual," Diane said.

Before Lorie had a chance to ask what she meant by that, Diane continued, "He seems to be pretty impressed with you also."

Lorie remembered how Rich had helped her with the tennis tournament and how he became possessive and clinging afterward. She didn't want a situation like that to develop again.

"Diane, please don't tell him that I called you," she said. "I would like to maintain a business relationship only. I just can't handle anything else at this point in time. Remember Rich and what a disaster that turned out to be. When I'm ready, I'm sure that things will happen naturally, but please don't play matchmaker. That only makes situations very uncomfortable. Plus, they never seem to work out."

"I know what you mean," Diane agreed. "Matchmakers create more problems. Relationships have to happen on their own, and only the two people involved can judge what is right for themselves."

"Diane, I'm so glad that you understand," Lorie said, relieved. "I've tried to explain this to Kate on several occasions, but it never seemed to sink in. After the last conversation we've had, I am hopeful she finally realizes this."

"Don't worry about anything, Lorie. Just try and enjoy the game. You're not going to be perfect. No one is. Just do the best you can. I'm sure after the tournament is over, you'll feel less tense."

Lorie sat at her desk, looking at the piles of papers, folders, and mails that had accumulated since Friday. She hated Mondays. The sound of high heels clicking down the hall caused Lorie to look up. She was always surprised to see what kind of shoes Monica had on each day and couldn't believe that anyone would be able to walk in them. *Studded zipper back heels today.* Her thoughts were quickly diverted when Monica spoke.

"Well, well, well, I saw you pulling out of Silver Lake over the weekend. Doing some practicing, are you?"

Lorie didn't answer.

Monica smothered a laugh. "You're going to need all the help you can get, I'm sure."

Lorie tried to ignore her and concentrated on the work on her desk. James arrived at that moment. "Good morning, James," Lorie said before continuing on with her work.

"That's more than I got this morning," Monica quipped. "She wouldn't even speak to me this morning."

"Lorie, is there a problem?" James said, puzzled.

Lorie felt like punching Monica in the face at that point. "No. She didn't give me chance to answer. That's when you walked in."

"That's a lie," said Monica, her face turning a bright red. "She didn't want to answer me because I saw her coming out of Silver Lake this weekend. She didn't want me to know that she was practicing."

"You girls are supposed to be practicing," James said. "There should be no secret about it. So what's the problem, Lorie?"

Lorie couldn't believe what she was hearing. Why was James acting like she was having a problem?

"James, I'm not trying to be secretive about anything, and I can't understand why Monica is so upset."

Monica started to walk over to Lorie's desk. Lorie actually felt like Monica was going to attack her before James intervened.

"Monica, could you come to my office?" he said.

They left and closed the door behind them. Lorie was still a little shaken by that exhibition when June walked in. Without saying a word to Lorie, June walked to James's office. Before she had a chance to knock, Lorie couldn't resist saying, "Take a number."

Giving Lorie a dirty look, she knocked on his door.

"I'm busy now," James said, thinking it was Lorie. "Use the intercom."

"No one speaks to me like that," June said under her breath, stomping out of the office.

Lorie shook her head in amazement, thinking that June would find some way to blame her.

Driving home after work, Lorie felt sick in her stomach. Suddenly, tears welled up in her eyes. *Jake, this is all your fault for dying. I could handle things until you decided to die on me. Now look. I have a crazy boss and have to work with a bunch of nut cases.*

Remembering the calm effects of prayer, she prayed, *Oh Lord, I'm so sorry for blaming Jake for the predicament that I'm in. I know it's not his fault. I also realize that it's not my place to judge when it is time to be called to our eternal home. Please forgive me and help me to get through tomorrow.*

James stopped by Monica's place after work. Hearing noises from the bedroom, he ran upstairs.

"James, you startled me," she said, dressed only in underwear. "I didn't hear you come in."

Seeing Monica half naked caused a stir within him. His arms encircled her.

"What are you doing?" he asked.

"What do you think?" Monica said, pointing to the outfits on the bed. "I'm trying on outfits for the golf tournament. Which of these do you like the best?"

"They look the same to me," he said, noting that both outfits were black and white.

"They look different when I wear them. I'll let you pick the one that you think is the most becoming."

Monica looked stunning in a black top with a side tie waistband, cinched V-neckline, and cap sleeves. Next, she pulled on a white ruffled skirt with a drawstring waist.

"Nice," James said, smiling.

Monica turned around a few times. "Okay, now let me get your opinion on the other outfit."

James's eyes widened with delight as she donned a deep open back halter top with a tie neck and dropped cowl front. The little white denim skirt had six black buttons on the front and a pleated hem in back.

"No contest," James said in awe. "I pick this one."

As their lips met, James pulled her down on the bed. His cell phone rang loudly through James's sport coat. He staggered out of bed and began looking through his coat. "Yes, what is it?" It was Anna.

"James, where are you? We're supposed to meet the Hadleys for dinner tonight at the club. Did you forget?"

"No, of course not. I got tied up at the office," he said, not admitting he did forget. "I'll be home shortly." Hanging up the phone, he threw on his clothes and raced for the door. "Monica, I have to go now. I'll see you tomorrow," he said, pulling on his clothes.

Before she could say anything, he was gone. Rolling over in bed, she muttered, "That damn wife!"

Lorie stared out her window, watching the rain fall. She enjoyed the peaceful surroundings of her home and the quiet time during which she could think and pray. She pulled out a photo album, reminiscing about the events of the past. *Jake, oh Jake. How I miss you and those sailing trips on our sloop, Sunrise. It is truly a classic. Even though I don't do much with the yacht club anymore, I'll never sell it. You loved it too much, and it's part of us, the three of us: you, me, and Sunrise.*

Deep in memory lane, Lorie drifted off to sleep. Spinning through ocean waves, palm trees, and white sandy beaches, she woke to find that it was time to get ready for bed. She put the photo's away, thankful for the many good times in her life, and she prayed that somehow, someday they would once again return. Turning out the lights, she softly prayed, *Thank you, God, for all your many blessings.*

With the golf tournament approaching, things were getting more hectic at work. Lorie worked overtime just to keep up, too busy to worry about Monica or June. She tried to overlook things that they would do or say and just focus on the fund-raiser.

Then James summoned Lorie to his office. She thought Monica or June had another complaint about her. Lorie walked in and sat down across from James's desk.

"Lorie, I see that you have been putting in a lot of overtime," he said. "The board does not want our employees to work overtime. You'll have to arrange your workload in order of importance and leave on time each day. Is that clear?"

"James, I don't deliberately work overtime," Lorie said, hating being put on the defensive all the time. "Actually, I try not to. You have to remember that besides my regular duties, when we have a fund-raiser, it's a lot of extra work. Besides the assignments you give me, I get assignments from Monica and June, which bog me down at times."

"What do you mean you get assignments from Monica and June?" James said, puzzled.

"When you give them an assignment, many times, they give the bulk of it to me to complete for them," she said, knowing James wouldn't like the answer. She was right. James didn't like that answer at all.

"When I give them an assignment, you are not to get involved. In the past, I have noticed that you were working on assignments that I would give to them, but when I questioned them, they said that you insisted on helping them since you have been at the company for a long time and know what is expected from each assignment."

"James, I have never offered to help them with an assignment that you specifically gave to them," said Lorie, surprised the girls would lie about such a thing. "They just wind up on my desk. The girls say that they are too busy and that it is my duty to help out. Of course, you told me to help them from the start since I had to train them for their positions."

Lorie realized that she had said too much. Not only was James mad at her now, but she knew the girls would be extra hateful when they learned what she told James. Again, she felt as if she was between a rock and a hard place.

"I have to take this call," James said when his personal line rang. "From now on, I don't want you working on assignments that I have given to someone else. If someone else other than me gives you an assignment, tell them that they will have to clear it with me first."

James picked up the phone, and Lorie left the room, shutting the door behind her.

"Why you little bitch," June retorted as she shoved Lorie against the wall.

Lorie looked bewildered.

"Don't give me that surprised look. You know what you did. If you think you can get away with trying to get me in trouble, you have another guess coming. From now on, you do what I say and keep your mouth shut. You don't want to wake up one morning and find that you can't make it into work because you have four flat tires, now do you?"

Lorie was shocked. June was actually threatening her. She knew about June's prison record and wouldn't put anything past her. Lorie tried not to panic.

"June, if you're talking about the assignments that James gives to you, all he did was inform me that I'm not supposed to interfere or help with anyone else's assignments unless they okay it with him first. If you have a problem with what he said, then you should talk to him about it."

"He wouldn't have said that without you complaining to him," June said.

"Look, he called me into his office to tell me that the board does not want any of us to work overtime. James wants me to only do the assignments that he gives me and to leave on time each day." Lorie pulled away from June and went back to her desk.

"This isn't over," June mumbled as she left the room. Lorie didn't expect it to be as she continued her work.

The world seemed bleak that afternoon when Lorie arrived home. She didn't know if she should take June's threat seriously or not. Of course, if she did do anything to her car, she would have to call the police. On the other hand, she was sure that June would have an alibi and thereby making Lorie look like a fool. She thought about giving two weeks' notice at work. But she needed her job and figured that James would not give her a good reference if she did leave, causing her to be unable to find suitable work for a while. Mixed emotions filled her head.

What should I do, Lord? she sighed, looking upward.

Her thoughts were quickly interrupted by the phone. She jumped up to answer it.

"Hi, Lorie, this is Dave. Would you like to play nine holes tonight?"

Lorie was tired and really stressed out from work but agreed. Maybe this was what she needed. Lorie ran upstairs to take a shower. Her game was improving, and a little exercise might get rid of some of her stress.

The smell of flowers and freshly cut grass already had a relaxing effect on Lorie as she waited for Dave to arrive. She liked Silver Lake. She didn't know where Monica was practicing but kept her fingers crossed that she would not run into her while she was there with Dave. A bright red Ford Mustang turned onto the driveway and into the parking lot. Lorie thought the car fit him as she walked over to great him.

"What a beautiful day," she said. "Thank you so much for the invite."

"I couldn't pass up a day like this," Dave said, smiling. "It's perfect golf weather. Shall we get started?" Lorie nodded as they headed out to the green.

"Did you know that the game of golf is centuries old?" Dave asked.

"You're kidding, of course," she responded, looking at him in amazement.

"No, actually, I'm not. Shepherds have played golf with pebbles and sticks in the fields way before the game was devised in Scotland some five hundred years ago. That's when they substituted a small ball for the pebbles."

"Maybe I should be practicing with pebbles," she joked.

"Strength is helpful in golf, but the most important thing is coordination," Dave said, "and that takes a lot of practice."

Lorie smiled, thinking this is what she needed this evening, a kind friend who would help her confidence.

The day of the tournament was drawing nearer. Feelings of self-assurance filled Lorie's mind. She made one last check on the new clothes she bought for the tournament. Pulling the items from her closet, Lorie looked them over carefully and wondered if she had made a good choice. She needed another opinion.

Picking up the phone, she called Diane.

"We must have mental telepathy, girl. I was just about to call you," Diane said.

"Okay, what's up?" Lorie asked, laughing.

"Nothing much. I just wanted to see how things were going since the tournament is just a few days away. I talked to Dave, and he said your game has really improved. He is impressed."

"Yes, I'm feeling a lot better now about the tournament," Lorie said, glad that Dave said something positive about her. "I think I will be able to hold my own. At least, I'm sure as heck going to try. Dave has been a wonderful instructor, and I am forever grateful to both of you for all the help and moral support."

"Hey, what are friends for?" Diane said. "You would do the same for me, I'm sure. So what did you want to talk to me about?"

Lorie looked at the new clothes she had laid out on the bed. "Well, I wanted your opinion and was wondering if you could come over. I bought a cute pair of khaki Bermuda shorts with studded zipper pockets. They're cotton and spandex and fit real well. Also, to go with the shorts, I bought a ruche V-neck tank. It has a surplice neckline and side ruche in sunny yellow. I wanted to wear something light and cheery. How does that sound to you?"

"Sounds sexy and flirty but comfortable," Diane replied. "I could stop by tomorrow after work for a bit. Maybe we could go out to eat afterward."

Lorie chuckled. Diane had a knack for brightening her spirits. Lorie thought for a moment. "Okay, but I don't want to stay out late. I really need to rest up for the weekend. I'll need much strength then."

"Okay, see you tomorrow."

The office bustled with activity as last-minute details unfolded and were put in place. Lorie was so busy; she hadn't given much thought to June's previous outburst. Still, in the back of her mind, she knew it was only a matter of time before the next display of anger would emerge the Dr. Jekyll/Mr. Hyde syndrome again. At times, she felt bad for thinking such thoughts, but if the shoe fits …

A sudden break in continuity hindered her train of thought. She noticed June treading heavily down the hall before she stopped at Lorie's desk.

"Because of your constant complaining to James about how busy you are doing 'my' work, I won't have time to take care of the things on this list tomorrow," June said. "As soon as the tournament is over, you are to report to the kitchen. You are also on the cleanup committee." She flung the list down hard on Lorie's desk, as usual, and walked away.

Lorie was disgusted. She knew that she would be completely wiped out after the tournament and wouldn't have the energy to work in the kitchen or do cleanup until the wee hours of the morning. Confusion was making her head spin. What could she do about this? If she told James, she'd probably wake up tomorrow morning and find four flat tires. If she said she wasn't feeling well and went home after the tournament, June would probably crucify her the first chance she got. But if she could possibly win the tournament by some miracle, she'd have to talk to the newspaper folks, and that would take some time. Thoughts were racing through Lorie's head at the speed of light. Her spirit seemed to be screaming "help!" Abruptly, Lorie stopped, forcing all the unsettling emotions out of her mind. She was not going to worry about this. When the time came, she'd deal with it as best she could. When she left for the day, she made sure the list was left out on her desk in hopes that James would see it. Even if he didn't say anything to her, he might ask June about it. Her comeback to June would be that she had no control over what James looked at or took from her desk.

Employees and volunteers arrived early Saturday morning. At least one thousand guests were expected to attend the fund-raiser. James insisted that everything be taken care of early before the arrival of guests.

"So what would you do if you landed in a sand trap today?" Monica said, glaring at Lorie.

Lorie thought that was a weird question to ask someone, so she answered back in a weird way. "Oh, I'd probably kick it out with my foot."

"I don't doubt it," Monica snickered, walking away.

As Lorie, Monica, and the other players headed to the green, guests were gathering at the clubhouse. Lorie was glad that the tournament was being held at Silver Lake since that is where she had practiced. She had given up the thought of overpowering the course but somehow was hoping to outwit it and Monica. Dave taught her that one of the most important things in golf was coordination. He instructed her to try and become efficient, placing each shot in a strategic spot, and wanted her to realize that each new day was a fresh challenge.

"You can't worry about what you did yesterday," he told her when she became discouraged. "What matters is what you do today."

"Let the match begin!" James shouted as they got ready to tee off.

Lorie thought, *When it came to irksome bosses, James would take first place.* She wished she had some magical power to make him disappear right now. Instead, she tried to put all negative thoughts out of her mind and concentrate on golfing. *Lord, help me!*

When it was Lorie's turn, she remembered Dave's words. "You've got to believe in yourself," he always said. Lorie smiled to herself as she remembered Dave saying, "Perfection is possible." She knew that didn't apply to her. Nevertheless, she'd enjoyed her practice sessions with Dave. He was upbeat and very patient.

Her eyes focused on the crowd for a few moments, looking for Dave. She thought she would be less nervous if he were here. A wave of an arm and a big smile caught her eye. He was here. Now she could play.

Lorie slowly placed her ball on the tee. She wanted to drive the ball far and straight down the fairway. A little case of nerves set in as she made her swing, and her drive hooked slightly. Her ball landed close to the rough. Monica snickered as she teed up her ball. Feeling confident, Monica was completely surprised when she sliced the ball and ended up in the rough.

Who's laughing now? Lorie thought.

Approaching her ball, Lorie saw that it was just at the edge of the green. The shot seemed to be an easy one. She reached into her bag and selected her putter. She gently hit the ball with just the right touch, and the ball stopped short of the cup. She was pleased and was confident her next shot would go in. Monica found her ball in the high grass. Two shots later, she was on the green. Another two shots and she sunk her putt. Disappointment turned to anger. As they walked to the next hole, James told Monica to "slow down a little and concentrate more." Monica looked at him coldly but said nothing. James wondered if she had hit the bottle again. He warned her about drinking before the game. Because he didn't want to get her further upset, he decided not to say anything more.

Having some knowledge of the course, Lorie tried to settle down and stay patient on every shot. With each good swing, she felt reassured. As the match progressed, Lorie overcame a series of missed tee shots and putts. It was definitely hard to keep up, but she was determined to hang in there and do her best. When the wind began to pick up, the breeze felt refreshing on her warm, damp skin. Lorie thought the wind might work in her favor if she didn't catch a stray gust and was determined not to let the conditions bother her. She felt Dave's presence, and that brought her some comfort. She recalled his amazing stories of miraculous golf shots and putts. He loved the game of golf and allowed no compromise in his game. Lorie knew that she would never be able to reach her full potential even with Dave's enthusiasm and guidance but realized that his help had been essential to getting her this far. She was not expecting any hoopla at the end of this fund-raiser but just hoping to get through it without causing undue embarrassment to herself. She did possess a certain amount of skill but knew that it would take a ton of luck to get her through the tournament.

 Al Chambers stepped up to the tee. Lorie watched his smiling face. It seemed to be contagious and always brought a smile to her face. She realized that unlike so many others, his smile was not just an outward gesture but radiated from deep within. With a twinkle in his eye, he hit the ball with his free and easy spirit. Lorie admired anyone who was able to be so relaxed all the time. She thought he had the personality of a happy kid. By his expression, Lorie knew that he felt pretty good about the shot. She also was pleased and hoped that Al would win the tournament.

 A sun-soaked and brutal day left James feeling somewhat drained as he desperately tried to stay in the lead. A few bad holes where he missed makeable putts brought out the worse in him. Lorie could sense the negative vibrations he emanated. His competitive spirit caused him to overanalyze each shot. Lorie giggled to herself as she thought, *It would be funny if Monica's score was better than his!* Everyone played hard and played to win.

 Monica was cruising along, trying not to let the other players bother her. Forcing herself to think positive, she was determined that she was going to do well no matter what. With all the force she could muster, she hit her drive. Once again, her ball curved way to the right. Expectations suddenly turned to disappointment, but she felt like she was still holding her own. Monica knew she wasn't far behind and was determined to catch Lorie. *If nothing else, I will beat Lorie*, she told herself. *I must beat her.*

Lorie eyed the trees, the rough, and the greens as wisps of blond hair gently blew across her face. She didn't count on any wind today and was beginning to feel tired, making it harder to concentrate. But luck seemed to be with her on this shot. Using a five iron, her ball stopped about seven feet from the hole. Lorie was pleased with the way things were going for her. Hopefully, she could stay focused a while longer. She wasn't sure if she was feeling more relaxed or more tired at this point, but contentment enveloped her as she moved on to the next hole.

The day sizzled on. As temperatures rose and the winds picked up, tempers flared due to wayward shots and missed putts. James and Al were tied, followed by several other board members. Lorie was slightly ahead of Monica, but they trailed the others. Monica refused to come in last, but the harder she tried, the more frustrated she became. Evil manipulations ran through her mind.

Lorie glanced over at Monica. An uneasy feeling swept over her as she wondered why Monica always thought of her as the enemy. Determined not to shadow Monica's strange ways or be forced into retreat, Lorie decided to move forward in a steady pace. *This was a fund-raiser. Why did Monica act like everything was a life-or-death situation?* Lorie tried not to let her frustrations get the best of her. She should be used to dealing with the crazies by now and prayed for wisdom and strength.

The tournament was coming to an end. Monica was entirely spent, causing her to play poorly. After blowing her tee shot into the woods, she was unable to find her ball. Now she was becoming mental and started to speak her mind. James realized that Monica was losing it.

"Cool it, Monica, or else," he whispered sharply, taking her arm and squeezing it tightly.

"Are you threatening me?" she responded harshly.

"Remember, there are board members here," he whispered forcibly. "You have to start acting a little more professional. It's for your own good."

"And for yours, of course," she said as she broke away from his tight grip.

The tournament ended with Al coming in first and James second. Everyone who participated in the match seemed to be pleased when it was over, with some players on the verge of heat exhaustion. Monica came in last, her hopes extinguished, and vowed to get even with Lorie. Exhausted, Lorie was just glad that the day was coming to an end.

Dave ran up to Lorie and gave her a big hug. "Well, how's my favorite little golf player feeling now?"

"I'm just very tired right now and glad that this game is over," Lorie sighed.

"You played rather well today. I enjoyed watching you," Dave said.

Bewildered, Lorie looked at him. "You're kidding, of course."

"Oh, I believe that you were always good. You just needed a little reassurance to bring out that confidence to notice it yourself," Dave said firmly, conveying power and knowledge when he spoke. This encouraged Lorie. She needed to feel that someone could piece together the torn pages of her life, wanting to find again the peace and contentment that she had shared with Jake.

"You have made a difference in my life," she said. "You helped me believe more in myself. Of course, there is always room for improvement. So I'll keep working on it."

"Seems like my prodigy is awakening!"

Walking back to the clubhouse, Lorie was surprised to see Matt Phillips, the reporter, approaching her. "Hi, Lorie," he said. "Really enjoyed the match today and was glad to get this assignment. You seem to be a jack-of-all-trades for sure. Glendale certainly is lucky to have such a loyal employee."

"Hi, Matt," she said. "Yes, I do seem to get chosen for the strangest things around here."

"Really though, you did rather well," Matt said. "A few of your shots seemed to be struck with Swiss precision."

Lorie looked at Dave, and they both laughed.

"No, I wouldn't go that far, Matt, but thank you for the compliment," Lorie said. "Yes, it took a lot of hard work and preparation since I had not played in a good while. With the heat and wind today, it was hard to stay focused at times, but I tried to stay strong until the end."

"Well, I have to find Al Chambers," Matt said. "His game was beautiful. He made it seem so easy."

"Yes, what he accomplished is amazing," Lorie agreed. "I'm so glad he came in first place. He deserved to win, that's for sure."

The clubhouse was brimming with elegance as guests were seated for dinner. June found her way over to Lorie. "Excuse me," she said to Dave. "I need to have a word with Lorie." Taking her aside, she snapped, "Don't forget, you are on the cleanup committee this evening. As soon as dinner is over, report to the kitchen."

"Wait a minute, June," Lorie replied sternly. "James said that I am not to work any more overtime."

"I've already talked to James, and he approved it." The look on June's face reminded her of the Wicked Witch of the West, making Lorie shudder.

Lorie was speechless as she watched June's hurried exit. How was she going to make it through the night? She was totally exhausted. Suddenly, Lorie was surrounded by her friends Kate, Bob, Diane, and Dave. Happy and upbeat, they congratulated her on a match well played. For a few moments, Lorie put June out of her mind. She enjoyed having her friends by her side and the wonderful dinner that followed.

With the evening coming to an end, Kate and Bob decided to call it a night but not before making Lorie promise to bring Dave to the next meeting at the yacht club. Dave looked at Lorie timidly and said maybe he needed to "broaden his horizons."

"If you are interested in boats, you'll love the club," Kate said. "During our next meeting, we will be discussing boating safety basics, which will include first aid and CPR, vessel safety checks, rescue twenty-one, which is mostly about the DSC radio, GPS, and nautical chart readings."

"Now you've got my attention," Dave said chidingly.

Lorie laughed and thought he was just so cute. She was pleased that they liked Dave and wanted to include him but was hoping that Kate would not push too hard with her matchmaking skills. She felt it was her duty to find matches for singles. *Lord, bless her. She means well.*

Dave told the girls that he would take them home.

"Dave, I drove my car today, so I'll go home after I finish up a few things here," Lorie said. "But you all go on ahead. I'll talk to you guys tomorrow. Thanks so much for coming today."

"Lorie, we had a great time," Diane said, giving Lorie a little hug. She suspected that June had it in for Lorie and was reluctant to leave. "You know, Dave, I really don't want Lorie to be going home so late at night by herself, so I think I'll stick around until she is ready to go, but you go on now. And thanks for helping my best friend with all your golf advice. You really helped her get through the day."

"Girls, since you are kicking me out, I guess I'll take off," Dave said. "I'll call you tomorrow, Lorie."

After he left, Lorie said, "Diane, I didn't want you to stay because June says that I have to work on cleanup tonight. I will probably be here all night."

"I figured as much," Diane said. "I have a plan. When June is out of sight or gone for the night, I'll pitch in and help you. Remember how we used to work together in the old days? I'm really good at organizing and working fast. You know that, remember?"

"Diane, if she sees you or suspects that you're helping me in any way, the shit will hit the fan."

"Well, we won't let her see me. Now go and get started. June, being the lazy type, won't stick around very long after she gives you 'the list.' I doubt the other people on the committee will say anything, but if they do, you say that I was waiting for you to take me home. Not working, just waiting."

"You're impossible!" Lorie laughed. "Okay, wait here."

Lorie headed back to the kitchen to get started on the long night ahead.

CHAPTER 5

Beams of bright sun showered her face when Lorie awoke. She rolled over and looked at the clock. She'd slept most of the day. She got up and headed for the kitchen to make much needed coffee. Lorie felt like she was walking in her sleep and tried hard to get her eyes to focus. When the coffee finished brewing, she took it out to the back porch. She relaxed, watching the colorful birds and comical squirrels. Her thoughts returned to the day before. She did enjoy playing golf yesterday. The dinner was great, and her friends were supportive. Maybe if she tried harder to concentrate on the positive, it would help her get through the negative. Lorie tried hard to convince herself. Then she realized that no one had called her today. It was so late. Someone should have called by now. She quickly found her phone.

"Diane, hi, it's me. I just woke up. Did you try to call?"

"No," Diane said sleepily. "I haven't been up very long myself. How are you feeling this morning?"

Lorie wanted to ask her about Dave. She was wondering why he hadn't called yet but was reluctant to mention him. She didn't want to seem anxious.

"Oh, I'm fine. I just can't believe that I slept this late, and I wanted to check on you. You were such a big help to me last night. I just wanted you to know how much I really appreciated it."

"Hey, what are friends for? By the way, I knew we would be sleeping late today, so last night after I got home, I called Dave and left him a message about how we got stuck cleaning up and that we would be sleeping late today. Hope you don't mind that I told him, but I thought that you would need your rest today. Tomorrow it will start all over again, dealing with the office monsters."

"Yes, you're right, as usual," Lorie agreed, glad she found out why Dave hadn't called without actually asking about him. It was like killing two birds with one stone, checking on Diane and obtaining information on Dave as well.

June was puzzled when she looked at the hours Lorie turned in for the fund-raiser. She didn't work as long as June anticipated. *It should have taken Lorie twice as long.* June had checked to make sure everything was done to her satisfaction the first thing this morning, and all the tasks were completed. Everything looked clean. *But it should have taken her longer.* June decided to question other employees and volunteers on the cleanup committee. Most of them didn't pay attention to who was working. They wanted to finish quickly and go home. One of the employees, however, did remember someone who seemed to be helping Lorie.

Lorie jumped as June's loud voice summoned her over the intercom. She hurried to June's office. "Yes?" she said as she walked in the door.

"You had someone do your work Saturday night," June said, staring at her with glassy, cold eyes. It was an accusation, not a question.

Somehow Lorie figured that she would find out. "No one did any work for me. I did what you gave me to do on the list." Lorie once again felt daggers from June's eyes.

"Don't lie to me. Someone on the committee saw one of your friends helping you."

"I was supposed to take a friend home after the fund-raiser," Lorie said. "She didn't have another ride, so she was waiting for me to finish the chores. Maybe she got tired of waiting and picked up a dish or two, but I didn't ask her to help with anything. We all just wanted to get done and go home. I don't see where this is a problem."

"Wait a minute, sister. You don't tell me what is a problem and what is not a problem. First of all, for insurance reasons, only those employees or our volunteers assigned to certain stations during a fund-raiser are permitted on the premises or to do certain tasks. When I give my report to James, this is not going to look good for you."

Lorie didn't feel like arguing with June. June was a hopeless case, and nothing Lorie said or didn't say would make a difference. Lorie rolled her eyes and said, "Okay, fine," then walked out.

"I didn't dismiss you yet!" June shouted. But Lorie just kept walking back to her office.

Lorie glanced up at the clock. She had been working for hours and really needed a break. It was almost lunchtime. Suddenly, the sound of high heels clopping down the hall reached her ears. Monica plowed into the office, looking terrible. Lorie figured she had been drinking. Almost afraid to say anything at all, she mustered a small "hi," then continued to work. She didn't expect a reply but heard a muffled "yeah" as Monica staggered to her desk. If Monica was hung over or maybe even drunk, perhaps she wouldn't bother Lorie today with teasing remarks.

Lorie watched as Monica rummaged through her purse, then her desk, wondering what she was looking for. Suddenly, James emerged from his office. It was the first time Lorie saw him today. She didn't remember seeing him come in. She wondered how early he got here this morning. He glanced over at Monica with a sour look on his face. Was there trouble in paradise? Lorie tried to hide a smile. James walked over and helped Monica get out of her chair. As he passed Lorie's desk, he looked at her with cold piercing eyes and said, "Going to lunch." Lorie watched as they left the office.

Unbelievable, simply unbelievable! After her lunch break, Lorie felt refreshed. Maybe she'd be able to get through the rest of the day. Returning to her office, however, she noticed José standing by the coffeepot. An uncomfortable sensation surged through her. She wished that coffeepot was in another part of the building.

"When will James be back?" José said, turning toward Lorie as she entered the office.

"He should be back soon," she replied.

José walked over to her desk, and Lorie felt he was too close to her. Uncomfortable, she worked hard to control her breathing. José stared at her with penetrating eyes before speaking, "Heard you are going out of your way to aggravate my wife. If I were you, I would back off. You don't want to aggravate me."

"I haven't done anything to aggravate anyone," Lorie said, looking at him with repugnance. "If you or your wife have a problem with me, then it would be best to talk to James. He informed me that he is my boss, and I am only to take orders or direction from him and no one else."

Lorie looked away and tried to continue working. José stood at her desk for a few moments that seemed like hours but said nothing. Never had she imagined wanting James to be present. Fortunately, James and Monica returned.

"José!" James shouted as he entered the office. "You're just the one I want to see."

They entered James's office and shut the door. Monica, now somewhat sober and more in control of her faculties, stared contemptibly at Lorie before returning to her desk. Lorie just shook her head. She knew Monica was mad because Lorrie beat her in the golf tournament. Monica did not seem to want to forgive that.

Lorie's spirits usually perked up by quitting time, always relieved when it was time to go home. *Thank you, Lord, for getting me through yet another day,* she would say to herself as she left the office each day.

Relaxing at home in her favorite chair with a cup of tea, she stared out the window. Looking at the house across the street, Lorie remembered how she and Jake were such good friends with Irene and Frank. They were an odd couple. Irene was rather large and heavyset. Frank was very short and thin. But they were such good neighbors. They watched the house when she and Jake were out of town, retrieved the mail in, and watered the plants. Lorie and Jake would do the same for them when they were out of town. She thought of all the times when they would bring each other funny little gifts back from their vacations. Lorie's smile faded as she remembered how Irene turned on her as soon as Jake passed away. In Irene's mind, Lorie became a rival for her husband. Lorie was extremely hurt when she discovered how Irene felt as thoughts of Frank had never entered her mind. Frank was the kind of guy who seemed to be afraid of his wife. She was the one who wore the pants in the family, and when she said "Jump," he'd say, "How high?" An exaggeration, yes, but that's how Lorie perceived them to be. Jake and Lorie always found their relationship to be quite amusing but were truly fond of both Irene and Frank. They were great neighbors. Now when Lorie saw Frank outside working in the yard, he would only speak to her if Irene was not home. Otherwise, he was afraid to say anything and would quickly go into the house.

How sad, Lorie thought as she stared out the window. *Is Irene becoming senile? I miss the friendship that Jake and I had with them. Why does Irene think that I could possibly be interested in Frank sexually? Yes, he is a nice guy but definitely not my type. Besides, I wouldn't want to have anything to do with a married man. I wish I could convey this to Irene somehow, but she does not want me in her life or around her husband.*

But judging by the way the other neighbors treated Lorie, even if Irene did talk about her in a negative way, they must not have believed her. Plus, the idea bordered on the ridiculous. Anyone with any common sense at all would know that was not the case.

Taking a sip of tea, Lorie closed her eyes as she remembered a sermon that Father O'Malley gave one Sunday. He said that the primary emphasis should be placed on the unselfish love that should animate us and will result in love and concern for all. She remembered the First Letter of John and picked up her Bible. "Beloved, since

God loved us so much, we also ought to love one another" (1 John 4:11). Lorie thought that was easier said than done. Her thoughts still focused on Father O'Malley's many sermons. He was a good speaker, and many times Lorie would come home from church and make notes in her weekly journal. Paging through her journal, she came across the topic of pride. "One of the most dangerous temptations for traditional Christians is an easy assumption that they have responded to God's invitation and are now comfortably seated at the banquet, waiting for their final and inevitable heavenly reward." She noted his definition of pride: "It's not so much the tendency to think too much of oneself as it is to think too little of others." Father O'Malley emphasized the importance of having respect for others regardless of their social status or perceived unworthiness. Lorie gently closed her journal while praying silently for the grace to open her heart with kindness to all people.

The loud buzzing of the phone quickly dissipated Lorie's thoughts as she reached to answer it. "Hello," she said softly.

"Hi, Lorie," Dave said energetically. "Just checking in with you this evening to make sure you're okay."

Why is he wondering if I'm okay? Lorie thought before replying. "Yes, of course."

"Diane was telling me about the difficult people that you work with," Dave continued. "I want you to know that if you ever need anything, even if it's just a shoulder to cry on, I'm here for you."

"Thank you, Dave," Lorie said, smiling. "I appreciate your friendship. You are very kind."

Dave was reluctant to ask how her day went. Not easily finding the words, there was a pause in the conversation. Lorie noticed the silence and asked, "Dave, are you still there?"

"Yes," he replied. "I was just thinking about the golf tournament fund-raiser and wondering how things went for you at the office today."

Not wanting to delve into the many facets of this complicated situation, she replied, "Dave, I'm really tired this evening. It has been a rather hectic day. I'm going to turn in early tonight, but thank you for calling."

Dave got the hint. She didn't want to talk about it right now.

"Okay then. I'll let you go for now, but I would like to take you out to dinner sometime this week. Would it be okay if I called you tomorrow?"

Lorie smiled to herself once again and thought, *I think this one is a keeper.* "Of course, you can call me anytime. Good night and thank you."

As she got off the phone, a slight jog in memory caused her to glance out the window again. *You don't have to like me, Irene. It's such a waste of time to have so much bitterness in your heart for no apparent reason. You have created a finite situation, and for that, I truly feel sorry for you.*

Turning out the lights, she headed upstairs for the evening while thinking it was time for another visit with Father O'Malley before any more unpleasant situations occurred.

James sat at his desk, huddled over illicit receipts, pretending that they'd been received via the fund-raiser. He realized that in due time the company had to pay its taxes. As long as he could make it look like the company was having an unusually profitable year, the tax man would be happy. Plus, the board of directors would think he was doing an excellent job. He thought it was a win-win situation for everyone.

A knock on the door caused James to jerk abruptly. "Yes," he called out, relieved to see it was José.

"I'm meeting with the supplier tomorrow night," José said. "You have any instructions before I meet with the buyer?"

James thought for a moment. "No, business as usual," he said, leaning back in his chair. "But, José, I need a lump sum of cash, not too big of course but adequate. I won't be able to account for the money if it just shows up. Could you go to a few casinos with me one night this week?"

"Sure, what's your plan?"

"I'm going to do a little low-risk gambling: blackjack, craps, slots. I'll bet each chip, one at a time, on red. If I do that twenty or thirty times, I'll have about the same amount I started with. We can go to a few different casinos and repeat the whole process. Eventually, I'll cash in all my chips and go home with a story about how I won a bunch of money."

"That's one way to get at your stash without anyone being the wiser," José said, impressed. He pulled out a cigar. But before he had a chance to light it, James yelled that it was a smoke-free building.

"It's late afternoon. Everyone will be leaving soon. Who cares?" José's casual manner really irked James at times.

"If a board member waltzes into this office right now and sees you smoking a cigar, we both would be in trouble. We can't do anything that would cause any suspicion, José. There is too much at stake right now, and you know it."

José put the cigar back in his jacket. "In a few days, I'll be turning US dollars over to my peso broker," he said softly. "He'll purchase the goods. When received, we'll get paid, minus his usual commission."

"You're dealing with a black-market peso broker, José," James interrupted. "Just watch your back."

"James, he's like an old friend," José said calmly. "We understand each other. Besides, he charges a lower fee to conduct transactions, and we don't have to worry about government intervention."

"I guess you know what you're doing. So far, everything has run smoothly. So what else have you got going?"

José got up slowly and looked out the window as he spoke, "Amphetamine hydrochloride, a powder, doled out in two-ounce packets. Each packet is cut with one ounce of powdered sugar, making three ounces of the adulterated drug."

James nodded his head in agreement. "And the marijuana, how much is usually stuffed into the tires?"

"Up to seven pounds, at least," José said, a sly smile crossing his face. James looked surprised. "You stuff the loose weed into a tubeless tire, then place an inner tube in it, inflate it so that it holds the weed against the inside of the tire. Simple!"

"And what about the spare tire?"

"It works on any tire. If customs officials shake it, they would hear nothing."

"We'll have to keep our financial transactions complex in order to throw off anyone who might become suspicious," James said. "We have to make sure that tracing the origin of the money becomes very difficult."

"I applaud your skill, James," José agreed. "You have done well accounting for the illegal funds by adjusting legitimate transactions."

"Yeah, working with these invoices is driving me crazy," James said gravely. "But hey, someone's got to do it!"

They both laughed as José walked out the door. José was still laughing as he passed Lorie's desk. She pretended not to see or hear him, not wanting to feel creeped out. Lorie wondered why José spent so much time talking privately in James's office. She knew something was amiss but didn't have any definite proof. Someday they'd get careless and she'd find out. Lorie looked up at the clock, relieved it was quitting time and thankful that she made it through another day. She freshened up quickly before leaving for her appointment with Father O'Malley.

"Father, I'm so glad that you could see me today. I need a few tips on how to have a peaceful coexistence with some of the people that I work with. They can be very difficult and try my patience."

Father O'Malley always smiled before speaking, making her feel relaxed and as if she was not only talking to a priest but to an old friend. "Lorie, many people avoid confrontation of any kind because it makes them very uncomfortable. Sometimes that is appropriate, but generally, compromise and collaboration are better. First, it's important to separate the issue from the person. Disagreement is a normal part of life. We can disagree with co-workers and still manage to get along."

"Not in my office." Lorie frowned. "If you disagree with them, it's off with your head."

Father O'Malley looked concerned as he spoke, "Something important for all involved is to fight respectfully. That means don't attack one another's weaknesses and no name-calling. You must also take into consideration the feelings of others and work toward a mutually beneficial solution."

"Father, I don't think you understand the type of situation that I face each day," Lorie said sadly. "Everything you're telling me is good, if you're dealing with normal people."

"Lorie, God sees beauty and light in all of us, but we usually don't see it in ourselves or in others. He wants us to keep searching for it until we do find it within ourselves and also in others. To him, no soul is insignificant. So, my child, deal with trouble calmly. You can be assertive but without the aggression that is likely to alienate your co-workers. A suggestion that I give to everyone who comes to me with a bad situation is to take a deep breath and slowly count to ten before any confrontation. Remember, every conflict has consequences."

Lorie agreed with Father O'Malley but doubted that he really understood how bad her situation was at work. She already practiced many of the things that he suggested but seemed to get nowhere. "Thank you, Father," Lorie said, standing up. "Your advice is very helpful."

"No matter what happens to us, be it good or bad, it's all part of God's plan," Father O'Malley said, looking at her kindly. He again gave her a blessing before she left and handed her another holy card. She thanked him as he walked her to the door. Upon stepping outside, they were surprised to see a radiant double rainbow, a rare occurrence, with the colors of the outer rainbow arranged in reverse order.

"God is so amazing!" Father O'Malley said as Lorie stood in awe, gazing at this breathtaking sight, unable to speak. "God's wonders can leave you speechless."

Getting ready for her date with Dave, Lorie was happy that he was so insistent about taking her to the Radcliff Inn for dinner. It was one of the better restaurants in town, tastefully ornate and marked by refinement. Hearing the doorbell, she hurried down the stairs to answer it. She had to keep from running. All she needed was to break a leg trying to get to the door. With one quick look in the hall mirror, she opened the door slowly. "Why, good evening, sir," she said with a seductive smile.

Surprised but delighted, Dave thought Lorie was absolutely gorgeous. He handed her a lovely bouquet of flowers and said, "For you, my lady." They both laughed.

"Please come in," Lorie said dreamily as the soothing scent of the flowers flowed through the air. "They are so beautiful. Thank you so much. Let me put them in a vase. I'll only be a minute."

"Please take your time." Relaxing on her sofa, he noticed her reading material strewn about the room: *Sail, Blue Water Sailing, Boating World, Boating Life*.

Lorie noticed him leafing through the magazines. "Are you taking an interest in sailing?" she asked.

"Maybe," he answered. "All these different magazines seem to be identical on the inside."

"Not so," she said, laughing. "*Sail* features articles on boat equipment design, boat handling, and navigation. *Blue Water Sailing* is a monthly magazine about cruising and offshore sailing. *Boating World* is a boating lifestyle magazine for people who enjoy boating, and *Boating Life* is dedicated to recreational boating, activities, and destinations. So you see, even though they are very much alike, they are all different."

"Okay, that explains it," Dave said with a bewildered look on his face.

"Yes, sailing does have a reputation for being a boring spectator sport," Lorie continued, "but that is not true. Just for conversation's sake, did you know that in 1857, the philosopher Henry David Thoreau was the first to convey the enjoyment of both spiritual and lifestyle aspects of cruising while canoeing in the wilderness of Maine?"

"Interesting," Dave said. "By the way, would you be able to give me a few sailing lessons?"

"I'm not an instructor, but if you're serious, I'm sure we can set something up for you. There are a lot of things that you will have to master. My late husband, Jake, was a natural. For instance, the air moving across the sails of a boat creates various forces. If the sails are properly oriented with respect to the wind, then the net force on the sails will move the vessel forward. But boats propelled by sails cannot sail directly into the wind. The boat must be turned through the eye of the wind back and forth in order to progress directly upwind."

Dave's expression was one of utter confusion. "Okay, I'm lost. I can't think on an empty stomach anyway. Let's continue this conversation over dinner."

Lorie grabbed her purse, turned out the lights, and headed out the door, thinking Dave would do well as a sailor. *He definitely has winning qualities.*

Arriving at Radcliff's, Lorie was embraced by an air of sophistication. Seated by the window and waiting for their drinks, she looked over the menu. "My, the cuisine is certainly a vibrant mixture of traditional favorites," she said. "It's hard to choose."

"Yes, and all vying for a solo performance on this table," Dave joked.

The waiter brought their drinks and asked if they knew what they were ordering or if they needed more time.

Lorie looked at Dave and said, "I'm ready if you are." Dave nodded in agreement. Lorie ordered consommé julienne, hearts of lettuce with blue cheese dressing, broiled steak, browned potatoes, and green beans with mushrooms.

Dave smiled and said, "Looks like you read my mind. Make that two please." The waiter asked them how they would like their steaks cooked, then hurried away.

"This is a wonderful table," Lorie said, noticing the view from the window. "You can see forever."

"Well, it didn't happen by accident," Dave replied. "I specifically asked for this table. I wanted you to really enjoy this evening. I know things are rough for you at the office, and everyone deserves a relaxing evening from time to time. Wouldn't you agree?"

"Dave, you must be an angel in disguise," Lorie said, smiling.

Dave laughed and whispered, "Don't tell anyone."

Shortly, the waiter arrived with their dinner, and Dave reminded Lorie she was going to tell him more about sailing. Lorie thought for a moment. "Well, I learned a lot from Jake. He even enticed me into taking a few sailing lessons. I'll have to introduce you to my sloop, *Sunrise*."

"I'm looking forward to it." Dave laughed.

Lorie took a sip of wine as she looked out over the horizon. Distant thoughts of sailing trickled back into her memory. "Sailing is the art of controlling a boat with foils called 'sails.' Mastery of the skill requires experience in varying wind and sea conditions, as well as understanding one's surroundings. Jake and I used to do something called 'gunkholing.' That consists of taking a series of day sails to out-of-the-way places, swimming or snorkeling, and anchoring overnight. For us, it was a relaxing weekend getaway. Also, it was much less expensive than a normal vacation on land."

"Where did you mostly sail?" Dave asked.

"Gee, there were so many places," Lorie sighed, "but mainly the northeast, Chesapeake Bay, Long Island Sound, and the Great Lakes."

The evening grew late as Dave's interest in sailing increased. Noticing the time, Lorie promised to continue the conversation another day. Dave took her hand as he walked her to her door.

Lorie turned to him. "Dave, I had a great time tonight. Thank you so much. I wish I didn't have to go to work tomorrow."

"I know it's usually hectic for you at work," Dave said, hearing the stress in her voice as she mentioned work. "You need your rest. I'll see you over the weekend." With that, he gave her a little kiss then walked to his car.

Lorie waved goodbye before going in. She was so glad Dave was an understanding guy. With her mind at rest, a peaceful sleep engulfed her that night.

Busily typing away, the loud buzzing of the intercom startled Lorie.

"Lorie, could you come to my office?"

She knew what James wanted to talk to her about as she entered his office. James looked at her with his usual cold stare. "Have a seat."

Lorie sat down quietly across from his desk.

"Lorie, June tells me that you are becoming completely insubordinate. This report states that you had a friend help you with work that you were required to do alone. June said that she explained to you why people who are not employees or volunteers cannot work here but that you walked out of her office before she was finished speaking. If you don't straighten up, I'm afraid I will have to let you go."

Lorie knew that James was bluffing. He had to be. After all, she was the one who constantly had to help Monica on everything and also did a great deal of work for June. Those women would not be able to hold their positions favorably if it were not for Lorie holding things together at the office.

"James, as I told June," Lorie said calmly, "a friend of mine asked if I could take her home after the fund-raiser. I agreed because I wasn't told that I had to be on the cleanup committee until the last minute, just before the golf tournament started. My friend was sitting there afterward and waiting for me to finish working. I did not ask her to help me. If she got tired of sitting there, maybe she picked up a few things, but I did not see her do anything. If June would have informed me beforehand that I was to work afterward, then I wouldn't have agreed to take anyone home."

"Lorie, you are going to have to try and get along better with the other employees," James said, a look of disgust on his face. "I am sick and tired of these complaints. Consider this your first warning."

Lorie felt like quitting. She knew that James would be in a heck of a spot if she did, but she needed her job. She stood up and walked out of his office, not caring if she was dismissed or not. As she sat down and continued her work, the sound of screeching high heels stopped at her desk. She looked up. Of course, it was Monica.

"In trouble again, I presume?"

Before Lorie could think of anything to say, Monica walked back to her desk. Lorie felt her blood pressure rising. She had to tell herself to calm down, that getting angry wasn't worth it. Monica and June's day would come. She was sure of it.

Later that day, Lorie noticed that she was alone. Monica and James were on break and, no one else seemed to be around. Lorie casually walked into James's office. A desk drawer he usually kept locked was open. Lorie figured that he probably didn't lock it because he was only on a short break. She thought this was her chance and slowly peered into the drawer. Pulling out a small writing tablet, she quickly leafed through it: cocoa leaves, opium, cannabis, unlicensed LSD, car tires. *What did car tires have to do with anything?* Suddenly, she heard Monica's high heels coming down the hall. She immediately put the tablet back the way she found it, closed the drawer silently, and practically ran on tiptoes to the coffeepot in the office. Lorie was pouring herself a cup of coffee when James and Monica walked in. He went into his office and shut the door. Monica strutted over to her desk and nonchalantly thumbed through a few files on her desk. Lorie looked at Monica and thought it would be great if she actually knew how to work.

That evening, as Lorie relaxed in her favorite lounge chair with a cup of tea, she thought about the notebook she saw in James's desk. Curiosity got the best of her. As she suspected, cannabis was marijuana. But what about the car tires? Could it be that they were smuggling drugs in the tires? Lorie felt her stomach tighten and had to tell herself to calm down. There was no need to get knots in her stomach over what they are doing. It was their problem. Still, Lorie didn't know what to do or how to handle this. Criminal behavior was foreign to her, having been raised a devout Catholic, but she did know that possession of any hallucinogenic drugs with the intent to sell was a felony. Reluctant to say anything to her friends, she decided that she would take some time to figure things out first. She knew she was treading on eggshells and needed to accumulate enough evidence before going to the authorities. If not, she could wind up at the bottom of a lake with a cement block tied to her leg. That terrified her. As she laid her head on her pillow that night, tears welled in her eyes, and sleep became a distant reflection.

Tired from a sleepless night, Lorie dragged herself out of bed the next morning and began getting ready for work. She tried to focus, but her mind kept wandering back to the notebook she found in James's desk. Lorie considered her options. If she found out too much, James might get wise and put her in harm's way. Lorie argued with herself as she drove to the office. She was so accustomed to her routine at work that she performed her duties each day robotically. Taking time out, of course, to deal with the likes of June, Monica, and James. *If it wasn't for them, she would actually enjoy work, she thought as she prepped the office coffeepot.*

Lorie was startled when James's voice came loudly over the intercom.

"Lorie, could you come to my office?"

She didn't realize that James was already in since she had just gotten there herself. She glanced at her watch. She knew she wasn't late as she hurried to his office.

"Good morning, James. Did you need something?"

He was busy stuffing something into an envelope.

"I need this to go to the post office right now, but before you leave, bring me a cup of coffee," he said as he sealed the envelope.

Lorie was glad that the coffee was not finished brewing yet. "I just put coffee on. It should be done in a few minutes."

"Well, just go now and get this in the mail," James said, looking aggravated.

Lorie took the envelope, got her purse, and headed to the post office. Heading back to her car, she ran into Al Chambers.

"Well, good morning young lady," he said with his usual big smile.

"Good morning, Al."

"So what brings you to the post office this early?"

"I had to mail something for James."

"I'm heading for the coffee shop across the street," Al said. "Would you have time to join me?"

"I really would like to join you, Al," Lorie said, wishing that she could. "But I have to get back to the office."

He saw the disappointed look on her face. "I'll call James and tell him that I insisted." Before Lorie could object, Al was on his cell phone. She knew that James went out of his way to please the board members, so she figured that she was going to be able to join Al for a cup of coffee. But Lorie also knew that James would not be happy about this, and she would pay the price when she got back to the office. Just another normal day with someone mad at her for something.

"I guess you are wondering why I asked you to have coffee with me this morning, Lorie," Al said. Lorie was surprised by that question. She didn't know how to respond. Al could see that she was lost for words, so he continued, "Some of the board members are questioning Monica's abilities to hold the position James has given her. She rakes in a pretty good salary, but she seems to have a problem with alcohol. In your honest opinion, does she ever show up intoxicated for work?"

Lorie was astonished by the question and completely caught off guard. Once again, she was lost for words. After a few moments, she said, "Al, as you probably know, James and Monica are rather close. Since I have to work with both of them, I prefer not to comment."

"I guess you feel like you're being put in the middle of a rather awkward situation," Al said, noting Lorie's stress.

Lorie smiled but said nothing.

"Your silence speaks louder than words," Al said. "My advice to you is to hang in there."

Lorie felt like she could trust Al. She also wanted to know some things herself. "Al, did you know Monica before she started working at Glendale?" Lorie said, trying to be casual.

"Yes, but not real well. I knew her husband. He was a nice guy. He was killed in a car accident. After that, her whole personality seemed to change. She used to dress and act with dignity when I would see her with her husband at various business dinners. I notice now she sometimes looks like, well, I'd rather not say."

Lorie laughed out loud but quickly put her hand over her mouth. "I'm sorry, Al. Please excuse me for laughing. It's just the way you said it."

Al seemed to read her mind and said, "Looks like we're on the same page."

Lorie thanked Al for the coffee and headed back to the office. She wondered just how much he and the other board members knew. Monica did drink way too much at the fund-raisers, and it was obvious that she and James were having an affair. Lorie wondered if anyone on the board saw that or if they even cared. Lorie was a natural at reading people and was aware of the fact that some of the board members also had mistresses. At times, she wondered if all rich men had someone on the side but figured that there had to be a few good ones. She wanted to believe that people were basically good but occasionally got caught in various situations. She would scold herself harshly when she felt that she was getting too judgmental. Only God should judge anyone. She tried to give everyone the benefit of the doubt.

As soon as she walked into the office, James summoned her. Reluctantly she went to his office.

"So, Lorie, tell me what's going on."

"What do you mean?" she asked, perplexed.

"Why did you have coffee with Al?"

"James, it was not my idea to have coffee with Al. He insisted and called you to okay it."

"What did you talk about?" James said angrily.

Lorie thought that was a very strange question to ask someone, and she repeated it out loud. "What did we talk about? It was just small talk, James. I don't see why any of this is upsetting you."

"Your duties do not include having coffee with the board members," James said, trying to control his emotions. "Make sure this does not happen again. You can go now."

Lorie couldn't believe the conversation that had just taken place. It was almost as if James was afraid of something. As soon as she got back to her desk, Monica walked over and slapped the message pad down hard.

"While you were out running around with Al, the phone was ringing off the hook." She quickly turned and walked away. Lorie was confounded. Even when she tried to be nice and please everyone, she still found trouble. As she tried to calm down and focus on getting back to the work at hand, Al's remark popped into her head. "My advice to you is to hang in there." Lorie contemplated that for a few moments. *Maybe there is light at the end of the tunnel.*

That evening, as Lorie settled down with her usual cup of tea, thoughts of her childhood slowly emerged. She remembered how her parents and sister Emma looked forward to their yearly summer camping trips. She could still see her dad's face as he excitedly explained what he had planned for vacation. The women in the family spent weeks getting things ready to pack. She admired her dad for working so hard during the year and saving for their annual trip.

A trip to Yellowstone National Park left a lasting impression. She remembered the many geysers, hot springs, and cauldrons in the park and the excitement of waiting for Old Faithful to erupt, shooting water and vapor straight up into the air. Etched in her mind was a particular morning when she awoke before the others. Peeping out of the tent, she noticed a fine haze in the air gently settling on the trees. As the sun rose, the leaves sparkled in the early morning mist. She focused her eyes again through a clearing and noticed the glistening yellow color of the steep canyon walls. It was just like seeing a little bit of heaven. Then she laughed as she thought of the bears. They were both cute and comical as they constantly scavenged for food. She remembered the two little bear cubs on the side of the road. Her dad stopped the car but told the girls not to get out because the mother bear was not far away and would be very protective. Lorie and her sister opened the car window just a little and were throwing cookies out to the cubs. The cubs were so playful as they devoured the cookies. Suddenly, the mother bear came out of nowhere. She was huge and laid her upper body across the hood of the car. Lorie remembered her mom yelling at her dad to do something.

"Girls, open the window on the other side of the car and throw out the whole bag of cookies," her dad said calmly. "Then close the window tightly."

Lorie and her sister followed their father's instructions. Then everyone sat for a few minutes, wondering what the mother bear would do. As quick as a flash, she stood up on her two hind legs then dashed toward the bag of cookies. Retrieving the cookies, she ran into the woods with the cubs hurriedly trailing behind her. Her mom was relieved, claiming that it was too close a call for comfort.

Her dad laughed and said, "Won't we have some stories to tell when we get back home?"

Returning to the present, somber feelings filled her spirit as she thought of her family. She missed them so much. Lorie and her mom grew closer after her dad passed away. But when her mom died, it was unbearable. Both she and Emma began to feel like orphans. They got together as much as possible, trying to assure each other of better and brighter tomorrows.

While sipping her tea, Lorie noted the design on her tea cup, which had belonged to her beloved grandmother. Her granny was a respectable woman, her white hair pinned in a bun and her dress always covered in a neatly pressed apron. She spoke broken English at best, but her manner was loving and generous to all. Every Sunday, she would have the family over for a delicious feast of pierogi, homemade chicken soup, stuffed cabbage rolls, and her wonderful Polish bread, Babka. Her granny had a heart of gold. During the Great Depression, when the itinerant rail riders would pass by the farm, she would always make sure the hungry men were fed before traveling on. She knew hunger as a child in Poland, and because of those difficult times, she felt blessed to live in this country where food was plentiful. She acknowledged that all blessings are a gift from God and must be shared.

Golden memories of so long ago but still so fresh. If only Emma were still here to reminisce. Lorie could almost see Emma running through the field and laughing, her long blond hair glistening in the sunlight. *Those were happy times.* Although Lorie loved her sister, Emma's life became too complicated for Lorie to handle. Both she and Jake tried to be there for Emma after her husband, Pete, passed away. Emma struggled trying to hold down a full-time job while constantly bailing her son, Rod, out of trouble. Lorie started to cry as she remembered the stress that Rod gave his mother. *That stress is what caused her to have a heart attack.* She wondered what life was like for Rod now that he was in prison. She felt obligated to go see him but could never get on the visitors' list. She and Rod were never close, and he did not want to see anyone. Lorie prayed for Rod each day, saddened by the fact that she could not even visit her one remaining relative. Maybe it was for the best. What could she say to him? She would always have love in her heart for him because he was her nephew, but it was a sad love because of all the hurt he caused the family, especially her dearly departed sister.

She remembered Rod's wife, Leah. From what Lorie saw, the woman was a very bad influence on her nephew. Her drinking, drug use, and criminal actions in general were a major factor in bringing Rod down. Leah seemed to be a class act when it came to scamming people and companies that she worked for. She cheated on everything, from taxes to unemployment benefits and even workmen's compensation. She knew the law inside and out and always seemed to get away with all her crooked dealings. The most amazing thing Lorie noticed about Leah was the fact that every time she was sure that she got away with a scam, she'd go to the local bar and, while on a drinking binge, would brag about how she got away with it. The woman had no morals or scruples. Rod tried to leave Leah many times, but invariably, she tracked him down like a bloodhound and, through drugs, made him take her back. It became a vicious cycle that ultimately ended in a life sentence for Rod. Of course, none of this seems to faze Leah, who was still scamming everyone she met and still bragging about her scandals at the local bars. Lorie thought Leah was living on the edge and wouldn't be surprised if someone knocked her off someday. With her lifestyle, she was asking for it.

Lorie remembered a statement in a book that she had read years ago: "Life is sad." Lorie thought that was true but was also convinced life was a blessing. She picked up her Bible and opened it to John 16:33 and read aloud, "I tell you all this that in me you may find peace. You will suffer in the world. But take courage! I have overcome the world." With that, she found peace in her heart. Trying to dismiss all negative thoughts, she headed upstairs for the evening.

CHAPTER 6

Trying to get through the pile of folders and mail on her desk, it seemed to be business as usual on this gloomy morning. Lorie looked up as José and Monica came out of James's office. She tried to listen carefully as James told them about buying a vacation package to the Cayman Islands. He lowered his voice considerably as he talked about investing money overseas. Lorie thought there had to be an ulterior motive for James to do anything, even go on vacation. The detective within her started to surface. If he did go away, maybe she could find out what really was going on.

After meeting with José and Monica, James called Lorie into his office. "Lorie, I'll be going on vacation next week. While I'm gone, June and Monica will be in charge. Make sure they have everything they need and don't give them a hard time."

Lorie was surprised. She always did most of their work and refused to argue with them, even when they pushed her to the limit. "Okay, James, if you feel like I'm the one who causes the problems around here, then I'll hand in my resignation right now," Lorie said with fire in her eyes.

James was taken aback by her response. He knew June and Monica depended on Lorie to get things done appropriately. If she left as he was about to go out of town, it would be a disaster. "Lorie, you apparently took what I said the wrong way," he said quickly. "The problem is that you are a little too sensitive. I'm sure you also take things the wrong way when June or Monica say something to you as well. You would probably get along with them much better if you could just chill out a little."

"James, I have always gone out of my way to placate them," she said, anger in her voice, "and I refuse to argue with them. I'm at a loss as to how to deal with them."

"If there is any arguing in this office while I am gone, I will take disciplinary action when I get back," James said, now angry himself. "That will be all for now."

James looked down at the papers on his desk and began shuffling through them. Lorie realized that the meeting was over, and as usual, nothing was accomplished. A hopeless feeling came upon her as she slowly walked back to her desk.

June walked into the office. "Some of the board members are having a meeting later this morning," she said loudly. "See that everything is set up for them. Do it now."

Lorie couldn't believe her ears. "June, I have to take care of this mail right now."

"You have one hour," June said, looking at her watch. "You'll have to clean up from last night's event before you can set up. If you think you can do that, fine. But just make sure it gets done."

June left quickly, and Lorie went back to James's office. Knocking on the door, she walked in before he had a chance to answer.

"What is it now?" he said, with aggravation.

"June wants me to clean up from an event that was held last night before I set up for a meeting that some of the board members want to have in an hour. I don't have time to clean because of the workload on my desk. I haven't gotten to the mail yet, and that needs to be distributed. Do you want me to clean or do what is on my job description?"

James's face turned bright red. "Monica can handle the mail. Do whatever June tells you."

Lorie realized talking to James was a complete waste of time. She went upstairs to the meeting room and saw it was a mess. Quickly, she straightened up, ran the sweeper, and set up for the next meeting, finishing in record time. Her years of experience at the company paid off. She had learned long ago how to multitask. Heading back to her desk, she wondered if Monica had sorted and distributed the mail and how many people would complain that they got the wrong mail. Reaching her desk, she was relieved to see that Monica was still trying to sort the mail. Lorie smiled to herself, recognizing that Monica had no idea how to distribute the documents. Monica looked up, cross.

"The phones have been ringing off the hook while you were taking your time tidying up." She stood up, grabbed her purse, and walked out the door, saying, "I'm taking a break. You can finish sorting the mail."

Now Lorie had to clean up another mess. While she had been working upstairs, Monica did absolutely nothing with the mail. Everything was opened and scattered on her desk, but nothing was really sorted. This even made it harder for Lorie as she had to figure out what went together since most envelopes contained more than one document. Lorie was used to handling the mail, so in no time, she had it sorted and distributed. Some employees in various departments commented on the mail being late, as they tried to stay on schedule. Lorie was not about to let this go by without adding a comment of her own.

"Monica handled the mail today while I completed another assignment," she said sweetly, smiling. Just saying that made her feel better.

Glad another day was coming to an end, Lorie couldn't get out the door fast enough. She enjoyed relaxing at home with a good book or visiting with friends. While she was fixing herself something for dinner, Diane called.

"Hey, girl, would you like to run out to get something to eat?"

Lorie thought for a moment. "You know, I was just fixing a veggie stir-fry for dinner, but you're welcome to come over and join me."

"Okay, I'll be there soon."

Lorie knew that Diane loved veggies even more than she did, so she got a few more packs of frozen veggies out of the freezer. Soon, the girls were chowing down. Lorie always enjoyed having dinner with a friend but was especially glad that Diane could join her this evening.

"Diane, I would like to talk to you about something puzzling," Lorie said.

"What gives, girl?" Diane said attentively.

Lorie hesitated for a moment before speaking, "Diane, I feel that James is up to something illegal."

"I'm not surprised," Diane said. "That place is becoming a real zoo. Remember the good old days?"

"Yes, it was a great place to work before the current crew arrived," Lorie said, smiling, but quickly her smile turned to a frown.

"What is it, Lorie?" Diane said. "If something illegal is going on, you have to go to the authorities. If you don't, you might wind up being caught in the middle, which might in some way implicate you."

"No, no, they are very secretive," Lorie said, shaking her head. "I haven't a clue, but I suspect something is not right."

"What do you mean when you say 'they'?"

Reluctantly, Lorie said that she also suspected José and June to be involved. Diane asked if Monica was part of the scheme.

"I don't know what to think about Monica," Lorie said. "I know she and James are having an affair, but there is something deeper going on, and I'm just not sure what or who is involved."

"Why do you think it has to be something illegal?" Diane said, digging deeper. "What do you have to go on?"

"Diane, maybe I shouldn't even say this because I don't have the necessary proof to back up anything I tell you, but from the bits and pieces that I've put together over the past year, I feel strongly that James might be involved in money laundering and possibly drugs," Lorie said, knowing she could trust Diane. "And today I overheard him tell José and Monica that he bought a vacation package in the Cayman Islands."

"So what's illegal about going to the Cayman Islands?" Diane said, confused.

"Nothing, it's what he said after that, about wanting to invest money overseas. Why would he go through all the trouble of investing money overseas if it was legitimate?"

"Well, there must be reasons people do that. Maybe it's not always illegitimate. But on the other hand, James doesn't seem like the kind of guy who would have an extreme quantity of money to invest overseas, at least, not legally."

"Now you see what I mean?" Lorie said, glad that Diane was now getting the picture. "Plus, I have come across some strange-looking invoices in James's desk."

"You mean that you actually snooped through his desk?" Diane said, a surprised look on her face.

Lorie laughed. "This is what happened. James and Monica took a smoke break. I casually went into James's office since no one else was around. He usually keeps his desk drawers locked when he's not in the office, but I found one that was unlocked. I carefully looked through the drawer. That's when I saw the strange invoices. I managed to get everything back and get out of his office before they returned."

"Well, that's evidence. Did you make a copy of the invoices?"

"Diane, I barely got out of his office before they returned," Lorie said, sighing. "It was really a close call. When I heard them coming down the hall, I just had enough time to get to the office coffeepot. I was pouring a cup of coffee as they walked into the office."

"When James goes out of town, maybe the invoices will still be there. Other than James, who has the keys to his desk?"

"Gee, I don't know," said Lorie, deep in thought. "I don't think he would trust Monica with his keys. She can't do anything right. He would probably think that she would lose them or something. But James does have a lot of closed-door meetings with José, so much so that I'm beginning to think that they are partners in crime. Maybe, just maybe, June might have a set of keys to his desk."

Diane had a frightened look on her face. "Lorie, that woman is a real monster. I'm sure that if she caught you snooping around her things, it would be 'off with your head.' She seems to have a violent personality. At least, that is the impression I get."

"Diane, I did some snooping a while back. I looked at their resumes and did some checking on my own. How June and José ever got jobs at Glendale is really uncanny. Did you know that they both have prison records?"

"You're kidding! How in the world did they get hired?"

"You tell me," Lorie said, shaking her head. "Talk about weird. If someone committed a crime years ago and was sorry, give them another chance. But those two are street-smart and have terrible personalities. June didn't have a clue where to begin when she was hired. I taught her everything she knows now, plus I still do most of the work that she gets paid to do. The whole thing is absurd."

"Lorie, my advice to you is to get out of there. If there is something underhanded going on, you may be in danger."

Lorie almost agreed with her when she remembered what Al had told her. "Diane, I think maybe some of the board members might suspect something. When I had to go to the post office for James one day, I ran into Al Chambers. He insisted that I have coffee with him before going back to work. I reluctantly agreed, knowing that James would have a fit about it. Anyway, Al was asking me questions about Monica and mentioned her drinking problem. I was afraid to say anything negative about her because I knew the consequences would be severe, so I told him that I could not make a comment since I had to work with her. Al could see that I was afraid to speak, so he didn't push it."

"So what did he say when you couldn't answer his questions?" Diane asked.

"He told me to hang in there," Lorie said, smiling.

Diane seemed relieved. "Lorie, there are others now who are beginning to get the picture. If one board member realizes that something is amiss, the others will follow. Things will eventually come out."

Sitting in silence for a few minutes, the girls tried to think of a plan. Suddenly, Diane laughed as she thought of an article she read called "Avoid 'Awfulizing.'" Lorie looked puzzled.

"No, it's not funny," Diane said, shaking her head. "But the title of an article I read seems to fit the crew you are working with. The article stated that you should avoid 'awfulizing,' viewing your situation as a catastrophe. But you also have the stress of establishing a relationship with a group of people. The answer is not to make yourself miserable by worrying about what you should have done when things get bad or out of control. It also doesn't help to walk away from a problem and pretend it doesn't exists. To counter the effects of those destructive thought patterns, it suggests 'functional thinking.' Basically, it's having a positive attitude and not putting yourself down if things don't work out."

"I know what you're saying," Lorie sighed, "and I have tried every feasible approach at the office, but to no avail. The situation there is quite impossible, but if you can come up with some good functional thinking, let me know."

"Hey, it was just a thought." Diane shrugged.

Before Diane left for the evening, she asked if Lorie was going out with Dave Saturday night. "Of course," Lorie said, trying to hide a smile.

Diane gave her a little hug. "Lorie, he thinks the world of you, but you already knew that, right?"

"You know, I never thought I could again feel that special something that Jake and I shared," Lorie said, leaning against the wall, "but I've got to say, Dave is becoming a very special friend."

"You mean he's a keeper?"

Lorie punched her gently in the arm. "Get out of here and don't you dare say a word to Dave about anything we discussed tonight."

"Mum's is the word," Diane said, her finger against her lips. "I promise." She then drove away.

Lorie thought, *If anyone could understand, it would be Diane.*

The loud buzz of the phone startled her. Lorie quickly ran to answer it.

"Hi, Lorie. Guess who called me?" Lorie laughed. Kate always wanted her to guess something.

"Hi, Kate. No, I can't guess. You'll just have to tell me."

"Dave called and said that he was interested in taking sailing lessons." After a brief pause, she added jokingly, "I wonder what piqued his interest all of a sudden? Okay, give me the scoop. Are you two a couple or what?"

Lorie waited for Kate to take a breath before trying to answer, "Let's just say that we are becoming very good friends and leave it at that for now."

"Lorie"—Kate giggled—"the club is starting up a new class on sailing. Since Jake did most of the work in the past when you were sailing, I was thinking that it might be a good idea for you to retake the course with Dave. You're already familiar with it, and it would make him feel more secure being that this is a whole new field for him."

Lorie thought for a moment. "Yes, you're right. It might be a good idea. Sounds like fun. What will the course cover?"

"Let's see now," Kate said, pulling the list from her folder. "Okay, the introduction course includes the usual things like the history of sailing, physics, the effects of wind shear, basic sailing techniques, trim, tacking and jibing, reducing sail, sail trimming, hull trim and heeling, sailing hulls and shapes, sailing terminology, knots, rules and regulations, and, of course, licensing. So what do you think?"

"Sounds like it would be a lot for him to learn in a short period of time."

"It's going to be rather general. I don't think they will go into that much detail in this first course. Now the next one will cover approximately the same things but in more detail. Actually, some of the members are going to take the course again as a refresher."

Lorie thought for a moment before answering, "Okay, I'll give you a tentative yes right now, but let me talk to Dave first. I'm going to see him on Saturday."

"If you can, let me know by Monday, okay? And have a wonderful weekend. I'm sure you will."

"Thanks, Kate," Lorie said, thinking that Kate was the eternal matchmaker. "I'll call you Monday."

Just as Lorie was about to hang up the phone, Kate interrupted, "Lorie, I almost forgot. I have to tell you something else. This is so weird. Rich, Bob, and I were having lunch together the other day, and my, you won't believe this." Kate stopped to take a breath.

"What won't I believe?"

"Naturally, we were talking about sailing, but when I mentioned that you and Dave would probably take the sailing course together so that Dave would be more comfortable with it since this was out of his line of expertise, Rich seemed to get very aggravated. He asked if Dave was your new boyfriend. I told him that you all seemed to be rather close and have been dating lately. Well, Bob and I were shocked that Rich seemed to get so mad about that. After all, he is still dating that floozy from the strip club, and besides, you and Rich were never a couple. Anyway, all of a sudden, Rich told us that he was going to give Candy a ring. Bob and I were speechless. We actually couldn't speak. Finally, I asked him if he meant an engagement ring, and that is what he meant. After he left, Bob and I sat there in shock. We can't believe that he would actually want to marry someone like Candy, but what we are really concerned about is that it seems like the real reason he is giving her a ring is to get back at you. We can't understand why he is so upset about you dating Dave. It actually seems to make him angry. What gives?"

Lorie was speechless. She couldn't believe that Rich was still upset with her after all this time. "Kate, I don't know what to say. It's not like we were ever going together. Why is he acting like I broke his heart? And gee, we never even kissed once. I kid you not. Do you actually think that he is getting engaged just to get even with me?"

"I don't understand it," Kate said. "He used to be such a normal guy. When you told him that you weren't ready to get into the dating scene, his personality changed. He seems to get upset easily now and be in a bad mood. I thought after he started dating Candy, he would return to his old self once again, but apparently that hasn't happened. Maybe I should tell Bob to have a one on one with him to find out why you still bother him so much if he is planning to marry Candy. None of this makes any sense."

Lorie couldn't believe her ears. She took a deep breath. "I have to work with crazies all day long, and when I'm not at work, I'm usually happy and relaxed, especially now that Dave and I are dating. But if Rich is going to cause problems for me at the club, that will just add more stress to what I already have at work. My plate is not only full, at this point it seems to be overflowing with stress. I just don't understand it. I thought I was very nice the night I talked to him about not wanting to date yet. But maybe he thought that when I was ready to date, he would be the one. This may be like a slap in the face now that I'm dating Dave. Why does everything have to be so complicated?"

"I just thought maybe you would want to know about Rich's attitude," Kate said. "All I can say is that he must have fallen for you—hook, line, and sinker. So it might take a while before he really feels something for Candy. Until then, he probably won't be very nice to you or Dave, sorry to say."

"Kate, thanks for the heads-up," Lorie said, amazed by this unusual conversation. "Let's just play it by ear and see how it goes. Surely, things will get better eventually. One can only hope."

"Hey, you didn't do anything wrong. Maybe he will come around if we kill him with kindness. Actually, everyone thinks Candy is a joke, but if we all act like they are a great couple and make a fuss over them at the meetings, maybe he will take a turn for the better. Like you say, we can only hope. Got to run now. Call me."

Lorie sat there for a few minutes after her phone call from Kate. She felt like she'd been hit by a lead balloon. How in the world could she handle a situation like this? Hopefully, after Rich got married, he'd love his wife or at least accept things the way they are and move on. Maybe they could be friends again. Even as she tried to convince herself, she had her doubts.

Disturbed by Kate's call, Lorie tried to remember a relaxation technique she read about to reduce stress and bring more calm into her life. It was getting rather late, and the house was very quiet now. She sat back in her favorite chair and closed her eyes. She made a conscious effort to practice visualization. It's supposed to prevent stress from spiraling out of control. If Lorie focused her attention and visualized something calming, her stress should be reduced. Forming a mental image in her mind, she focused on relaxing at the ocean. She smelled the salt water and heard the sound of the waves gently crashing against the soft white sand. She felt the warmth of the sun on her body. As she relaxed completely, sleep swept over her, and peace filled her troubled spirit.

Saturday afternoon could not roll around fast enough. Lorie was excited about heading north with Dave to the vineyards and winery. Thoughts of the magnificent views of the vineyards produced a joyous sensation within her as she stepped out on her back porch to check the weather. It was an absolutely gorgeous day. *Thank you, Lord.*

During the long drive to the winery, Lorie listened intently as Dave related the many events that led to the planting of grapes in the area.

"The area is also great for apples and nut trees," he said, smiling. "But the most intriguing attribute is how the waters from the area were sought back in the Victorian times for their medicinal powers."

"Sort of like the Fountain of Youth in Florida?"

"I don't think so, but we can give it a try."

Laughing, they approached the vineyards. It was as beautiful as Lorie remembered. "It's been quite a while since I was up this way," she said, looking at the panoramic view. "But I can't say that I'm disappointed."

They were offered an exclusive private tour of the wine-making facility and enjoyed an informative talk about growing grapes and the wine-making process. A sit-down wine tasting of the award-winning wines followed, and a wonderful tray of assorted cheeses and crackers were served as the vineyard manager talked about wine appreciation and food pairings. He ended by quoting Benjamin Franklin: "Wine is constant proof that God loves us and loves to see us happy." After purchasing several bottles of wine, Dave and Lorie thanked the manager and the staff for the unique experience and headed home.

Driving home, Dave asked if Lorie had enjoyed the day.

"Oh yes, it was wonderful," she replied. "Thank you so much."

"I've made a reservation at Radcliff's tonight, if that's all right with you," Dave said. "We should be there in a few hours."

"Yes, the food is great, and so is the atmosphere." Lorie said, nodding in agreement. "It's one of my favorite restaurants."

Arriving at Radcliff's, Lorie was pleased to be seated at the same table as before, by the huge window. The view was great, and she loved to watch the sunsets. Lorie pondered over the menu.

"What sounds good to you tonight?" Dave asked.

"Well, the meal I had last time was excellent, but I'd like to try something else tonight. I think I'll go with the chicken ala Mornay with sweet potato balls and buttered peas with pimiento."

"You've read my mind again. How about that!" Dave laughed.

"Dave, you don't have to order the same thing as I do every time we dine out!"

Dave looked disappointed. "Well, you do have good taste. Would you mind if I ordered the same thing?"

"No, of course not," Lorie said with a laugh. "I was only kidding."

"The sunset is exceptionally beautiful this evening," Lorie said, sipping her after-dinner drink. Dave agreed.

"Didn't you once tell me that the name of your sloop was *Sunset*?"

"No," Lorie corrected. "Just the opposite, we 'baptized' it *Sunrise*."

"How do you baptize a sloop?"

Lorie looked serious. "With a bottle of champagne."

"Of course," Dave said mockingly, hitting himself in the head with his hand.

"Hey, I hear you want to take a sailing course," Lorie said. "Mind if I join you?"

"My, word travels fast in this town," Dave said, looking surprised. "Well, yes to both questions. Actually, I was going to ask if you would like to join me. Truthfully, I don't know a thing about sailing, but I would like to learn."

"Great!" Lorie shouted but put her finger to her mouth when all eyes were looking her way. "You know how it is, sometimes I just get carried away."

Dave ordered another round of drinks. "Kate sent me a list of what would be included in the introductory course. Maybe you could elaborate a little for me."

"Okay," Lorie said. "What would you like to know?"

Dave pulled a sheet of paper out of his sports coat. Trying to hide a smile, he asked, "What in the world is a 'jibing'?"

"That's why I think I should take this course with you," she said, trying to stop laughing. "Okay, let me explain about tacking and jibing. There are two ways to change from port tack to starboard tack. You can turn the bow through the eye of the wind, which is called tacking, or the stern, which is called jibing. If you are traveling upwind, tacking is the safer method. Jibing is often necessary when sailing downwind."

Dave looked overwhelmed. "Hey, if there's a test, I'm sitting next to you."

"No way!" Lorie said, shaking her head. "Seriously, we can use my sloop, *Sunrise*, for practice. It holds five to seven people, has sleeping berths, is excellent for coastal cruising, and, because of its size, has easy access to most mooring areas. It's no problem to live on board for a few days."

"When was the last time you had her out?"

"I haven't since Jake passed away," Lorie said, her smile fading. "When I go sailing anymore, it's usually with someone from the club.

Actually, I was thinking about selling *Sunrise*, but so far, I haven't been able to go through with it. She was my 'baby' for so long."

Dave understood how hard it was to let some things go. Trying to cheer her up once again, he added, "I wouldn't throw in the towel yet. I have a funny feeling that *Sunrise* is going to get busy real soon."

"She's never let me down yet," Lorie said. "You'll like her when you get to know her. And let me tell you, in case of a 'no wind' situation, she even has oars."

"That will be your job." Dave laughed.

Driving to work on a gloomy Monday morning, Lorie was deep in thought. She had an extremely wonderful time with Dave on Saturday. It was absolutely perfect. She dreamily wished every day could be Saturday. Pulling into the parking lot at Glendale, the happy daydreams abruptly vanished, and the weight of stress settled heavily on her shoulders. As she got out of her car, she remembered something she had read recently: "Every saint has a past. Every sinner has a future. Judge not!" The words seemed to shout in her mind. She decided to make the best of today, no matter what.

She was the first one to arrive. After making a pot of coffee, she peaked into James's office. Lorie thought it was strange that it seemed a little untidy. *Maybe he was here over the weekend working on something.* Lorie looked around. She noticed papers sticking out of the trash can. Looking out the window to make sure James's car was not in the parking lot, she looked at the discarded documents. Not really knowing what she was looking for, she tried to figure out what they were. She wasn't sure, but it looked like James was trying to create some sort of bogus document. She also noticed some invoices that looked suspicious. Lorie knew she did not have much time before the others came in, so she quickly made copies. Replacing the originals exactly as she found them, she hurried from the room.

Hearing voices approaching, she poured a cup of coffee and headed back to her desk. Monica and June arrived at the same time. As they walked into the office, Lorie looked up, smiled, and said, "Good morning, ladies!" Not expecting a reply, she looked back at the papers on her desk. Without warning, the harsh sound of June's voice sent chills down her spine.

"Doesn't she remind you of a Miss Goody Two-shoes?"

"Yeah, why are you so happy this morning?" Monica laughed.

Lorie didn't bother to answer. It was useless to try and have a normal conversation with these women.

"She must have gotten 'some' over the weekend." June laughed. "Poor guy." After getting a cup of coffee, June left the office.

Lorie noticed Monica sitting at her desk, looking as if she was hung over again. Even her makeup seems a little crooked this morning. Lorie tried to cover her smile with her hand. Then James walked into the office. Again, Lorie offered a pleasant greeting. James was not in a good mood.

"Morning," he said in his usual ill-tempered way, walking into his office. A few minutes later, he called for Monica. Lorie watched in disbelief as she slowly moved to James's office. She was definitely hung over again this morning. *And how could she walk in those zippered T-strap heels? They must be at least four-inch heels, maybe four and a half. And that asymmetrical side-slit dress was certainly not appropriate for the office.*

Lorie suddenly stopped and scolded herself. *You can't sit here and judge. It's not right. Like my dad used to say, "What is, is." I just have to make the best of it while I'm working here, and if I don't understand something, it might be best to just ignore it.*

In the back of her mind, she knew that she couldn't ignore things. Something was going on at Glendale, and it wasn't business as usual. Lorie knew that she would never stop searching for the truth. Maybe that is what kept her there, or maybe her friends were right. Maybe she was a glutton for punishment. Regardless, her determination took center stage. James, at some point, would get sloppy with financial records. If she could stay vigilant, she might be able to trace the origin or history of his transactions. With enough evidence, she could go to the board. Until then, she'd say little and pray a lot.

James stared at Monica's tight red dress as she entered the room. A pernicious smile crossed his face. "You certainly know how to fill out a dress," he said. "Come here." The tight embrace left her breathless. "I tried to call you last night," he whispered. "Where the hell did you go?"

"I was out with my girlfriends," Monica said, pulling away just enough to catch her breath. "After all, you always tell me that it is impossible for you to get away on Sunday nights."

"Christ, Monica, look at you," James said, looking perturbed. "You're hung over again. You don't even have your makeup on straight. Suppose a board member came in this morning. They're not blind, you know."

"Relax, James," Monica said, pulling away from him and sitting down. "You worry too much about the damn board. I'm real nice to them. They like me. Hey, how about a cigarette break? We could both use one."

"What you need right now are a few cups of coffee. After you sober up a little, come back in here. We have some business to discuss this morning. Now get going."

Aggravated, Monica hurriedly left his office. Standing by the coffeepot sipping his hot cup of coffee, José eyed Monica covetously as she approached.

"Watch it, José, or you're going to have two black eyes to explain to June," Monica snapped.

"Hey, sister, why are you so uptight this morning?"

"I'm not your sister, and I do need a cup of coffee," Monica said, her blood boiling. "Do you mind?"

José backed off. He knew that she and James were an item and didn't want to make any waves. Walking away, he said, "Women, they're all the same come Monday morning."

José walked into James's office and slouched down carelessly in the chair. James looked at him oddly.

"Don't tell me you're hung over too," James said.

"So that's why Monica almost bit my head off." José laughed. "She does like her booze."

"What she does is none of your concern, José," James said angrily. "We have more important things to think about."

"If the drinking gets out of hand, it could cause you problems," José shot back. "Like you said before, we can't afford to make any mistakes. There's too much riding on our deals."

James stood up. "I'll take care of Monica," he said, a stone-cold look on his face. "You just make sure you take care of everything on your end."

José could see this subject was not open for discussion, so he got down to business. "One of our counterparts has been under investigation and is now charged with corruption and forgery. This was on other deals he was working on and has no ties to us. I don't think any of this will hinder our operation."

"I don't like it," James replied. "You know how the Feds are. They'll keep digging and digging. Is there any way your people can be tied to this?"

"James, I've been over this many times in my head," José said, shaking his head. "No, don't worry. We have the perfect cover here. We're good."

"Okay, I've moved more money into the company," James said, accepting José's explanation. "I've created a series of complex financial transactions to make it difficult for anyone to suspect anything. Then by adjusting a few legitimate transactions here and there, I will be able to account for the profits. Of course, I have a separate bookkeeping system that accounts for both the legitimate profits and the illegal funds, but that's between us."

"Looks like you have things under control," José said. "I don't see any problems. By the way, maybe we could hit the casino again one night next week or so."

"Sounds like a plan," James agreed. "I'll get back to you on that. Now we better do a little Glendale business. I've got another board meeting to get ready for, so I'll be busy for the next few days. Here is a maintenance schedule that the board wants done. Maybe you can get this list completed before the meeting."

José looked agitated as he went over the list but said nothing.

"Hey, we have to keep the board happy," James said. "We don't want to do anything to jeopardize our jobs now, do we?"

"No problem," José replied, walking out the door.

Lorie felt José's eyes on her as he walked by her desk. She felt like he looked right through her, and it gave her the creeps. José and June were such a strange couple, and Lorie couldn't figure out what in the world they saw in each other and why they would ever want to be together in the first place. Stranger things had happened, she supposed. At that thought, she happened to look over at Monica's desk. *And that's one of them!*

That evening, as Lorie tried to make sense out of the papers she'd found earlier in the day, she realized that James was using Glendale as a front for some kind of illegal activity. Lorie suspected all along that he might be involved in the drug trade, but until now, it was speculation. Seeing the words "cocaine" and "methamphetamine" scribbled on the wrinkled papers only substantiated her theory. Lorie tried to imagine the street value of these drugs and how this explained James's travels to the Cayman Islands and his offshore accounts. Soon, she'd have enough evidence to go to the board. Al Chambers suspected something. Lorie was sure she could trust him. Thoughts raced through her mind, accelerating at great speed. Feeling somewhat dizzy, she held her head in her hands. She was not a detective and not that familiar with the law. If she was wrong about any of this, it would be a disaster. But Lorie felt like she was really on to something. She also realized that one of her talents was reading people, and she felt that she had James pegged from the start. She couldn't turn back now.

Before heading upstairs for the evening, she glanced over at the phone. She'd forgotten to call Kate today about the boating course. Smiling, she dialed Kate's number.

"Hello," Kate said softly.

"Hi, Kate, it's me," Lorie giggled.

"Lorie, I was just thinking about you. Did you talk to Dave over the weekend regarding the boat course?"

"Yes, I did, and it's a go. He is actually looking forward to it. Of course, he wants me to take the course along with him, but as you know, I had planned to do that anyway. I have a feeling that he will enjoy it."

"Hey, what's not to like?" Kate said. "I don't know of anything more refreshing or invigorating than sailing out to sea with the wind in your face and a splash of salt water on your feet."

Lorie giggled, thinking that Kate really had a way with words. "Okay, so we're in. Actually, I'm so glad that Dave wants to take on a new sport. I've missed *Sunrise*. You know how I feel about her."

"Lorie, I'm so glad you decided not to sell her. I know you were seriously thinking about it, but I also knew that she was so much a part of your life and the life you had with Jake. I figured you just wouldn't have the heart to sell her."

Lorie's thoughts suddenly drifted back to a sailing trip she had taken with Jake. Tears filled her eyes. Squelching the thoughts almost as quickly as they emerged, she added, "Life goes on, Kate."

Kate could sense that Lorie did not want to talk about Jake. She knew Lorie was really making an effort to get on with her life now. Kate broke the silence and said, "Well, I'll put you two down for the course, and I'll see you next week."

"Sounds great," Lorie replied. Hanging up the phone, Lorie thought how easy life would be if this was all she had to think about.

Trying to look as busy as possible at work, Lorie was especially vigilant, casually listening to conversations and gathering as much information as possible for her file. She didn't enjoy playing detective but couldn't look the other way when she felt something was terribly wrong. The more facts she acquired, the more she could see that James was not flying solo. José and June were definitely involved. She wasn't surprised. But what about Monica? She and James were having an affair, and she was an alcoholic, but Lorie couldn't connect her to the drugs or suspected money laundering. If she smoked pot with James, did that make her a partner in crime? Thoughts began to swirl tirelessly through her head. She looked up at the clock. Just a few minutes more and she could go home. Clearing her desk for the day, she quickly exited the premises.

Sitting in her favorite chair that evening, she reached for her Bible and watched it fall to the floor, opening to a passage she'd read many times over the years. "Have no anxiety, but in every prayer and supplication with thanksgiving let your petitions be made known to God. And may the peace of God which surpasses all understanding guard your hearts and minds in Christ Jesus" (Philippians 4:6, 7). Lorie felt certain that somehow she would get through all the trials before her. She knew that God didn't create everything in one day, that things and time were on her side.

Al slowly turned into the parking lot of Curtis Glass Works. He wondered why Curtis Thompson wanted to meet him at his company since they talked regularly during board meetings at Glendale. Did Curtis also suspect that things were not on the up and up at Glendale? Al was good at reading between the lines, and he felt Lorie knew more than she was willing to share at this point. He remembered how reluctant she was to speak during their conversation at the café. He figured she was afraid of losing her job if she repeated any gossip or even if she told him of her suspicions working closely with

James and Monica. Al could see that Lorie carried a heavy workload. Yes, Monica was James's assistant, but what did she actually do? From what he could see, Lorie took care of the many assignments that were originally given to Monica. James said Lorie was Monica's helper. But Al could see through that comment.

Al knocked softly before entering Curtis's office. Curtis stood up to shake Al's hand and told him to take a seat and offered him coffee. Al noticed a large carafe and cups on a side table. "I take it black," Al said with a huge grin.

"Ah, the only way to truly enjoy a great cup of coffee," Curtis said as he poured a cup for Al. But the mood suddenly became serious as Curtis sat down behind his huge oak desk.

"Al, I'll get right to the point as to why I wanted to see you today. While Marjorie and I were going to dinner at the Hyatt last night, we saw James and Monica in the parking lot. At first, I thought they were working late and decided to have dinner before going home, but then I noticed that Monica was dressed rather sleazily. I also noticed that James's arm was around her waist. Marjorie noticed it also, but all she said was 'oh dear!' I didn't want to alarm my wife, so I said that maybe there was a logical explanation. But when we entered the restaurant, they were nowhere in sight. I realized that they didn't go there for dinner. Marjorie seemed shocked and lost her appetite, so we left. I told Marjorie not to say anything about the incident until I got to the bottom of it. Christ, Al, James has a beautiful wife who seems to be intelligent and has a wonderful personality to boot. I can't see why he is running around with his assistant. I think she certainly lacks any refinement, to say the least."

Al shook his head as he stared down into his coffee. It was obvious his suspicions were being confirmed. "Curtis, from what I have seen at Glendale, especially during the fund-raisers, I suspected that Monica was an alcoholic. Now I'm willing to bet on that. And yes, the way she dresses, even on a regular workday, well, it's not business attire, that's for sure. But I have a hunch that there is more going on behind the scenes than James's affair with his so-called assistant.

I did a little investigating on my own, and his frequent trips to the Cayman Islands are making me a little suspicious.

I ran into Lorie one morning as she was taking mail to the post office. I insisted that she have coffee with me at the café before heading back to the office. Do you know that she actually had to get that okayed with James? I could tell that she was reluctant to call him, so I made the call. Lorie seems to have a good sense about her. She is very observant. Since she works closely with James and Monica, I wanted to see if I could get any information out of her. Lorie impresses me as not being the type to gossip. I figured that if she would say anything at all, it would be something totally truthful."

"What did she say?" Curtis asked.

"She was very reluctant to say anything. I could tell that she definitely was aware of things not being on the up and up, but she said that since she had to work with James and Monica, she had no comment at this time."

Now Curtis was shaking his head. "Do you think it would do any good if I spoke to her?"

"No. When Lorie is ready to talk about anything, she'll come to me. She trusts me enough to give me particulars on any given situation. But she is very careful. I think she is just watching, waiting, and gathering facts. There is one person she's talking to though. Remember Diane Holden who used to work in marketing?"

"Yes, a real nice girl," Curtis said. "She left to take another job some time ago. She was a lot like Lorie, very businesslike. How in the world did we ever get something like Monica to take her place?" Al could see the disgusted look on Curtis face after making that statement.

"I heard through the grapevine that Monica and James were friends before she came to work for Glendale," Al said. "Of course, when asked, James will tell you differently. According to him, she was the person best suited for the job."

"Hogwash!" Curtis shouted, standing up, his face bright red. "Looks like it's time for some investigation into these atrocities.

Glendale has always been a very respected and upstanding company. How these seedy characters wormed their way into this once-fine pillar of the community is beyond me. Have we been so lax that we actually left our guard down, or do we just assume that everyone has good intentions and cares about the people in this community?"

"Look, Curtis, calm down. Call a special board meeting. Maybe hold it at your place so that James doesn't get wind of it."

"Don't worry," Al said, patting Curtis on the shoulder as he got up to leave. "This will get straightened out. I have some friends in high places, so to speak. I'll get them to start looking into things."

"Thanks, Al," Curtis said, finally smiling as he shook Al's hand. "I knew I could count on you."

Leaving the office, Al realized there was a rough road ahead. He just hoped that when all was said and done, Glendale would survive an inquiring media and general public opinion.

That afternoon, Al called another board member, Kelley Barnes, attorney. Kelley—a tall, gaunt, and unemotional man—was a reputable lawyer and a trusted friend. Al figured that during the initial investigation, the board would have to come up with detailed and accurate facts before going public. He knew Kelley would be discreet. Kelley listened carefully as Al disclosed his suspicions and concerns before commenting.

"First of all," Kelley said, "like a good friend of mine once told me, we've got to start putting the emphasis on justice rather than game playing. It might be a good idea to give James a chance to explain himself before any formal accusations are made. Maybe the key element here would be a judicious use of a polygraph. Usually, a man who has been cleared by this test will almost never be prosecuted."

"But is it reliable?"

"Reliability is not a real issue. There is no question of the polygraph's scientific reliability in the hands of a competent operator. In most cases, an innocent man will want to take the test. If guilty, he'll raise all sorts of objections. Upon our findings after further investigation, we would make James aware this could mean an unpublicized absolution of suspicious behavior. If he is innocent, we wouldn't want to blacken his name with a formal accusation or cause any unfavorable publicity for Glendale. On the other hand, if James is in over his head and a trial is necessary, the polygraph results would not be admissible in our courts."

"Let's give James every opportunity to spin the roulette wheel so that the ball will fall on the red instead of the black," Al said.

"You know"—Kelley chuckled—"even if he is innocent and gets acquitted because the evidence against him is thin, a majority of the public will always feel that he is guilty but got off on a technicality. So in the best interest of Glendale, we will have to look for a new president or CEO regardless of what happens." Al agreed.

Al leaned back in his office chair, pondering his phone call with Kelley. The ball was now rolling, and the next step was talking to Lorie. Al was sure she knew a lot more than she let on. Once she knew that Al had talked to Curtis and Kelley, he was sure she'd become more cooperative.

Lorie persuaded Dave to attend the monthly yacht club meeting with her. Arriving twenty minutes early, they decided to have a drink at the bar before the meeting started. Rich and Candy were already there. Judging by Candy's demeanor, she already had one too many. Lorie thought Candy's behavior would be an embarrassment to Rich but tried to dismiss that thought as she walked up to them.

"Well, hello!" she said, smiling. "How are you this evening?"

Rich looked at Lorie without smiling. "That is the worse hairstyle I have ever seen," he said.

"It's very unusual for guys to worry about other people's hair," Lorie said, trying to make light of his rude comment. "Are you trying to tell us something, Rich?"

Everyone within hearing distance burst out laughing, including Dave. Rich was aggravated but instantly tried to change the subject. "I see you brought a friend along this evening."

Lorie made the appropriate introductions. All Candy could muster was a dry "hey!" Rich immediately informed Lorie that he and Candy had gotten engaged. Candy thrust her hand in front of Lorie's face and shouted, "How do you like them rocks?" Lorie looked surprised and stepped back quickly as Candy's hand almost hit her in the face.

"My," she said, a little stunned by the maneuver. "It really is lovely. Congratulations to you both."

Rich smiled slightly while Dave shook his hand.

"Yes, congratulations and best wishes to you both," Dave said. "Let me buy you a drink. What's your poison?"

"Champagne!" Candy said loudly. "We are celebrating, and champagne is delightfully festive."

"Bourbon for me, Old Fitzgerald," Rich added.

After a round of drinks, they headed into the meeting. As Lorie expected, Rich was not exactly friendly to her, but he wasn't rude either, just cold. Lorie couldn't understand why he would still have ill feelings toward her since he had gotten engaged. If he really loved Candy, he would be in a good mood. And he hadn't been in a good mood since Lorie told him she wasn't ready to date. Of course, when she started dating Dave, that only added fuel to the fire. But why? Lorie was confused, but as the meeting began, her thoughts shifted to sailing and to her baby, *Sunrise*.

"How did you enjoy the meeting this evening, Dave?" Lorie said, holding Dave's arm as they left the meeting.

"I really did enjoy it," Dave said, smiling. "It was quite interesting. Thanks for the invite. Now I'm looking forward to the sailing course."

"I have a feeling that you will be a natural at it."

"Why do you say that?" Dave said, looking at her in amazement.

"I'm pretty good at reading people," Lorie said softly, moving closer to Dave and looking him in the eyes. Their lips touched gently.

Happy thoughts sailed through Lorie's mind as she got ready for work the next morning. *I think I'm in love. I can't believe this is happening to me.*

Suddenly, she told herself to stop and slow down. She couldn't let herself get overwhelmed about anything right now. Things were happening too fast, and it was crazy at work. Still, Lorie felt happy, a happiness that she hadn't felt in a long time, and it was hard to hide.

When she got to the office, June was standing by her desk with a pile of folders in her hands.

"Well, I see you finally decided to show up for work," June said coldly.

Lorie looked at the clock. She was twenty minutes early. "June, what are you talking about? I'm not late."

"From now on, you are to show up at least a half hour before it's time to start. That way, you can get situated, get coffee made, answer the early phone calls, and be ready to start promptly at eight thirty in the morning. Is that clear?" June did not give Lorie a chance to respond. "Now I want all these contracts done before noon and on my desk." Slamming the folders down on Lorie's desk, she promptly exited the office.

Lorie stood there for a few moments until the shock wore off. She'd be discussing this with James today whether he liked it or not. Looking around, she noticed that Monica wasn't in yet. Lorie had a few minutes before Monica or James arrived, time enough for a little snooping. She was headed to James's office when the phone rang. It wasn't time to start answering the phones yet, but if June heard it ringing, she'd come in bitching.

"Glendale! Lorie speaking. How may I help you?"

"Lorie, it's Al Chambers. How are you doing?"

"Hello, Al!" she said, glad to hear a happy voice after her encounter with June a few minutes earlier. "I'm fine. Thank you. What can I do for you today?"

After a brief pause, he said, "Lorie, could you possibly swing by my office on your way home from work today?"

"Yes, I could do that," Lorie said, confused by the request.

"This is confidential, Lorie," Al added. "I'll explain when you get here."

A chill ran through Lorie's body. She thought she knew what Al wanted to talk about, but was she ready to speak up?

"Sure, Al, I understand. See you later." Lorie hung up the phone slowly. As she sat there pondering the situation, James walked in. Startled by his presence, she almost jumped out of her skin.

"You seem a bit edgy this morning. What gives?" James said.

"Good morning, James," Lorie smiled, trying to ignore his comment. "How are you doing today?"

"You didn't answer my question. Why were you so surprised to see me? After all, I do work here." James stood there with cold, glaring eyes.

"I guess I didn't hear you coming down the hall, so when you were suddenly standing in the doorway, it must have startled me." Accepting that answer, James headed for his office. Lorie then remembered her conversation with June earlier. "James, I need to speak with you. I'll only take a few minutes of your time. I need some clarification on something."

"What is it?" he said, perturbed. She realized that saying anything about June was a sore spot with James but continued nevertheless.

"James, I know that you do not want any of us to work overtime, but this morning June told me that I must be here at least a half hour before we are officially open for business so that I could catch all the early morning calls, make coffee, and other things. If I have to be here and start working a half hour earlier each day, I'm going to have over forty hours on my time sheet. Did she clear that with you?"

"I'll talk to her about that," James said, not really looking agitated. "Meanwhile, no overtime is approved." He abruptly went into his office and slammed the door behind him.

Lorie thought she couldn't win. Someone in this crazy crew was always mad at her.

Lorie kept busy the rest of the day and avoided talking to anyone. She always tried to be polite and businesslike but still found her situation to be rather impossible. From time to time, she glanced at the clock. Lorie made sure she was out of the office on the dot each day.

Heading over to Al's office, she suddenly had a queasy feeling in her stomach. She told herself to be brave, but she didn't feel like she was up to answering questions. What did she really know anyway? She suspected and speculated about many things, but where was the proof? Lorie needed evidence, hard evidence.

Arriving at Al's office, Lorie took a deep breath. She would be as honest as possible but had a feeling that the shit's going to hit the fan very shortly. She wasn't comfortable with that. *God help me.*

Lorie walked into the building and up to Al's office. She hesitated before knocking softly.

"Come in," Al said in a rather weary voice. He was still working on some papers as Lorie entered. After a few moments, he looked up and smiled. "Have a seat, Lorie. Would you like a cup of coffee?"

"No, thank you. I'm fine." She sat there as Al got up to pour himself a cup.

"I guess you are wondering why we are having a confidential meeting this afternoon."

"You apparently have questions about something," Lorie said calmly, "and you're hoping that I can provide the answers."

"Ah, you are very observant, my dear," Al said, leaning back in his chair. "That's precisely why I asked to meet with you. You see, the board thinks there is more going on at Glendale than meets the eye. Many of us have been aware of some rather unethical business strategies. Now I'm not trying to put you on a hot seat, Lorie. You impress me as a sincere, conscientious young lady. If I had to guess, I would say that you are the backbone of the office but treated more like an underdog. Am I right?"

"You are very observant indeed," Lorie said, surprised. "But how did you know?"

Al grinned. "Just like you, Lorie, I know more than I'm willing to let on."

Lorie bit her lower lip. *Here it comes.*

"Lorie, level with me," Al said, leaning forward, his expression turning serious. "If what I suspect is happening, Glendale may find itself enmeshed in a threatening situation. I've watched you and feel that you really care about the company. That's one reason why you are still there. Am I right?"

Lorie looked down at her hands before mumbling a quiet "yes." Al understood Lorie's reluctance.

"Lorie, let me tell you what the board is aware of at present. We know about the affair James is having with Monica. We also know about Monica's drinking problem. Something that is even more of a concern to us are his frequent trips to the Cayman Islands and alleged offshore accounts. For the honorable reputation of Glendale, could you shed any light on any of this?"

Lorie mustered her courage as she reached for her handbag. "Al, I too have had some suspicions, so at times I would look around James's office. Here are copies of some of the things that were in his trash can."

"Just as I suspected," he said, impressed by Lorie's ingenuity as he looked over the papers. "There are definitely drugs involved. This requires further investigation. We'll need more facts before we can approach him."

Al studied Lorie's face, wondering if she had more information. She felt as if Al was trying to look inside her head. She wanted to tell him more but was reluctant to say anything without hard facts.

"Continue to keep a close watch on what goes on in the office," Al said finally. "And as I'm sure you are aware, our meeting today is strictly confidential." Lorie nodded her head in agreement as she stood up to leave.

"Lorie, I know this is very difficult for you, but you understand that not to do anything about this situation would be disastrous."

"I'll see what else I can find out," Lorie said.

"You be careful now, you hear?" Al said, concerned for Lorie's safety. "Don't take any unnecessary chances. It takes time to get to the bottom of things like this. We watch and wait for now, and of course, be ever so vigilant."

With one last nod, Lorie was out the door.

CHAPTER 7

As soon as she got home, Lorie was on the phone calling Diane. "Diane, Diane, you won't believe what happened today."

"Hey, calm down, Lorie," Diane said, hearing the terror in Lorie's voice. "Now slowly tell me what is wrong."

"Diane," Lorie said, taking a deep breath, "apparently, the board is aware that things are not on the up and up concerning James. Al Chambers called me this morning and asked if I could stop by his office on my way home from work. I had an uneasy feeling that he wanted to ask me something about James."

"Lorie, put some coffee on. I'll be right over."

Lorie was busily preparing snacks in the kitchen when she heard the doorbell. Looking at her watch, she thought Diane must have flown over. As soon as she opened the door, Diane gave her a big hug.

"Lorie, what a difficult situation you find yourself in," she said. "I can't let you go through this alone. I'm here to help in whatever way I can."

Lorie returned the hug. "Thank you for being a true friend, Diane. Come on in. I made some snacks and coffee."

The girls settled at the kitchen table, and Lorie proceeded to fill Diane in on all the things she had seen and heard since James started working at Glendale. After a bit, she paused. Diane sat there in amazement.

"I knew James and Monica were having an affair," Diane said. "That seemed obvious to me, so I'm not surprised that the board found out about it. I also knew Monica and June treated you badly, not only from what you've told me but from what I've seen at the fund-raisers. I don't envy you working with those witches. But, Lorie, the drugs, the offshore accounts, the Cayman Islands, I believe this goes way beyond your expertise. Snooping around could be dangerous if they suspect anything. From what you've told me, they sound like a cutthroat bunch."

"I really don't trust any of them," Lorie sighed, "but I promised Al Chambers that I would help. I'll just keep doing what I've been doing all along, nonchalantly watching, listening, and maybe a little snooping when I get a chance."

"It's the snooping part that's scary, Lorie," Diane chided. "Promise me that you won't take any unnecessary chances. Please be careful."

Lorie gave Diane a little hug while walking her to the door. "Hey, don't worry. I'll be fine. Now that the board is aware of the situation, I think they'll be watching things a little more closely."

As the weeks rolled by, Lorie was constantly on guard for any unusual maneuvers in the office. Because June and Monica did not know shorthand, she took notes of anything suspicious by this method and transcribed them as soon as she got home each day, keeping a special file. Lorie wanted to share her findings with Dave but decided that she would wait until after he took his sailing test. She figured that if he was worried about her, his concentration would be limited.

After weeks of study, Dave was finally ready to take the test the next day. Lorie wondered if he was really comfortable with the task or if he was just trying to please her. Before turning in that night, she decided to give him a call. "Hi, it's me. Are you still studying?"

"Hi, Lorie," Dave said. "Yeah, but burning the midnight oil is not going to be much of an advantage tonight. I think I basically know enough to take the written test. I'm not worried about it." He sounded positive, and that made her feel more at ease.

"Okay then, get a good night's sleep, and I'll see you tomorrow."

"I'm looking forward to it."

At the yacht club, Dave looked around the classroom. There was a half-dozen people taking the test. Some of them seemed worried. Dave figured it would be taxing but felt that he would get through it okay. The test lasted several hours. Dave breezed through it and got up to hand in his papers. Before leaving the classroom, he realized that everyone was still taking the test. He thought he either missed something, or they were just slowpokes. Walking down the hall, he thought he was ready for the hands-on version. There was nothing like starting a new sport. If Lorie was happy, so was he.

Dave looked forward to attending the meeting with Lorie. Word had spread that he aced the test. Congratulations were in order, and Dave was greeted by everyone. Even Rich gave him a friendly handshake, which almost floored Lorie. *Maybe Rich was finally coming around.* Then Lorie wondered if Kate and Bob had a talk with him. That might have some bearing on his actions. Looking at Candy, Lorie thought maybe Rich was actually starting to like her. If that happened, then Rich might be nice to Lorie and Dave. Lorie didn't care what the reason was so long as there was peace between the club members. She didn't want hurt feelings to be an obstacle to Dave's membership and enjoyment in the club. During the meeting, plans were discussed and approved for a sailing weekend. The open-water test would be given at that time. Dave was looking forward to it, and his confidence elated Lorie.

Lorie sat at her desk, trying to look as if she was oblivious to her surroundings as she strained to hear the conversation that James and José were having across the room. She knew they were up to something. She had to find out what it was, but how? Finally, everyone went to lunch. James and Monica left together. She looked out the window to make sure they were gone. Then she saw June and José heading out. She watched as they walked down the hall together.

Passing a supply closet on their way out, Lorie noticed that June helped herself to a big box of toilet paper, handed it to José, then quickly headed out to the car. Lorie ran to the window. *Why did June need a box of toilet paper?* As José shoved it into the trunk, it suddenly dawned on her. They were actually stealing toilet paper! *Of all the low-down things to do to the company you work for.* Lorie was amazed that anyone would stoop that low as she headed toward James's office. *If toilet paper was all I had to worry about, the situation here wouldn't be so severe.*

Careful not to disturb anything, she slowly began looking through James's desk. Judging by the false invoices and bogus documents she found earlier in his trash can, Lorie figured that they could probably get him on corruption and forgery. But she knew there was more, and she was determined to find more evidence. *Sooner or later, he was bound to get sloppy or slip up with his financial records.* She remembered Al's words: "We just have to watch and wait."

Al and Kelley decided to talk to a friend from the police department, Cid Hartmann. The men were convinced that Cid's antidrug tactics and strategies would lead to arrests and casement of the problem. Cid listened as Al and Kelley talked about their suspicions and showed him the copies that Lorie had retrieved from James's office trash can.

"Gentlemen, this calls for a special drug task force," Cid said as he looked over the documents. "To approach the problem, we'll need to define our strategy in operational terms. I'll make it a high priority. We need to get this situation stabilized as soon as possible for the good of Glendale and the community."

"So what is your strategy, Cid?" Al asked.

Cid thought for a moment before speaking, "We'll definitely need to start work behind the scenes. There are no plausible solutions. Each case differs significantly from one another: protocol, employing various tactics, sophistication of strategies. It looks as if there is a sufficient empirical basis from which conclusions could possibly be drawn. Currently, our primary focus point is Lorie Simms. From what you've told me, I feel she would be invaluable as far as observing, recording, and reporting any suspicious behavior. Of course, she would have to keep a low profile and avoid any confrontation. I wouldn't want her to become a target or expose her to retribution by drug retailers."

"Gentlemen, I'm afraid I have to take leave at this time," Kelly said, glancing at his watch. "I will check in with you again tomorrow."

"I'll walk out with you, Kelley," Al said as he stood up. He extended his hand to Cid. "Cid, thanks for your time today. As you can see, the situation at Glendale is dangerous. There are many variables here."

"I assure you, the situation will be taken care of," Cid said.

"Drugs have become one of the major problems confronting our civilization," Kelly said as he and Al walked to the parking lot. "The incidence of drug use among people of all ages and social ranks has reached alarming proportions. Unfortunately, it's easy money if you have the right connections. It would be a shame if James has fallen into that trap."

"Yes, you're quite right, Kelley," Al said, nodding. "Drug dealers feel an overpowering need to continue in the business. If James is on any kind of narcotic, he will try to obtain it by any means. Of course, the end effect would be detrimental to his career, not to mention the possibility of ruining Glendale."

As the two men parted, a solemn look of despair mirrored their faces.

Deep in thought, Lorie tried to relax in her favorite chair that evening as she pondered the events that had taken place at the office. She knew Al and the other board members were counting on her, but was she up to taking such a lead role? She wasn't a spy or a detective. She wouldn't even know where to begin. Her thoughts were suddenly interrupted by the doorbell. It was Dave, right on time. As soon as she opened the door, he gave her a big hug.

"I'm happy to see you too," she said with a big smile. Looking down, she noticed two bottles of wine near him.

"Now you don't suppose those are for tonight?"

"Hey, you can't blame a guy for trying," Dave said.

Lorie looked at him slyly.

"Okay, we'll just open one tonight. Take your pick."

"Cabernet Sauvignon!" she shouted, heading to the kitchen.

Embers burned slowly in her fireplace, casting a cozy glow throughout the room. Lorie nestled in Dave's arms, feeling secure and safe. She wondered if she should tell him about James and the others. Feeling somewhat carefree from the wine, she decided that it was now or never. "Dave, I have to talk to you about something." She looked at him hesitantly for a moment.

"Lorie, what's wrong?"

She didn't know where to start but felt like it was time to talk about it. Taking a deep breath, she proceeded to relay her suspicions and those of the board. Dave listened intently, completely caught off guard by this most unusual tale. When Lorie finished, she stared into the crackling fire, feeling both relieved for confiding in Dave and skeptical as she awaited his reaction.

"Lorie, for goodness sakes," Dave said, urgency in his voice. "I knew things were not great for you at Glendale, but this goes way beyond your duties. If the board suspects that James is into narcotics or money laundering, let them take this to the proper authorities. Having you spy on James is not only ridiculous but could be downright dangerous."

"Dave," Lorie said, squeezing his hand tightly, "the board has already approached the police. They are aware of the situation, and they are not asking me to do anything dangerous. They just want me to keep my eyes and ears open, that's all. When I do see something unusual, I take a few notes in shorthand. No one in the office knows shorthand, so I'm safe. Now get that worried look off your face."

Dave's stern expression did not change. "Lorie, I don't like any of this. No matter what you do, you're in harm's way."

"Like I said, the police already have a pretty good idea as to what is going on, and they will be working on things from their end," she said, snuggling closer to Dave. "Now stop worrying and just kiss me."

His thoughts swirled like strong surf breaking upon a beach as she moved into his arms. At that moment, for them, nobody else existed.

Arriving at the dock early Saturday morning, Dave wondered how he would do on his open-water sailing test. He had aced the written test, but now he had other things on his mind. The uneasy feeling he tried to squelch surfaced at an alarming rate. He glanced over at Lorie's sloop, *Sunrise*. *If anything should ever happen to her, I ...*

Suddenly, Lorie came running down the dock to meet him, interrupting his train of thought.

"Sorry I'm a little late. The others are on their way. Hey, here they come now."

Dave pulled Lorie close to himself and held her tightly. His embrace seemed to take her breath away.

"Do I sense a bit of stage fright this morning?" she said, looking deeply into his eyes.

Dave didn't answer.

"Remember, you aced the written test," Lorie continued, "and we've been practicing on open water. You are doing great. I want to see your positive attitude right now."

Dave finally smiled, kissed her on the cheek, and waved to the other members approaching.

"Now that's my Dave," Lorie said approvingly.

Dave, along with his instructor, Randy Taylor, did a quick inspection of the boat's equipment. After prepping the boat, they cast off the mooring and headed out, deploying the running rigging and hoisting the main sail and jib. There was very little wind as they made their way across the open water. Dave trimmed the sails and picked up as much wind as he could but battled to maintain a compass bearing at all times due to the time differential in the boat's reaction to the rudder. He was tacking back and forth, losing wind. Randy suggested that he pick a landmark on the horizon, line it up with the forestay, and steer by that alone. Once Dave mastered the technique, everything went smoothly, and the boat held both course and wind beautifully.

After a long day, they approached the dock. Lorie watched as he brought the starboard side to the dock. Easing up on the throttle and kicking the port screw into reverse for just a little restraint, he gently eased to the dockside.

"Yes, yes!" she shouted, waving.

Dave laughed as he watched her joyful outburst. Randy also seemed pleased with Dave's performance and congratulated him on a job well done.

A celebration was in order that evening starting with cocktails, a group dinner, and the exotic sounds of kettle steel drums. A buffet dinner of grilled lobsters, baked potatoes, mixed vegetables, salad, assorted breads, and pies were enjoyed by all. After dinner, Lorie and Dave stepped out to enjoy the refreshing night air.

"Look at all the stars, Dave," Lorie said. "It's just like magic."

"Yes, and there are so many constellations," Dave said. "It's just mind-boggling."

Just then, Lorie's mind drifted back to a time when she and Jake would look at the stars, and he would tell her about Orion and the dippers, Ursa Major and Minor.

Dave noticed a change in her demeanor. "Lorie, are you feeling okay?" he asked.

Lorie looked at him and smiled. She knew it was time to move on. What is past is gone forever, and Jake wouldn't want her to sit around crying about anything. He always said, "Life is for the living." He lived his life to the fullest, and she knew that he would want the same thing for her. She took Dave's hand and squeezed it.

"I'm fine," she said, trying to sound convincing. "I was just trying to think of some of the constellations that I've studied in class many years ago."

Dave thought for a moment then said, "Let's try to name some of them."

"Okay, I'll start," Lorie said.

"No fair. You will name all the easy ones."

"Ladies first!"

Dave agreed.

"Let me see," Lorie said as she put her finger over her lips as if deep in thought. "We all know Orion; the Bears, dippers; Ursa Major and Minor; Monoceros, the Unicorn; Taurus, the Bull; Gemini, the Twins; Pegasus, the Winged Horse. I also know that there are sailing stars, but I can't remember their names. Okay, I guess that's it for me. Now it's your turn."

"You're pretty good," Dave said, shaking his head. "Most people don't know that much. But since I was taking the sailing course, I do remember reading about the sailing stars. I can remember several of them: Puppis, Stern; Vela, Sail; and Carina, Keel. Well, that's about it for me."

"Hey, I think we did real well," Lorie said as they slowly walked back, arm in arm to the party. Before they entered the clubhouse, Lorie asked, "What did you think of the sailing test today?"

"It was definitely tougher than the written part," Dave said. "You really need a firm background in navigation. But I have to give Randy credit. He's a great instructor."

Lorie agreed. The festivities lingered late into the evening. Thinking of what lay ahead for her at work, Lorie wished the fun-filled weekend would never end. That night as she drifted off to sleep, she prayed, *Oh God, I need strength to get through work tomorrow. I trust that you will help me.* In the back of her mind, she thought it might be time for another visit with Father O'Malley.

Lorie struggled through each day, trying her best to look aloof as she kept her eyes and ears opened, paying particular attention to any comments James made to José or June. By now, it was obvious that there were deceptive business practices going on at Glendale. She continued to keep notes in shorthand, taking them home with her each evening to transcribe. Al Chambers checked in with her daily for updates.

One evening, as Lorie worked on her report for Al, a phone call interrupted her train of thought.

"Hi, Lorie, it's Kate. I just had to call and tell you the latest news."

Lorie seemed puzzled as she had just seen Kate and Bob at the party over the weekend.

"Okay, Kate, the suspense is killing me," she joked.

"Well, did you find it strange that Rich and Candy were not at the party last weekend?"

Lorie tried to remember. She had been so excited about Dave passing his sailing test, and with the party being especially festive, she really hadn't given it any thought.

"You're right, Kate. There was a huge crowd at the party, but I really don't remember seeing them."

"They broke up!" she exclaimed happily.

"You're kidding! What happened, and why are you so happy about it?"

Kate tried to tone down her exuberance. "Well, Bob and I have always felt that Rich dated Candy because, in his weird way of thinking, he was trying to get even with you for dumping him. And it seemed that when he found out you and Dave were dating, he got really angry and wound up giving Candy the engagement ring. As you know, everyone in the club was shocked that he would date a sluttish barfly like Candy. The way she carried on with other guys after having a few drinks, especially at the club, well, I just think that she finally embarrassed Rich to the max. The engagement is off, definitely, and Rich is moving out West now. He has some friends that live in California, so he will stay with them until he finds a place of his own."

Lorie was speechless. Did Rich do all this because of her? "Kate, I can't believe any of this had anything to do with me. Yes, Rich did act weird when I told him that I wasn't ready to date and then began to date Dave shortly afterward. Also, he did seem extremely hateful at first, but at the last meeting we attended, he was friendly to me and even shook Dave's hand and congratulated him on passing the written part of the sailing test."

"Lorie," Kate interrupted, "I don't care what you say. Bob, I, and others think that he just couldn't handle the rejection of a girl that he wanted to spend the rest of his life with. *You.* That's why he jumped into that relationship with Miss Silicon Valley."

Lorie burst out laughing. "Kate, that is a very unkind way of describing Candy."

"Lorie, I have to tell you something that happened at the club a few nights before the party," Kate said, stifling her laughter. "Bob and I were on our way home from his mom's place when we decided to stop by the club to have a nightcap. Rich and Candy were at the bar. Surprise! Surprise! Anyway, Candy was pretty well lit by the time we got there, and she was actually talking about her breast augmentation surgery. Everyone was in hysterics. You can just imagine how funny it was hearing a drunken woman talking about such a thing. Of course, Bob and I thought it was gross, so we left, but we laughed all the way home. I believe it was stuff like this that Rich finally got sick and tired of. Originally, Rich probably thought that if he got a girlfriend that looked and acted sexy, it would bother you. But when he saw how happy you and Dave were together, he realized that all his efforts to hurt you were not working but instead were serving as an embarrassment to him. That's the story from my point of view."

Lorie thought anything was possible. Finally, she said, "Whatever the reasons for the breakup, it's probably for the best since Candy apparently has a drinking problem. I'm sure Rich will be happy in sunny California. From what I hear, it's a whole different world out there."

Kate hesitated before speaking again.

"Kate, are you still there?"

Kate's voice suddenly took on a serious tone as she slowly said, "Lorie, Bob and I saw something else that night as we were coming home. Now it may not mean anything, but we thought maybe you should check on your sloop."

"Why do you say that?" Lorie said, puzzled.

"Remember when you were telling me about how Betty would take advantage of you every opportunity she got and how you finally got wise to her and wouldn't lend her any more money?"

"Yes, but what does that have to do with my sloop?"

Kate didn't want to accuse anyone unjustly, but what if her instincts were right? She was afraid not to tell Lorie her suspicions. "Lorie, it was dark, so we can't be sure of this. But while driving back home, we past the docks, and a woman was hurrying away as we got closer. It looked very much like Betty, and it looked like she must have been coming from your sloop."

A cold chill ran down Lorie's spine as she listened intently to Kate's description. Then a sudden thought hit her like a ton of bricks.

"Oh, Kate!" Lorie shouted. "I just had the most horrible thought. Betty knows that I am on to her and that she can't get anything else out of me. You don't suppose she might be trying to get even with me in some weird way, do you?"

Kate thought for a moment. "Anymore I'm just not sure about her. You're not the only one she has been trying to take advantage of. What I don't understand is the fact that she is not hurting for money by any means. Yet, like you say, she seems to want everyone else to pick up the tab all the time. I don't like to think the worst about people, but it certainly wouldn't hurt for you to at least check out your sloop to make sure everything is okay."

"Thanks for telling me about this," Lorie said. "I know you only like to think the best of everyone, and I do appreciate your concern. I'll have Dave run out with me tomorrow, and we'll look it over carefully. God, I hope I don't find anything wrong."

"I'll let you go now," Kate said. "I just wanted to tell you the latest."

Lorie slowly hung up the phone. Thoughts flew through her mind as she tried to digest the latest news. *You don't suppose ... No, she wouldn't ... She couldn't ... But wait ... Maybe.* Feeling drained, Lorie flopped into her favorite chair, her hands tightly gripping her face. She was getting the impression that if Betty couldn't use her, she might try to get even. Lorie forced herself out of her chair. She had to settle down. Maybe a nice hot bath and a glass of wine. Worrying about every little thing was making her crazy. Maybe Kate was wrong. She wouldn't know until she checked the sloop. Nor could she believe she played such a big part in Rich's life since she barely realized he existed in the first place. She started to get the impression that she was a magnet for weird people. She hoped she was wrong. Life was certainly strange.

After another hectic day at work, Lorie went to Al Chambers's office. Al seemed particularly eager for this meeting.

"Lorie, we're getting close to finding out what James and his crew are up to. This is what we know: James apparently has gone into the drug business. From what we can tell, he structures all bank transactions to avoid mandatory reporting requirements and always keeps his transactions under ten thousand dollars to avoid drawing investigation from the Internal Revenue Service. I also have reason to believe that we may be able to catch him on wire fraud, conspiracy to commit wire fraud, and forgery. The list keeps growing."

"Al," Lorie said, nodding her head in agreement, "from what I'm seeing at work, I believe that José and June are involved in some way. I'm not sure about Monica. Although I suspect they aren't smoking cigarettes when they take their breaks outside on the grounds."

"Why do you say that, Lorie?"

Lorie was almost afraid to answer because she didn't have actual proof and did not like to speculate where a crime was concerned. "Al, people who smoke cigarettes usually don't roll their own, do they?"

"Not usually, especially nowadays. Do they often roll their own?"

"Yes, most of the time, they do. But they always seem to cover their tracks well, so I haven't been able to gather any material evidence."

Al stood up before speaking. "Lorie, you are doing a great job. Continue to keep your eyes and ears open but please be careful. Your safety is important to all of us on the board."

"Al, you can count on me," she said, standing up and shaking Al's hand. "And don't worry, I'll be fine."

But driving home, goose bumps ran down her spine. Although she tried to sound convincing to Al, she wondered how much more she would have to endure before all guilty parties would eventually pay their due. She wasn't a detective. *Lord, help me get through this.* Feeling her stress level rise, she reached for her cell phone and arranged to stop and see Father O'Malley.

Arriving at the rectory, tears welled up in her eyes as her kindly mentor greeted her.

"Ah, Lorie," he said with a gentle smile. "I see some anxiety in your face. Come to the kitchen with me. I was just fixing some tea when you called. Would you like a cup?" Lorie nodded as she followed him. "Now, now, Lorie," Father lightly scolded, "wipe those tears from your eyes. Tell me what has you so upset."

As Lorie sipped the hot mint tea, a calming effect set in. She knew that she could tell Father O'Malley anything. Whenever she felt distressed, this was her refuge, a safe place. Father O'Malley listened intently as Lorie recited the events of the past weeks. Lorie studied his face as she spoke, trying to read his thoughts. She knew he often thought "outside the box," which many times gave her a new perspective on how to think or deal with issues she was facing. When Lorie finished speaking, they both sat silently for a few moments.

Then gently, Father O'Malley began to speak. "You know, Lorie, sometimes we fear our uncontrollable world. We tend to reject anything that we cannot control. We forget that all the really important things in life, and life itself, is a gift to be received, not a problem to be mastered. Faith gives us the courage to trust the world of God's promises and to open ourselves to these uncontrollable realities. When we are afraid to take such a risk, we have no choice but to deny everything that lies beyond it. Faith puts us in touch with God's love. It is this experience that leads us through trials and adversities. God can work wonders through us, provided that we trust in him." He paused before continuing, "The events you describe are quite significant. You are looking for the means to accomplish the mission you have been given. You feel inadequate for the task. So we have a mission, and we are looking for the means. You have to remember, Lorie, there are resources other than your own that you can draw on. Apparently, you are important to the board of directors. They would not deliberately put you in harm's way. You are only to watch and report any suspicious activity. You cannot control the situation, but with your help, the authorities will be able to control it."

Lorie smiled as she listened to Father's analysis. Leaving the rectory, she felt renewed strength as she headed out to meet Dave. She realized she couldn't do anything alone. But Father O'Malley was right. God can do wonders though her, provided she trusted in his power.

After meeting Dave, they rode together to the dock. Lorie sat in silence. Dave could see the worried expression on her face. He knew that she had a special love for *Sunrise*. As soon as they arrived, she ran to the sloop. Dave followed and yelled, "Wait up!" He caught Lorie by the arm and gave her a little hug.

"Hey, don't worry. We will check the sloop carefully. If the least little thing is wrong, we will find it. Also, I've asked Randy to help us today since he knows boats inside and out."

"Thanks, Dave," Lorie said, taking a deep breath.

Just then, Randy pulled up. "Hey!" he shouted as he walked briskly over to them. "I just talked to Kate and Bob. Let's give this sloop a good checkup before we jump to any conclusions. You really hate to think the worse when it comes to a club member." Lorie agreed.

After several hours of careful searching, the only thing they could find was a small cut in the life raft. Randy said that even though the cut was relatively small, it was significant enough to cause a problem when used in an emergency. Lorie tried to evaluate the findings in her mind before giving her opinion.

"This is what I think," she said. "I could be wrong, but judging from everything I have gone through with Betty so far, I believe she realizes that I am on to her and that she will not be able to get me to pay for any more of her meals, airport parking, or other items. I feel that she did this as a last straw. It's her way of getting back at me because she knows that I won't let her use me anymore. But she has gone too far this time. Suppose I needed that life raft at some point? My life could depend on the condition of that raft. The way I see it, this is a crime and should be reported to the police."

Although Dave and Randy agreed with her, they said that without positive proof, she didn't have a case. The three of them stood there, perplexed by the situation.

Finally, Dave spoke up. "If we report her to the police, she would just deny everything," Dave said. "Plus, it might make her so mad that she'd try to do something else to get even with Lorie. Let's not say anything. We can replace the raft. As long as she thinks the damaged raft is still in the boat, she will think she won. Of course, before using the boat, we will check things over carefully. Lorie's well-being is my main concern."

Agreeing, the three of them, along with Kate and Bob, decided not to tell anyone else in the club about what happened on the sloop, although extreme vigilance became their key concerning Betty.

Morning came all too quickly for Lorie. Sitting quietly at her desk, she began arranging her workload for the day. Suddenly, June appeared with an armful of folders and slapped them on Lorie's desk.

"Of course, you know that we are having another fund-raiser," June said. "Some overtime has been approved because of this. I want all these lists completed by the end of the week. Get on it." She stomped out of the office.

Lorie sat, bewildered. How could she play detective if she was swamped with work?

After working several hours at her desk, Lorie strolled over to the coffeepot. The door to James's office was cracked slightly. She could hear James and José talking in hushed tones. She slowly moved toward the door, brushing against it ever so softly, trying to catch some of the conversation. James happened to look up and saw a piece of her skirt against the door. She noticed him running to the door and swiftly returned to the coffeepot. He swung the door open rapidly and stared at her with glassy, cold eyes.

Lorie tried to look nonchalant as she continued to pour coffee into her cup, but sudden fear and panic gripped her like a vice. She then remembered a Bible verse: "I can do all things in Him who strengthens me" (Philippians 4:13). Trying to remain calm, she looked James in the eye. "Do you need something, James?"

As she spoke, José walked over and stood beside James. They looked ruthless. Neither of them spoke. Without warning, James slammed the door shut as they retreated back into his office. Lorie took a deep breath, feeling scared. Her hands were shaking as she carried the coffee back to her desk.

Just then, Monica walked into the office, late as usual. "Good morning, Monica," she said with no emotion.

"Hey," Monica replied as she flopped on her chair.

Lorie was amazed when she noticed Monica was wearing an ombré-printed minishirt dress with a low-cut notch neckline. *Certainly not office attire.*

"Hey," José said smugly, noticing the pale look on James's face. "Why so upset?"

"I think Lorie knows more than she is letting on," James said, glaring at José.

"James," José said, shaking his head in disagreement, "she's just a secretary, a nobody." He reached into his pocket. "Here, you need a snort." He was surprised that James took it without giving him the regular speech about not having coke at work. But instead of calming down, paranoia seemed to set in. James didn't trust anyone. He needed to get away, far away. José stepped out of James's office and closed the door behind him. Lorie noticed him heading to the coffeepot. She could feel his eyes on her without looking up. José walked over and stood in front of her desk. Lorie didn't bother looking up and continued working.

Finally, she mustered up her courage to look him straight in the eye. "Did you need something, José?"

Before he had a chance to speak, her phone rang. It was James buzzing her. Fearing the worse, she picked up the phone. "Yes?"

"Has Monica come in yet?"

"Yes, she's here," Lorie said, trying to steady her voice.

"Send her in," he snapped as he threw down the phone.

Lorie felt something must be dreadfully wrong this morning because James seemed more on edge than normal. José and June didn't seem too happy either. And Monica was just Monica. "Monica, James wants to see you in his office right away."

Monica gave Lorie a dirty look as she rolled out of her chair and staggered toward James's office. Lorie thought she was hung over again. José also watched as she slowly made her way to James's office. Entering, she slammed the door behind her.

Hearing heavy footsteps rumbling from the hall, Lorie looked up. Of course, it was June. José knew that June did not like him hanging around Lorie's office, so he headed out, taking his coffee with him. Lorie was relieved that June showed up when she did. That relief only lasted a moment. Sounds coming from James's office stopped June in her tracks as she stood in the doorway. Lorie looked at her with utter amazement. June was wearing a printed kimono-sleeve mini dress with an orange multicolored pattern, which made Lorie dizzy by just glancing at it. *June and Monica must shop at the same store!*

"What's going on?" June asked.

Lorie was surprised that June would ask her anything, especially about James or Monica. Lorie realized June was testing her to see how much she knew. Without saying anything, Lorie just shrugged her shoulders. June then slapped down some lists on Lorie's desk and said, "Take care of this before the end of the week." She left almost as fast as she arrived.

"Okay, Monica!" James shouted. "What in the hell do you think you're doing by showing up drunk?"

"I am not drunk," Monica said smugly, trying to compose herself.

"Look, anyone in their right mind can see that you have a hangover. From now on, don't come to work until you sober up. Is that clear?" He didn't give her a chance to answer before shouting, "Now go get some coffee! I'll talk to you later." He turned and tried to focus on the documents in front of him.

Monica felt that he was overreacting, but without making a comment, she stomped out of his office, slamming the door once again.

James sat at his desk, pondering the scenario. What could he do about Monica? Between the booze and the drugs, she was getting a little careless. Having her around any of the board members could be dangerous. Then there was Lorie. She was starting to give him the creeps. He was sure she knew more than she was letting on. Maybe it was time for him to leave the country. José had connections. He could get a passport in another name. Suddenly, a knock at the door brought him back to reality. James tried to compose himself.

"Yes!" he shouted. He was relieved to see that it was José.

Hey, man," José said with a chuckle, "just checking in to see if you're okay. You seemed a little stressed out earlier."

"No problem," James said, leaning back in his chair and trying to look relaxed. "After all, you have everything under control, right?"

A smirk crossed José's face. "You got it, man. We make a pretty good team. Your import company and me in charge of sales, arranging trips, and, best of all, collecting payments for the jobs. What's to worry about, right?" James nodded in agreement. Just before leaving, José looked back over his shoulder. "Just don't get flaky on me."

James sat in silence for a few moments. His thoughts turned quickly to his various bank accounts in the Cayman Islands. He could have that money transferred anywhere. Anna knew nothing about his activities. She was not a problem. He could just take off and leave her behind. On the other hand, Monica was becoming a problem. But she could be taken care of with a drug overdose. José could make it look like an accident. But what to do about Lorie? Maybe José was right. She's just a secretary, a nobody. Secretaries seem to have that snoopy gene. They acted like they knew it all and ran the show. She couldn't possibly know what's going on. Besides, her to-do list was endless. She was so bogged down with work she didn't have time to worry about anything else. The only thing left to do was to persuade José to back off some. Let things cool down a little. Don't cause any suspicion.

No one was in a good mood the rest of the day, and Lorie was relieved when it was time to leave. Stopping by Al's office before heading home, she reported the strange occurrences.

"Well, it doesn't surprise me, Lorie," he said, shaking his head. "Actually, we are getting pretty close now. The heat is on, and I believe James is getting a bit nervous. Can't go into anything with you at this time, Lorie. Your safety is paramount. The less you know, the better. Just continue to keep your eyes open and be vigilant. We don't want him to suspect that he is being watched."

Lorie agreed and reassured Al that she would be careful.

While driving home, Lorie only wanted to block out the events of the day and find some peace. *Lord, help me!* Then her thoughts turned to Father O'Malley. He was always there for her. His calm demeanor and kind words seemed to help her find the strength to get through the many difficult times she had endured over the years. Without hesitation, she headed toward the rectory.

Father O'Malley greeted her with his usual exuberant smile but noticed the distant look on her face. "Lorie, I can tell you are troubled once again. Let's talk about it."

Lorie wanted to tell him everything but knew the authorities did not want her talking about the current situation since it was still under investigation. "Father, many things are happening right now at Glendale, things that I'm not at liberty to discuss at this time. Soon, you will know. I guess the reason I came to see you today is to hear your kind words. Whenever I feel overwhelmed or confused, you have a way of bringing peace to my soul."

"Lorie, I don't think I'm the one who brings you peace," Father said, smiling, "but our discussions do center on the King of Peace. He lives within all of us, in our hearts and minds."

"Yes, Father, but sometimes I need to be reminded, and you help bring things to the surface."

A thoughtful expression crossed Father O'Malley's face as he spoke, "Lorie, faith and life in Jesus is a special gift. If we truly have faith, then we can live without fear, knowing that the Lord is always at our side. He welcomes us with joy and love."

Lorie could feel the love that Father O'Malley had for the Lord. It radiated through him naturally. After their meeting, she felt much better. Driving home, she thought that his love for Jesus must be contagious. Her spirit was so uplifted after their talks. She'd be able to sleep peacefully tonight and face tomorrow bravely knowing she was not alone.

Going through the endless lists that seemed to accumulate on her desk, Lorie wondered how she would ever get things accomplished before the end of the week. This fund-raiser was a Bocce tournament. She hoped she wouldn't be asked to participate. She had to make out the menu for the buffet dinner and dessert bar, call area businesses for donations for the silent auction, and arrange for the pickup of donations. Lorie's thoughts were interrupted when June walked in and started shouting.

"Did you get that menu completed yet?"

Lorie was startled by the shrill sound of June's voice but not surprised by the question. "I'm working on it right now. I'll have it to you shortly."

"Just don't give me that same old crap," June said, her hands on her hips. "We want this menu to be vibrant, something different. People get tired of the same types of food. And don't take all day to get that to me." She stomped down the hall.

Lorie sat in amazement for a few moments. She'd never heard of "vibrant" food before. *She must be on drugs.* Slowly, she wrote down her thoughts as she completed the menu. She hoped this was "vibrant" enough for June as she quickly typed up the list.

In no time at all, June was back. Before she had a chance to say anything, Lorie handed her the menu. June grabbed it quickly and read it out loud, "Wedding soup, stuffed banana peppers, artichoke romano, stuffed mushrooms, shrimp cocktail, antipasto salad, penne ala vodka, sausage and peppers, chicken marsala, New York-style cheesecake, crème brûlée, assorted tortes, pecan ball drizzled with caramel or chocolate sauce." June looked pleased as she read the menu. Without saying a word to Lorie, she hurried back to her office. Lorie took that as a yes.

Finally, after months of investigating, things were beginning to unravel for James. Undercover officers were monitoring his drug deals. A sting was planned. That evening, Al Chambers, Kelley Barnes, and Cid Hartmann met to finalize their plans.

A thoughtful but serious frown crossed Cid's face as he addressed the men. "Gentlemen, at first, we suspected James to be involved in marijuana. Now we know that cocaine is playing a major role here. As you know, the sale of a kilo of cocaine is a felony. The wholesale price for a kilo of coke is about sixty thousand dollars. James has been doing rather well, moneywise. We also know that José is involved in negotiations with the Colombians and the transfer of coke to the States."

"And because Lorie has been vigilant and carefully monitoring things whenever James was out of the office," Al chimed in, "she found a few documents that he would need for traveling under a false identity. Seems like he may be getting ready to run."

"That's good detective work," Kelley said. "Maybe I should hire Lorie in my law firm." But their smiles turned serious when Kelley said the indictment for importing and possession of cocaine with the intention to distribute and conspiring with others to import and distribute, plus money laundering, could result in a life sentence."

"Okay, enough said, we have to move before he takes off," Cid said.

After weeks of planning and pushing herself to the max, Lorie sighed with relief when the big day finally arrived. Everything seemed to be in place for Glendale's Bocce tournament. Since the fund-raiser was to go on rain or shine, Lorie was especially pleased to see the bright blue skies. She carefully checked to make sure the silent auction items were arranged systematically. Everything was perfect. She went to check on the buffet before heading over to the admissions table. Walking past the elaborate buffet tables, she was impressed by the professional staff that seemed to be connoisseurs of fine food. Even before she got to her table to collect tickets for general admission, June shouted at her. "Why aren't you at your table? You should be set up by now. People will be arriving any minute."

Thinking it was useless to reply to June's rudeness, Lorie quickly headed to her table and spent a good part of the evening there, greeting people. The players were first followed by the spectators.

As she started to close up her cash box to take inside, June appeared. "I'll take that," she said. "Now get over to the kitchen and help with the cleanup."

Lorie felt like she had enough of June for one night. It took every bit of her strength not to tell June where to go, but with silent restraint, she complied.

On the way back to her desk, June noticed a piece of paper sticking out from underneath Lorie's desk. She inadvertently picked it up, but before discarding it, a shock wave pierced her being when she saw what was written on the paper. "These are Lorie's notes to Al Chambers," she said to herself. Panic stricken, she ran to find José.

José was the type of individual who seemed to be prepared for anything. After the brief meeting with June, he silently faded into the darkness. Since the employee parking spaces were poorly lit, he began working his evil deed. "Now we'll see how far Lorie gets before she meets her maker," he whispered under his breath. "Fool with me, and pay the price."

As the last guests were leaving, officers moved in to arrest James, José, and June. Monica was intoxicated beyond reasoning and didn't realize what was going down or care for that matter. Lorie kept pretty much out of sight during the fiasco until Al came up to her and said,

"Lorie, until further notice, you are in charge here. Curtis will be in the office tomorrow morning. A few employees will be assigned to help you until a new CEO is hired."

Lorie stood there with her mouth open. Even though she knew that James and the others would eventually be caught, the sheer magnitude of the evening seemed to overwhelm her with disbelief.

Al noticed the shocked look on her face. "Lorie, are you okay?"

Finally, she was able to speak. "Yes, yes," she said softly. "I'm fine. I guess I just didn't expect everything to happen so fast."

Al smiled. "You know, you are a good detective. Thank you for all the help you have given us."

Lorie returned his smile. "I didn't really do anything, but thank you for the encouragement to hang in there. I really do care about the company and want to see it succeed. With James, I was starting to have my doubts."

Al shook her hand and said, "Go home now and get some rest. I'll be by tomorrow morning with Curtis."

As they were getting ready to leave, they heard the custodian yell, running toward them.

"Goodness, Phil! What in the world is wrong?" Lorie shouted.

"Lorie, I saw José around your car a little while ago but didn't think much of it at the time as I thought maybe you had asked him to fix something for you. But after the arrests were made, I told Cid Hartmann about it. Well, he had one of his men check your car. Lorie, José planted a small explosive under your car."

Lorie stood there as if she had been frozen in time. Al finally got her to sit down and take a breath. After the initial shock, Lorie was able to converse with the authorities but was not anxious to get back into her car that evening. As Dave drove her home, he assured her that everything was okay now. She was safe. The nightmare was over.

Lorie hurried into work early the next morning. She wanted to have some time to get her thoughts together before the others arrived. Slowly, she opened the door to James's office, not believing this nightmare had finally come to an end. As the other employees arrived, the office was buzzing with gossip.

When Curtis Thompson arrived, everyone became silent. He immediately walked over to Lorie and shook her hand. "Lorie, the members of the board and I would like to extend our sincere appreciation for all the help you have given us," Curtis said. "There will be major changes here at Glendale, and you can be sure that they will be for the better. I will send a memo regarding an employee's meeting in a few days. Meanwhile, please take care of things here in the office. The board and I will assist in any way we can until a new CEO is hired."

Not knowing what to say, Lorie reciprocated with a big smile.

Later that afternoon, Al came by the office. After everything that had happened, Lorie thought of Al more like a friend.

"Al, what's going to happen now?" she asked.

"James will be indicted on multiple counts—importing and possession of contraband and conspiring with others to import and distribute drugs and conspiring to implement money laundering schemes. José and June were coconspirators, so they will also be charged. Monica was not in on the drug deals. She was having an affair with James, but that's as far as her involvement went. The board has decided to let her go. During the next meeting, your promotion will be announced, and you will be given a qualified secretary."

Lorie's tried to speak, but no words came forth.

"Lorie, you're not supposed to know any of this until the board meeting, so could you please look surprised when Curtis makes the announcement?"

"Oh, Al, you are just too much." Lorie laughed.

"Remember, mum's the word," Al said, putting his finger over his lips. "You didn't hear it from me."

Dave noticed the faraway look in Lorie's eyes as they sipped wine and watched the sunset from their favorite table at Radcliff's that evening. "A penny for your thoughts," he said.

Lorie looked at him and smiled. "Dave, so much has happened. I guess I'm just trying to put it all together and make some sense out of it."

"You've been through quite an ordeal," Dave said, gently patting her hand, "and life hasn't been easy for you. But you were able to deal with it, and you've come out on top. That says a lot about your character."

"You know, my mom always said that life is a learning experience, and that is so true," Lorie said, smiling again.

Looking at her, Dave knew that she was the girl that he wanted to walk forever beside him. Her loving spirit reflected in the evening sunlight, surrounding her in a canopy of gold.

"So, Lorie, what did you learn?"

A thoughtful expression crossed her face. "Well, I've learned that most people, including myself, have no idea where they are going or what they are supposed to be doing in life. I can't see the road ahead of me, and I do not know for certain where it will take me or where it will end. But I believe that the high ideals that I've held throughout my life are worth striving for and worth fighting for. It has to do with basic loyalties and deep convictions. And of course, if you have faith, you're never alone."

As she glanced out the window once again at the brilliant sunset, she whispered, "It's time to look up!"

EPILOGUE

Of the office staff, James Lowden, convicted on multiple counts of drug trafficking and money laundering, brought a life sentence in prison. His coconspirators, José Tamayo and June Chrisner, landed similar fates. Monica was fired from her job at Glendale and entered a rehabilitation institution for alcoholics. Ann Lowden divorced James and moved to the West Coast where she started a small business in the clothing line. Harry Watson, finding himself alone after his wife left him, became a manager at a fast food restaurant, married a young woman with two children, but continued to have affairs and ultimately wound up alone again. Alice Watson moved to Florida, is retired, and spends most of her time shopping and beachcombing. Esther continued as a volunteer at Glendale and died at a ripe old age of eighty-six.

Al Chambers, a lifelong member of Glendale's board of directors, continues to lend his assistance to his friend, Cid Hartmann, and the local police department. Curtis Thompson, although a strong supporter of Glendale Corporation, has stepped down as chairman to oversee his business at Curtis Glass Works.

Lorie's friends, Kate and Bob, continue to be active in the yacht club. Kate teaches math at a local elementary school, and Bob started a new hobby, raising alpacas. Diane Holden earned her master's degree in business and became a supervisor at an advertising company. Lorie's estrange friend, Rich, moved to California, and now lives in a trailer with his new girlfriend, a dedicated surfer. Candy has become a fixture at the local bars.

Betty, Lorie's rival from the yacht club, made another attempt to mess with her boat *Sunrise*, was caught, and was sentenced to two years in prison. Lorie's old neighbors, Irene and Frank, have turned a new page in life. Irene apologized for her behavior toward Lorie after Jake had passed away, and they have become friends once again. Lorie's childhood acquaintance, Gail Zeller, never married, lives alone, and works as a housekeeper.

Lorie's nephew, Rod, continues to serve time in prison. He eventually became a model prisoner and developed a close relationship with Lorie. They continue to write to each other on a regular basis. His wife, Leah, a much older woman, has become bitter and resentful. With drugs and alcohol being a constant in her life, trying to outsmart law enforcement has become a hobby.

Father O'Malley, advancing in age, continues to be a close friend and inspiration to Lorie as her spiritual director. Dave and Lorie married and moved into a large ranch-type house on a lakefront property where they spend their evenings relaxing on the veranda, watching the sunsets, and counting their blessings.

ABOUT THE AUTHOR

A Western Pennsylvanian widow, Lorraine has long enjoyed and participated in a variety of sports and extensive travel. Her frequent journeys were the inspiration she needed to submit a photo to the International Library of Photography entitled "Key West" and was publicized in the historic photography anthology, "America at the Millennium."

Always on the lookout for a new adventure, she mastered the scuba rating of rescue diver late in life from the Professional Association of Diving Instructors (PADI).

A professional secretary by trade, she has the skills she needed to create newsletters for the various children's groups she volunteered with over the years. Now in retirement and seeking yet another new adventure, she has returned to a once cherished dream: writing a novel.

Confident that there is nothing in life you cannot overcome, Lorraine takes you to the extreme in *Office Monsters* featuring many facets: anxiety, despair, humor, contentment, and ultimate victory. The book is an inspiring story filled with life-changing effects, obstacles, and solutions.